The Fatal Five Minutes

R.A.J. Walling

First published: 1932 London

This edition published 2022 by

OREON

an imprint of

The Oleander Press
16 Orchard Street
Cambridge
CB1 1JT

www.oleanderpress.com

A CIP catalogue record for the book
is available from the British Library.

ISBN: 9781915475176

Cover design, typesetting & ebook: neorelix

The Fatal Five Minutes

Sign up to our infrequent newsletter
to receive a free ePub of

Fatality in Fleet Street

by Christopher St John Sprigg and get
news of new titles, discounts and give-aways!

One

SHEER accident mixed up a number of perfectly incongruous persons in the Midwood affair. They came out of three worlds as wide apart as the outer planets – fastidious people from Mayfair, plain middle-class people from the City, bizarre people from Bohemia. They had nothing in common but the universal liability of mankind, the obligation to die. It was Death that tangled them all up in a toil of trouble and for one agonising week ground them all under the heavy heel of a country policeman.

Before Midwood my mental picture of the country policeman was a stage illusion. Old Inspector Catterick dispelled it.

Even the subtle Tolefree had to admit that Catterick stood for something not only intelligent but fine – for the impregnable integrity of Justice as well as for the vindication of the Law. I suppose old Catterick was neither well educated nor well paid; but he was astute and incorruptible, and when a more penetrating intellect showed him the short cut to his goal he was grateful.

I went down to Midwood in Surrey that Saturday afternoon in November knowing only two of the persons whom Catterick, as the god in the legal machine, was presently to dominate. One was Wellington Burnet himself, the owner of the place. The other was Philip Tolefree. The rest of them were rather off my map.

Naturally no reader of newspapers could be quite ignorant of Cossor, either his appearance or his achievements. Among the best-known men at the bar, he had a big practice in the Central Criminal Court. His lean, angular features often decorated the front page, whence his keen eyes looked down his nose at one just as they did at hostile witnesses in the box. But before Midwood I had never seen Cossor in the flesh. He was game too high for a mere shipbroker to fly at. And so was Alison Burnet, his cousin – till the Midwood affair brought her down from the aristocratic empyrean where she breathed so rarefied an air.

As to Annesty, the polished Bohemian, and Denley, the private secretary at Midwood, they were not even names to me. Gillespie, the young nephew whom Burnet had brought into the City, was not much more than a name. I was ignorant of the very existence of the sister who kept house for him at Highgate. Burnet, however, I knew like a book; or thought I did. No two men were ever closer friends or deeper confidants than Burnet and I, as will appear.

But as to Tolefree. Long before I made my visit to Midwood, Philip Tolefree had taken my fancy. In a noisy, fussy, gossipy world like ours, he was a something unobtrusive and silent man. One has to put up with much clamour in the City Club where I made his acquaintance. One goes there chiefly at lunchtime, feeds, and takes his coffee and cigarette in a smoke room packed with sanguine people talking shop or politics at the tops of their voices. The place is a desert in the evening.

It was, nevertheless, of an evening that I fell into my first real talk with Tolefree. I had to be in the silent City that night, waiting for nine o'clock and a telephone call from my agent in New York. I took an almost solitary dinner in the Club, and when I strolled into the smoke room just after eight to find a place by the fire and burn a cigar to while away the half hour before going to my office, I found only one man there and it was Tolefree. He sat in a corner of the big hearth with a dispatch bag on the seat beside him and on his knee a big, black loose-leaf notebook in which he was writing.

He looked up, obviously surprised to see me, and nodded as I sat opposite him, turned over the log in the fireplace, and got out my cigar case. He returned to his writing. I held out the case to him with a word.

"These are good, I think."

He looked up, smiled, and shook his head.

"Do you mind if I fill a pipe instead?"

And he put away his papers and pulled out pipe and pouch.

"Pretty deserted here in the evening," I said.

"Yes," Tolefree answered, "it's the only tolerable place in London – for me."

He smiled again, a friendly sort of smile.

"Nasty jolt for the West End Clubs!" I observed.

"Haven't got one. I like this. Near my rooms. And I have the place to myself most evenings. You're the first man I've seen in the smoke room for three nights. And I suppose you wouldn't be here if you weren't going to telephone across the water about the Blue Anchor deal."

I stared, with my cigar in one hand and a lighted match in the other. That was exactly why I did find myself in the City after eight; but the business I had in hand was very private, I had not spoken to a soul about it, and secrecy was the essence of success for me. The match burned my finger, I said, "Damn!" and threw it into the fire.

"Look here, Tolefree, who's been— How the devil did you know anything about this?"

He seemed surprised.

"Sorry," said he. "No impertinence I hope? Certainly none meant."

"None at all. But how, man? How? I could have sworn no one in England knew I was specially interested in the Blue Anchor deal, and certainly no one could have known about my telephone call. And anyhow, you're not in the underwriting market, are you?"

As a matter of fact, Tolefree had a little insurance business, but so far as I was aware a thing like the Blue Anchor merger was entirely out of his reach.

"Underwriting?" He shook his head. "But there's no mystery about it, Farrar. Just ordinary putting two and two together. You're in ships. I have correspondents in New York. You never come to the Club in the evening: nobody ever does. But here you are tonight. You stroll into the room. Absent-minded. You've got a bunch of keys in your hand; you pick out a latchkey, swing the bunch on it, and put it away. You shoot up your cuff and look at your watch. Then you come along to the fire for a smoke. A man who's going to put away half an hour before he tackles the business that preoccupies him. In the West End, it might be a theatre. Or a woman. But in the City – well! Rotten habit of mine, figuring things out almost without knowing it. Seemed to leap to my mind this way: 'Farrar – ships – Blue Anchor – keys of his office – nine o'clock – four in New York – telephone.' But, forget it. It was undoubtedly impertinent."

I stared at him with some surprise, and, I suppose, a little annoyance in my manner, for he picked up his black book and fluttered the leaves, saying,

"Forget it if you please, Farrar."

The Blue Anchor affair cost me a few dollars in telephone fees and yielded me none. But I always reckoned my true acquaintance with Tolefree from that evening. Why he had made that dash at my business I could not fathom. There was certainly no impertinence, and not even an undue curiosity in his mind. I felt sure of that, and I did not think him the kind of man who would want to show me what a clever dog he was. It took me, in fact, a long while to discover the truth about Tolefree.

The revelation came about this way. There was a leakage of private information from my office. I had traced it as far as I could go. One of my four clerks was the culprit, but to fix him among the four utterly beat me. I mentioned it to a man who had met with the same kind of trouble and cured it. He said,

"It's easy. Try Tolefree. On the quiet."

And then it appeared that Tolefree's office was mere camouflage. Tolefree himself was an agent not for insurance, but for what they called "private inquiry." In other words, a detective who specialised in the kind of thing that City men wanted. In two days he telephoned me the name of the man who was giving me away. I laid a simple trap for him and he fell in.

Thereupon I went to see Tolefree in his office – two small rooms in Watling Street, barely furnished, and decorated only with the advertisements and calendars of Insurance Companies.

"How did you trip him?" I asked.

"I didn't. I just looked at him, Farrar. Let me look at any four fellows who don't know I'm looking, and I'll tell you which of 'em has and which of 'em hasn't a secret to keep. You couldn't hit on him because he was on his guard – that's all. Remember the night you came into the Club? Now, if you'd known there was a man in the smoke room who might be curious about you, and if you'd wanted to keep your business dark, you'd have been on your guard. You wouldn't have been fingering your office keys, you wouldn't have been looking at your watch and measuring out your time; you'd have been chiefly conscious that you were doing an unusual thing, and you'd have had an alibi ready. But, Farrar – you'll do me a favour? This is private, this business of mine. I'm nothing but a little insurance agent. The condition of my job is that as few people as possible know anything about it."

"Of course," said I. "But, Tolefree, this secrecy being an element in your success, why the deuce did you show me that night that you'd guessed what I was after?"

"Swank – sheer swank!" He smiled. "I simply couldn't hold out against the temptation. Here's Farrar, with his secret written all over him in letters a foot long, and he thinks nobody can see 'em. Well, – let's show the beggar... Something like that. It really was a piece of impertinence – and you took it like a sportsman."

Tolefree became the leading actor in the Midwood affair by accident – through being on the spot. Trailing criminals was not his line of country and I do not doubt that contact with a murder made him feel quite as pale as the next man. His proper business was the discovery of little secret things, petty wickednesses done in the course of business. But he owed this prime adventure of his life to the fact that my friend Wellington Burnet was a City man, and his success in it to the same factors that made him a success in the City: he had an extraordinary faculty for making deductions from a physiognomy.

Tolefree was a man of middle height, dark, clean shaven, with a rather pleasant face and when he was amused a really delightful smile. You might have taken him, with his neat, unobtrusive dress and his quiet manner, for almost anything – a lawyer, a member of the higher Civil Service, a schoolmaster. He had nothing about him of the detective either of fact or of fiction. Not that he was by any means colourless as a personality, but that he carried about with him none of the marks of a specific job in life.

After the episode of the disloyal clerk, we became friendly in a casual way. First we chatted when we met. Next I got him to spend an evening now and then with me in my flat in Manchester Square; then to come every Thursday: and once or twice I had supped with him in his queer rooms near Cannon Street Station. He was a serenely lonely man. He lived alone. He had not even a housekeeper. A woman "did for him" every day, and prepared his supper before she left. He ate it in solitude and silence, communing with some philosophical tome propped against the coffee pot, disturbed only by the occasional puffing of an engine under the great glass roof of the station thirty yards away. I used to say his bookshelf contained the only copy of William James's *Principles* within a mile – till he reminded me that the Deanery of St. Paul's was not so far off as that.

A curious mixture, Tolefree, with his bug of philosophical speculation and his exceedingly practical and realistic fashion of earning his daily bread.

But for Burnet's sudden defection from the ranks of the single, and his consequent departure from London to live in the country, Tolefree and I might never have reached such friendly terms. But he seemed to fit in – not exactly to fill the void Burnet had left, but at least to give me a companion for the Thursday evening Burnet had for years taken with me. The peculiar thing was that until the week of the Midwood affair, Tolefree had no knowledge of Burnet except that he was an old friend of mine, and had held a big position in the City.

"It's hardly likely," he said, when I spoke of it, "that a great lion like Wellington Burnet would ever hear of an insignificant mouse like Philip Tolefree or remember him if he did hear."

The lion and the mouse! – it was as if Tolefree had an unconscious second-sight when he used that figure.

Two

"What a dam' rotten sneak thief cut-throat game this is!"

Young Gillespie, having watched the balls to a standstill, stood up, made a few passes round his head with his cue and did a short step dance to release his glee.

"It's exactly like croquet, Mr. Farrar, don't you think? A dirty-minded game, croquet, without a spot of chivalry in it. And snooker – well, look what I've done to you!"

He chuckled.

"You are a pretty foul assassin," I admitted, studying the table.

We had played a close game. It hung on the last black. He had left me glued to the cushion at one end and the black tight at the other. Two to one I missed the ball. Ten to one, if I hit it I left him a shot.

"I give it to you, Mr. Gillespie," said I. "Have we time for another? Yes – why, it's not quite six-thirty. What time is the dressing bell?"

"Quarter past seven," he answered, clearing the pockets and sending the bright-coloured balls in a crowd to the top of the table where they made a futuristic symphony of red, yellow, pink, blue on the green cloth under the blaze of the lights. I watched him with pleasure. His fair hair shone and shadowed as he moved about; his bronzed face with the little moustache that was lighter than his skin, his grey, laughing eyes, his athletic slimness, his youth and irrepressible liveliness, and the kindly confidence with which he treated an older man and a comparative stranger, combined to make him a vivid and likeable person.

Burnet had often spoken to me of his young nephew, his only near male relative. But I had seen very little of him till two hours ago, when I entered Midwood House for the first time and broke in upon Mrs. Burnet's guests taking tea in her drawing room. The portentous accident that we were now playing snooker pool in Burnet's gorgeous billiard room, and remained there for another twenty-eight minutes came about in this way: When tea-drinking was over and everyone had said his and her utmost about the pestilential weather of this damp and gloomy late November afternoon, Burnet took Annesty off to his study to talk business; Cossor wished to go to his room to look over some papers; and Mrs. Burnet, Gillespie and I were left over the empty tea cups. Mrs. Burnet asked us to excuse her while she attended to her household affairs, and, as she was departing, said,

"George, – couldn't you and Mr. Farrar play billiards for an hour? Ring for Elford and tell him to get a man to mark for you."

"Righto, Alison," he replied. "That is, if you're game, Mr. Farrar? But we'll cut out the marker, Alison. I hate your supercilious footman looking on and his snub nose turning up at every stroke this poor mutt makes."

Mrs. Burnet smiled herself away.

"What a dam' Maskelyne's box of a house it is!" said Gillespie. "Everybody's disappeared. Your first visit, Mr. Farrar, isn't it? You'll like Uncle Wellington's billiard room. Though why in the name of Mike he spent about ten million on a billiard room seeing that he doesn't know the butt of a cue from the tip—"

I did like it. The room was beautiful and the table perfect – like everything else in this Palladian palace that Burnet had brought at so great a cost from the eighteenth century bang into the twentieth.

Gillespie eyed me with a polite curiosity as we looked round it and selected our cues and discussed whether it should be billiards or snooker. The youth had a taking way with him, half quizzical and half deferential. He was sizing me up, discovering whether I was really "game," whether he might let himself go with me, or whether I had to be numbered among the Outer Barbarians who had survived from the reign of Queen Victoria. I passed muster. We became friends before all the reds were off the table, and by the end of the first game his spirit, entirely liberated by friendliness and excited by the zest of the contest, soared as I have described.

When I had broken the pyramid the second time and he had picked off the first red with a delicate shot, taken one black, and neatly snookered me behind the spotted ball, he exclaimed,

"Oh, you foul tyke, Gillespie! Havers, Mr. Farrar! I never thought of it before, but snooker's just like life, eh?"

"How?" said I, getting the white tucked nicely against the pyramid. "Do you find life a dam' rotten sneak-thief cut-throat game – at your age?"

"Not me! But since I've been with Uncle Wellington in the City – what? Somebody's always trying to get in your way and you in theirs, and everyone's manoeuvring like hell for a soft shot at the black. What a snooker player Uncle Wellington would have made! He'd take two blacks every hand and always leave the other fellow under the cushion."

"But your uncle," I remarked, "would never foul a ball or break any rule of the game."

Gillespie nodded.

"You've known him since the Flood, haven't you?"

"Almost. Say about twenty years. Two men can't be in the same line of business anywhere in the Square Mile without getting to know each other. I see less of him now he's made his pile and slacked off to this grandeur – but I hope to see a good deal of you while you make yours. I haven't – well, I haven't taken quite as many blacks as your uncle yet. I've a great respect for his talents and an enormous liking for himself."

"Cheers!" said Gillespie. "He's the best scout I know. If I could only tell you all he's done for me and Margaret – that's my sister – you'd understand how I feel about Uncle Wellington. Don't know that Midwood's quite my taste – but it's his, and now that he's got Midwood he jolly well deserves to enjoy it anyhow."

"What's wrong with Midwood?" I asked.

"Oh, not the place. That's all right. It's the style. Those jays with the velvet breeches – great Cæsar! And Alison wanted us to have one here to overhear our backchat! And that foxy-faced butler – br-rr-rr! Look at him there: see what I'd do to him—"

And Mr. Gillespie slammed the yellow ball into the corner pocket with a noise like a bomb explosion.

"You have the advantage of me. I haven't seen the butler," I said.

"Your 'van, Mr. Farrar," he remarked. "Take it from me he's a nasty piece of work. I've told Alison, and she says he buttles well. I daren't say a word to Uncle Wellington. He's only just running himself in as a butler-owner, and sensitive. I could bet a million Mister Jolly-old Elford knows he's got hold of a pair of greenhorns and he's doing 'em down right and left. But bide a bit! – let Uncle Wellington get wise to it all by himself and Mr. Elford will wish he hadn't been born to buttle."

It seemed early days for me to take a hand in the domestic controversies of Midwood House. Therefore I let Gillespie run on till he had exhausted the topic.

Nevertheless I thought he might be right about Burnet's attitude – just groping his way into a new relation. And, also, I shared Gillespie's certainty that, if the presiding genius of his servants' hall was a crook, something excessively unpleasant was coming to him when Burnet found it out. For I knew Burnet as I knew the alphabet. I had watched him applying that devilishly methodical brain of his to one of the stiffest jobs in the world – making a steady fortune out of ship-broking and doing it without ever coming a purler. Nothing Burnet touched ever went wrong. Perhaps because he never touched anything he didn't know inside out. He had outpaced me from the day when we were clerks together in the City; but success did not spoil him nor did the ever-broadening gap between our fortunes crack our friendship. Even his departure from the sort of tacit understanding that we were doomed to be bachelors had made no moral difference, though in the last three years we had met less frequently. When I say "understanding" I do not mean any sort of pact. We had passed the forties and were well on towards the grand climacteric before time could be spared from business to think of domesticity. Men get that way when they do not marry young. As for me, I had never given a thought to marriage. Burnet was forty-five when he met Miss Alison Orton, then twenty-eight and a little out of the matrimonial market, just a thought above his world, but poor and very lovely. Out of a background vague to us in the City came whispers of a romance that had failed: she was still a young girl when the war ended, and one supposed some tragedy which had frustrated her. There were suggestions that the beauty which cast a spell about Burnet was sensitive to the magnetism of Burnet's riches. I knew nothing of that. What I did know was that Burnet, for a time, was a strangely transfigured creature with ideas entirely alien to all our ambitions. When he said to me as he smoked a pipe after one of the time-honoured Thursday evening dinners in my flat,

"I made twenty thousand last year, Bill. I shall make twenty-five this year. What a mug's game it is—"

Then I knew something had happened.

I acted best man at his wedding. He was like a being in a heavenly trance. She – well, she seemed a very gracious person; but I began to think there must be something in the whispered stories, and I doubted whether she could ever reconstruct that romance with the aid of Wellington Burnet. There were no reserves behind his eyes; I saw a whole world of reserves behind hers. What she did reconstruct, however, was Midwood House – and that on a scale far more lordly than anything even her world had ever held for her. What is more, she had fascinated Burnet with a plan for spending his superfluous wealth which I (in common with Mr. Gillespie) thought the most footling and unsatisfactory fashion of squandering money mankind had ever invented. But when Burnet got going on anything that interested him, an Oriental rajah could not excel his lavishness. It was always that way with him: a free-handed man, generous as the midsummer sun. Midwood had been a duke's toy in the eighteenth century; Burnet's Midwood would have made the duke's eyes drop out with envy. And the speed of the transformation! If Berkshire had been a county in the State of New York and Burnet had always lived in that electrical air it could not have been quicker.

Mrs. Burnet's new world was certainly not my world. I did not make fresh contacts easily, and I resisted all the pressure I got to become an habitué of Midwood. The City, the Club, and a weekly round of golf were enough for me, with an occasional theatre, and Tolefree to fill the gap in the Thursday evenings, and a carload of young nephews and nieces to take out on Sundays.

Just when it was that I perceived Burnet to be descending from Paradise to earth again I cannot say; but it was certainly not more than a year after his marriage. He had brought young Gillespie into his business, and at first had been content to leave things in the hands of a capable manager. But now I began to see more of him in the City and at the Club. He sought me out again, and though the old intimacy could not be restored (for Burnet married was a different man) he seemed to have a wistful anxiety to get it back while all the time some inhibition lay on him. He was no longer happy, and, much as I wished for his happiness, I could not put to him the blunt questions I should have asked a year before...

"Oh, good shot! Now you're on the black, Mr. Farrar—"

I was hardly conscious that Gillespie had finished his run, and that I was playing again, when his exclamation broke in on my reflections.

This urgency of Burnet's to get me down for this particular weekend seemed like a last effort to tear through the inhibition: he had almost suggested that refusal would mean a break in our friendship.

And then in an absent-minded way I had made a really excellent stroke and got into position so that Gillespie's enthusiasm became highly vocal and the train of thought about Burnet was severed. I settled down to the game.

Three

Five minutes afterwards Gillespie bethought himself of some duty which he had forgotten in the excitement of the game, and rushed off.

I sat down on a divan in the shadow at the side of the room, cue between my knees, and waited for his return. The door opened. One of Mrs. Burnet's jays with the velvet breeches stood there, holding it, and said,

"Mr. Halifax."

A man walked by him into the room and peered about. It was not easy to see anything past the brilliant lights over the table. As he hesitated I rose and stepped towards him.

"Good evening," I began. "Mr. Gillespie's gone out for a moment. Well, I'll be hanged —!"

A thin, dark-faced, clean-shaven man stood smiling at me and holding out his hand. I took it.

"What the devil are you doing in this galley, Tolefree?" said I. "I could have sworn that flunkey said Halifax."

"And you wouldn't have committed perjury, Farrar. He did. And what's more, a word to the wise, you know—"

I whistled.

"Good Lord!" I exclaimed. "You don't mean — ? Really here on professional business? Incognito, so to speak?"

He nodded.

"Who's the Gillespie you're expecting? And when? I'd no idea you'd be here – or anybody I knew. Nobody must know me. You mustn't know me. So keep your eye on the door."

"All right, then. Gillespie is Burnet's nephew. Nice boy. He'll be here any minute. So tell me straight away who Mr. Halifax is and where he lives and why he's at Midwood. I know all about Tolefree and his prying ways. If you were Tolefree I should guess there was trouble in store for somebody. But Halifax—"

"Old friend of Burnet's down for the weekend, that's all."

"Righto, Mr. Halifax; I understand. But now, Tolefree – what's the little game, eh?"

"I know exactly as much as you do, Farrar. I had a letter from Mr. Burnet at my office this morning. He said he wanted my help in a very difficult matter, and offered me a substantial fee to come down and see him about it. He told me there was a weekend party and he'd be glad if I would join it in the name of Halifax, because he was anxious that none of his guests should associate me – does he talk as formally as he writes? – should associate me with Watling Street. If the presence of a private detective in his house were known, it might produce a little awkwardness."

"I should jolly well think so!" I observed.

I had not heard the softest whisper of anything wrong in Moorgate Street. Burnet had lunched me at his West End Club two days before when he pressed home his invitation to Midwood and promised me an interesting party – Cossor, the booming young K.C., his nephew Gillespie whom he wanted me to know better because I could be useful to him, Annesty who was in theatres – but certainly never a word about Tolefree or any suggestion why he should want a person of Tolefree's profession at Midwood or elsewhere.

"I should jolly well think so, Tolefree," I said. "You're the nicest fellow alive as a friend of the family, but professionally you're just a Mother Carey's chicken."

"Anyhow, you're a godsend, Farrar. I suppose I can talk to you without breaking the rules after we've been formally introduced by somebody? These gilded halls of the great aren't my line of country, you know. I've got no small talk and no parlour tricks."

"You won't want either. I should say you'd be quite safe to talk psychology with Mrs. Burnet, and probably with Cossor—"

"Cossor? The King's Counsel? My hat—"

"And if they let you down, there's young Gillespie – a good type with no frills. Burnet's trying him out in Moorgate Street."

"Ah? But Cossor, eh? I wonder why Cossor? Is he a friend of Burnet's?"

"Presumably. I never met him before. Saw him for five minutes in the drawing room just now. You haven't seen Burnet?"

"No: the flunkey said he was engaged with somebody—"

"Annesty – theatrical bloke. And that seems to be all the crowd, Tolefree."

"Sh —! Halifax, remember."

Then the first significant incident of that fateful hour occurred. To all appearance it was perfectly banal.

The door swung open and a man stepped in and looked around. We had expected Gillespie, but this was not he. It was a tall youth with dark hair and eyes and a look of intense worry on his face. He could not see us where we sat in the shadow, at first, and he came forward into the light of the lamps and looked across the table. Catching sight of us, he said,

"Oh, excuse me. I thought Mr. Gillespie was here."

"Mr. Gillespie's gone out for a few moments," said I. "He'll be back directly, to finish a game."

"Ah... thanks." He took a long look at us and disappeared.

"Something's bitten the artist," said Tolefree. "Who is it? Annesty?"

But it was not Annesty. I had never seen this youth before. Almost immediately Gillespie returned, bursting in with,

"Sorry, Mr. Farrar. Didn't mean to keep you waiting. Oh—"
He stopped, seeing Tolefree on the seat beside me.

"This gentleman," said I, "er – Mr. Halifax, I believe — ?"

Tolefree nodded.

"Mr. Halifax arrived late, and, as your uncle was engaged, they showed him in here."

Gillespie held out his hand.

"How do, Mr. Halifax? My uncle mentioned today that he expected you. Rather an informal reception, I fear. Odd time between tea and dinner, and there didn't seem to be a chance of a hand at bridge, so Mr. Farrar and I came along here—"

Tolefree's best smile put an end to the apologies.

"You were playing," said he. "Do go on with the game. I'd like to mark for you."

"Well—" Gillespie looked at his watch. "It's not quite seven. There's just time enough – if you're sure you won't be bored? Your shot, I think, Mr. Farrar."

We had played perhaps three shots and Gillespie had his cue poised for another when he started, looked round, and said,

"Jehoshaphat! What's up?"

There was a sound of running footsteps in the corridor, the door flew open, and a man rushed into the room.

"Gillespie! – quick! Your uncle—"

It was Annesty, and he was a surprising spectacle. He had on a dressing gown and apparently not much else. His face was pale. He spoke in a choking voice.

"Uncle!" Gillespie cried, throwing his cue down on a divan. "What the devil's the matter, Annesty?"

"I'm afraid he's – ill. I've made Elford telephone for a doctor."

"Ill? There's something more, Annesty. Out with it, man! Where is he?"

"In his study, Gillespie."

"Excuse me, Farrar."

Gillespie strode to the doorway and collided with a man in evening dress who came in running.

"What's this, Elford?"

The butler glanced into the room at us.

"If you would be good enough to come outside a moment, Mr. George—"

Gillespie went through, the butler at his heels. Annesty, left panting and staring at the door, was a queer figure under the brilliant light as he leaned on the table to support himself. He looked round at me and Tolefree; then turned away again. Absolute silence followed the sudden upheaval. It did not last long. In not more than twenty seconds, just as I was about to ask Annesty what was wrong, Gillespie pushed open the door. His face was now as white as Annesty's.

"I'm going up, Annesty," said he. "Better tell Mr. Farrar and Mr. Halifax what's happened. I must see Alison. I'll be back—"

He was gone. The young man turned his white face to us and almost collapsed on the table.

"Look out!" cried Tolefree, and jumped to his side. I caught sight of a tray with spirit bottle and glasses on a table at the end of the room, and brought him a pick-me-up while Tolefree supported him to a seat. He gulped a mouthful of the whisky.

"Thanks," he said. "It turned me up. It'll be worse for Gillespie."

"What's happened?" I asked.

"Mr. Burnet – I don't know quite what – some accident – or an attack. He seemed to me—"

"Good God!" I cried. "You don't mean to say Burnet's—"

"He seemed to me – I can't say – Mrs. Burnet – she lay there like a dead woman—"

I gazed at him, speech paralysed for a moment. Tolefree took him in hand.

"Steady, sir!" said he. "You've had a shock. Go easy – take another drink."

Annesty gave him a grateful look. He raised the glass, clattering against his teeth.

"I must go back," said he.

"Not yet," said Tolefree, firmly. "There's plenty of help by this time, no doubt. Stay and recover a bit. Let him alone for a minute, Farrar."

I had begun a question. I choked it, and stood gaping at the two of them as though they were men in a dream. But in three minutes Tolefree had got out of him just what happened, nursing him along with adroit questions.

Annesty had left Burnet's study about a quarter of an hour ago and gone to his room intending to have a bath before he dressed for dinner. He was actually in the bath when the butler came knocking at his door. He slipped into his bath robe and opened. Elford apologised and said Mr. Burnet would be obliged if he would spare him another minute or two in his study before dinner. He said he would go straight there as soon as he was dressed.

Then in less than a minute he heard a terrible shriek. It seemed to be a woman's. He dashed out into the corridor. Cossor, whose room was close to his, had heard it too and reached the corridor at the same time. There was no other sound. They consulted about it. Then they heard quick footsteps on the stairs below and rushed down. The butler, coming up, arrived outside Burnet's study with them, and all three saw at once that the door of the room was open and that just inside lay Mrs. Burnet. Cossor dropped to her side and found that she was living but unconscious. Then the butler, who had looked into the room, cried out and pointed, and Annesty saw Burnet himself stretched out on the rug between his desk and the fireplace. He stepped over Mrs. Burnet's body and knelt down by Burnet. He placed his hand on Burnet's heart and could detect no beat. He thought —

Annesty pulled up with a shudder.

Four

Burnet was dead... old Burnet!

Annesty knew Burnet was dead. Annesty suspected something more than accident or seizure. Nobody could mistake that. Something dreadful had happened to Burnet, and here we were in his grand billiard room, in the midst of a game with the gay balls that shone on the bright table.

I shivered.

"Tolefree!" I exclaimed, "I must go up—"

Annesty's pale face turned from me to Tolefree in a puzzled glance.

"I thought," said he, "you were Mr. Halifax?"

"Both," said Tolefree. "But never mind that. If you're feeling better, don't you think we should all go up and see whether we can lend a hand about anything? Or Mr. Farrar and I will go if you still feel shaky."

"No," said Annesty. "I'm all right now. I'll go too. You see, it sort of hit me behind the knees. It was frightful. I'd been talking to him ten minutes or so before. Let me show you the way."

Burnet's study on the first floor was one of a range of rooms along the front of the house. As we hurried behind Annesty up a great staircase, there was a bustling above, and when we arrived breathless in the corridor at the top Cossor and Gillespie were on their knees beside the unconscious Mrs. Burnet. Presently they rose and carried her sagging form towards the door of a room which a maid held open. They went in. A footman stood beside Elford at another open door. Annesty pointed to it.

"There!" said he in a whisper.

In all the circumstances, I suppose, I ought not to have been surprised by Tolefree's conduct. He had been summoned to Midwood for some unknown professional purpose, and no doubt this sudden tragedy aroused all his professional instincts. At any rate, from the moment when Annesty pointed to the door of Burnet's study, and the butler looked towards us with an air of invitation to inquiry, Tolefree took charge.

"Leave this to me," he said in my ear, and I dropped behind with Annesty. Tolefree advanced to the butler.

"You're Elford, aren't you?" said he.

"Yessir."

"I wish to let you know at the first moment, Elford, that I am a detective who was engaged by Mr. Burnet to come down here to make some inquiries for him—"

Elford started back as though he had been stung.

"A detective!" he cried.

"A detective!" Annesty echoed. "Mr. Burnet engaged a detective? Could he have feared—"

Annesty's sentence tailed into nothing. Elford recovered from his shock.

"Yessir," said he.

"You quite understand?" said Tolefree. "Now, before I go in, have you or either of you been in that room since Mr. Annesty came downstairs?"

"No, sir, – we've been attending to Mrs. Burnet."

"Anybody been in?"

"Only Mr. George."

"You've telephoned for the doctor – what doctor? And how long will he take to get here?"

"Dr. Jacquelin, sir. His house is about three miles away, at Midwood Green. He should be here at any minute."

"Very well. Until the doctor comes, I take charge, Elford. I will explain to Mr. Gillespie. Stay where you are, all of you."

Tolefree went into the room. He was there perhaps two minutes.

"Farrar," said he, returning, "Mr. Burnet is quite dead. Elford, ask Mr. Gillespie to spare me a moment."

Gillespie came out at once from the room where they had taken Mrs. Burnet.

"You want me?"

There was astonishment in his look and tone.

Tolefree took a letter from his pocket, and handed it to the young man.

"You'll understand, Mr. Gillespie, if you read that."

Gillespie took the paper and hurriedly read.

"Good God!" he muttered, passing it back. "What could he have suspected?"

"If Mr. Farrar and I could see you in a downstairs room for a minute or two?" Tolefree suggested. "And if you would order the servants and request all other persons now on this floor to stay here till we return—"

Gillespie's face darkened as he looked earnestly in Tolefree's eyes.

"Ye-es," he said. "I see—"

"Mrs. Burnet — ?" I asked him.

"Alison's coming round, Mr. Farrar. Wait one instant while I tell Cossor. Elford, no one is to leave this floor till further orders, you understand?"

"Very good, sir," said Elford.

Gillespie eyed him thoughtfully during a second or two.

"Peters," he said to the footman, "you understand that no one must leave? These are absolute orders."

"Very good, sir."

"There's no key in the door," said Tolefree. "Who has a key? Elford?"

"Yessir, there are all the keys in my pantry."

"Ah, well, that can wait. In the meantime, nobody goes into the room."

Tolefree looked along the corridor to the West. Beyond a turn where the staircase to the second floor ascended was a green baize door. Tolefree strode to it, locked it, and gave the key to Gillespie. The servants stared hard at him as he passed. Then the three of us went down.

Among all the queer things that happened on that horrible evening, none was queerer than our brief meeting in Mrs. Burnet's drawing room. Gillespie led the way there, switched on the lights, and turned inside the doorway to face Tolefree. During a strained moment they seemed to be measuring each other up.

Gillespie shook himself together.

"What does it mean?" he asked.

"It was a violent death," said Tolefree.

Gillespie shuddered.

"Have you sent for the police?" Tolefree asked.

"No – I ought to have thought of it. But we were worried about Alison – Mrs. Burnet, I mean. Couldn't tell what to make of her."

"But she's all right now? Who's with her?"

"Her maid – and Cossor's there."

"Then, Mr. Gillespie, I think you should telephone at once for the police."

That was all. But behind this spasmodic dialogue there were a hundred things unsaid, and the two watched each other as if every word was a flash of lightning.

Gillespie immediately started for the hall and we started after him, for there was no telephone in the drawing room. There we found servants grouped around the foot of the great staircase, at whose head stood Peters the footman on guard. They broke apart as Gillespie appeared.

"Please go back to your work," said he, and waited till they had trooped away before he took us into a small room and telephoned the Police Station at Midwood village.

The worst of the horror for me was yet to come, but to stand there silent alongside Tolefree while Gillespie waited for the connection, and while he told the Inspector that Burnet had been killed, and while he said, "Yes – we think it is murder," was horrible enough. When we came out into the hall again, the doctor had arrived and was waiting, with a footman standing by him, to speak to Gillespie.

"An accident? ... Worse? ... Police?"

I heard the words in a sharp voice, coming clear. Dr. Jacquelin was a young man, keen and certain in his manner.

"Take me there," said he, grabbing the bag which the footman was holding.

Tolefree warned the man Peters as we passed him still to let nobody up or down, and, when we reached the door of the study, he checked us with a word.

"I think we should disturb nothing in the room, Mr. Gillespie, don't you? The doctor understands the importance of touching nothing. We will remain here."

Dr. Jacquelin gave him a quick look.

"Excellent," he said; and while we three stood close inside the door he strode across to the spot where, projecting beyond the pedestal of a writing table, I saw a pair of shoes, toes upwards, shining under the light.

And this was all of Burnet I could see – old Burnet, my friend of twenty years or more. My pulse beat very hard as the doctor dropped to the carpet and, in his turn, was concealed by the writing table. We heard the little movements he made. We heard the quick indrawing of his breath, like a whistle. Within a minute he had risen and returned to us.

"You, sir," he said to Tolefree, "are you the police?"

"I have no official connection with the police. They will be here directly. Perhaps Mr. Gillespie will explain — ?"

"No matter," said the doctor. "This is an affair for the police. Mr. Gillespie – your uncle is quite dead. He has been killed by a crashing blow on the top of the head – a blow of immense force. His skull is crushed. Is anything known of—"

"Nothing at all," came Gillespie's choking whisper.

"Then the sooner the police get busy the better. It's – well, it's an unspeakably brutal crime. Strange, too – here. It was here, I suppose?"

Gillespie nodded.

"I see nothing – I mean, no signs of violence except on the body. You, sir—" he addressed Tolefree again.

"This is Mr. Tolefree," said Gillespie. "The circumstances are very curious, Jacquelin. Mr. Tolefree is a private detective who was invited down here by my uncle today for a consultation and was actually waiting to see him when—"

The doctor's breath was drawn in again with that little whistle.

"By Jove!" he exclaimed. "That's suggestive. I understand what you meant just now. Well, I've touched not even the body. You see nothing here, do you?"

"Very little," said Tolefree. "But there's been no time for a real examination. And anyhow the police must see everything first exactly as it is."

"Quite so."

"Jacquelin," said Gillespie, "the terrible thing is that he was discovered by Alison—"

"Good Lord! Mrs. Burnet? – it must have knocked her out!"

"It did. We took her to her room. Will you come along and see her? That is, if Mr. Tolefree—"

"Don't defer to me, Mr. Gillespie," Tolefree said. "Of course, the doctor should see Mrs. Burnet. Mr. Farrar and I will stay here and wait for the police."

Five

They went out. Tolefree and I were left in the company of old Burnet. I trembled so with emotion and nausea that I could not speak to Tolefree.

"This isn't much good to you, Farrar," said he, kindly. "We won't stay in the room. But before we go, take a good look round, will you? The doctor saw nothing; I saw little; but we may have both missed a good deal. Think you could bear to have a look at him?"

"Just a look, for an instant, perhaps—"

"Tread in the middle of the room. Touch nothing," Tolefree urged me, and I went with him the few paces that took us within sight of Burnet. I staggered and caught Tolefree by the arm.

In visual fact it was not so dreadful as I had thought. Burnet lay on his back, stretched straight with arms out and hands clenched, and his face was paler than ever I had seen it. But at a glance he was not greatly disfigured. A stain of blood was on his forehead – not very conspicuous; it might have been a scratch. The thick thatch of greying hair, which had been one of Burnet's physical distinctions, concealed the real damage.

But the thing behind this visual fact was appalling. The sudden death of Burnet would have afflicted me anyhow. Death in this way – I turned aside. Tolefree was looking at me thoughtfully.

"Who—" I began and did not continue the question.

"Ah," said Tolefree, "it's going to be hard – dam'd hard, Farrar. But we've only a minute. Try to fix the room in your mind as it is now. Note everything. I'd like to be out of it before the police come."

The room was not large – almost square and rather high in the ceiling, in the eighteenth century style. The door from the corridor was in the right hand corner of the wall. Looking left along the wall on that side there were bookshelves; in the end wall to the left a door apparently leading into another room, and a fireplace in which, however, an electric fire glowed instead of logs of coal. In the wall opposite the door two windows were cut almost from ceiling to floor. Heavy curtains were drawn across them, almost but not quite meeting in the middle. Tolefree went over and peered through the slits, but did not move or even touch the curtains. On the left of the windows stood an ordinary steel safe; on the right a tall cabinet in rosewood. Almost in the middle of the room was the large writing table on two pedestals with knee space between. This bore two letter baskets, two telephones, an electric table lamp with a green glass shade, an inkstand, a blotting pad and a neat pile of papers. Burnet was always a very tidy and methodical man. On the floor in the kneehole was an electric heater, with the current still on. To the right of this table, and between it and the fourth wall, a small table had been placed, with a small chair – apparently for the use of secretary or amanuensis. The only thing on it was a little tray containing a pencil or two. Bookshelves filled the fourth wall. A dark blue carpet covered the floor.

This was the plain room of a business man. It had nothing of the air of luxury that pervaded Midwood in general. It was Burnet rather than Mrs. Burnet – Burnet as I had known him in the City.

My eyes went slowly round the place once and then again while Tolefree stood contemplating that figure on the floor which my glance now avoided.

"Come," said he. "We'll leave him alone till the police get here."

We found Gillespie and Dr. Jacquelin talking in the corridor.

"Mr. Farrar and I will go down. You won't want a crowd when the officers come. We shall be on hand if we are wanted."

Gillespie looked an inquiry from Tolefree to the servants standing by.

"I think," said Tolefree, "the police will be grateful to you if you keep that order in force."

"It's a little difficult to explain to—" Gillespie began. "But never mind."

Tolefree and I went down to the hall and were there when the police arrived almost immediately.

There were three of them, an obvious Inspector in mufti at their head. A business-like man. A footman having admitted them, he looked sharply around, saw me and Tolefree standing by the door of the drawing room, and gave us a long stare. His companions were a sergeant and a constable in uniform. His first step was to post the constable at the door.

"No one leaves or enters without my permission, Collins," he said.

His next order was to the Sergeant.

"Take this man, and seal up all entrances and exits, Sergeant. You go with him, my man. Where is Mr. Gillespie?"

Thirty seconds after his entrance the Inspector had passed up the grand staircase out of our sight.

"Well," said Tolefree, opening the drawing room door, "that's energy anyway. Shall we go in and sit down?"

There was a chiming clock somewhere in the great salon. Just as we entered, its soft gong rang three of the Westminster chimes: it was a quarter to eight. If Burnet's house party had gone according to plan, we should now have been talking to Burnet in our tails and white waistcoats and waiting for Mrs. Burnet to come down and for the popinjay in the velvet breech-es to open the door and announce that dinner was served. But

Burnet was not going to eat any more dinners and we were to have none that night.

Tolefree had no sooner shut the door than he said to me,

"Farrar, hold the fort. I want to have a look round before too many cooks spoil the broth. The sergeant may think of the drawing room windows, but it's just as likely he won't."

Before I could make any reply, he had switched aside a long curtain, drawn a bolt, and disappeared. He was away an unendurable time. The golden chime sounded eight and a quarter past and another quarter, with intolerable spaces of silence between, so that my nerves were creaking desperately when I heard a voice say,

"Good evening, gentlemen."

I leaped out of my seat. Any sound would have been a thunder-clap to me, and the Inspector had a good resounding voice.

"Good evening," I replied, wondering how I was to account for Tolefree; but he was suddenly in the room, saying, "Good evening, Inspector." He threw down an illustrated paper and came towards us.

"Which is Mr. Tolefree?"

"I'm Farrar," said I, "an old friend of Mr. Burnet's. This is Mr. Tolefree."

The burly, sanguine officer and the thin, studious-looking Tolefree took stock of each other. A perceptible moment passed before they spoke.

"I'm Inspector Catterick." The policeman broke the silence. "I believe you are a private detective, Mr. Tolefree?"

The shadow of a smile crossed Tolefree's face: there was a certain tone in Catterick's voice.

"Nothing so grand as that, Mr. Catterick," said he. "I have a tiny practice as an inquiry agent in the City. I'm not a sleuth, and I don't do any criminal work: I leave that to people trained to the job. Let the shoemaker stick to his last, you know."

"Ah!" Catterick's tone changed noticeably. "Then I don't quite understand what Mr. Gillespie told me."

"At the same time," said Tolefree, "if I can be of the slightest service—"

"Shall we sit down?" The Inspector deposited his big frame in one of Mrs. Burnet's soft chairs. "I think you can be of very great service, Mr. Tolefree – as a witness, I mean."

"As a witness? Very well. All I know is very little; but it's at your disposal, of course."

"That little may be vital. I think it is, Mr. Tolefree. It may confirm the theory I have formed."

"Theory? That's quick work!" Tolefree exclaimed. "You have a theory already?"

"I said a theory – not a solution. We've been at it an hour, and that's quite time enough to form a theory, which may be right or wrong."

"Quite so," said Tolefree.

"If my theory works out," Catterick went on, "I shall have you to thank for my success—"

"That's very generous of you, Inspector. But I'm not conscious of having done anything to help you yet. I've been in the house only – let me see – about three hours."

"Nevertheless, by taking steps to prevent anyone from leaving the upper part of the house after the discovery of the crime, I believe you have prevented the destruction of a very important piece of evidence."

"Ah?" Tolefree stared at him, puzzled. "What's that? But, of course, I have no right to ask you."

The Inspector's glance flitted between us.

"This gentleman, Mr. Farrar – one of the house party, I believe? No association with you?"

"Only as a City acquaintance and a member of the same club," said Tolefree.

"But apparently in your confidence."

"Oh, yes – I have nothing to conceal from Mr. Farrar."

"Mr. Farrar arrived here at about half past four, I think, went straight from the drawing room to the billiard room with Mr.

Gillespie, and remained there until after the discovery was made, and was with you at the time. That's correct?"

"Perfectly exact," said I.

"There was some talk about your being here anonymously, Mr. Tolefree. You couldn't have been anonymous to Mr. Farrar?"

"Certainly not."

"And did you tell him why you were here?"

"Naturally – seeing that Mr. Burnet's intention would apparently have been defeated if my real name had been known. I simply had to explain to Farrar why I was incognito."

Catterick considered me for a moment. He turned to Tolefree.

"I should like to see the letter you received from Mr. Burnet if you care to show it to me."

Tolefree took it from his pocket-book and passed it over. Catterick put on his spectacles to read it. He went through it slowly again and again.

"You'll produce this if and when it is wanted?" he said, folding up the letter.

"Better keep it yourself," Tolefree answered. "You'll be sure to want it at the inquest. I've got it all in my mind."

The Inspector, with a nod of thanks, inserted it in a wallet of papers.

"Would you mind telling me what sort of inquiries you usually do – the sort of thing Mr. Burnet might have had in mind when he asked you to come down?"

"They're generally financial inquiries. Observations on people. Information about their way of life. Evidence of peculation – that sort of thing."

"Ah! peculation—"

Catterick took out the letter and read it again.

"Mr. Burnet had a great business in the City. I see he speaks here of wishing to consult you – only a consultation. It might have been about anything. Something in the City. Not necessarily here?"

"It might have been anything," said Tolefree. "I'm quite as much in the dark as you. This is the only communication I ever had from Mr. Burnet."

Catterick was keen. I watched his processes with a certain fascination.

"The coincidence is remarkable," he said. "Mr. Burnet is apprehensive of something. What we don't know. He calls in a private inquiry agent. Before even he can see the inquiry agent, he is killed. It's impossible not to link the two things in one's mind."

"Quite impossible," Tolefree agreed. "On the other hand there may not be the remotest connection between them."

"Not the remotest. But did you ever actually see chance working like that – to the very tick of the clock?"

"I can't say I did, Mr. Catterick. But who can put any limits on chance?"

"No one. But I find it a good rule to exhaust the probabilities before I consider the improbabilities."

Tolefree, smiling, said it was a good rule.

"Anyhow, I've acted on the probability," said the Inspector.

"Acted! Already?"

"Yes – I've detained a man for inquiries. Sergeant Martin is now on his way to the station with him."

Tolefree whistled. Catterick did not immediately volunteer the name of his suspect. I shuffled on the edge of my chair with excitement. But Tolefree did not put the question. Instead, he asked,

"Have you freed the staircase?"

The Inspector chuckled.

"You ought to be in the service," he said. "Yes – I've freed the staircase. But you're going to ask me whether I went through the upper part of the house with a broom first. I did."

"Could I know whom you found there?"

"As you kept 'em there, I think you might."

Catterick pulled out his notebook and read.

"There were above stairs the following persons," he said: "Mrs. Burnet, Mr. Cossor, Mr. Annesty, Mr. Denley—"

Tolefree had been pencilling the names on the back of an envelope. He stopped.

"Denley?" said he. "Who's that?"

"Mr. Burnet's private secretary. He has a room on the first floor."

"What's he like?"

"Tall young man, very dark; wears his hair rather long."

I caught a lift of Tolefree's eyebrows.

"Denley – yes." He put down the name.

"Mr. Gillespie, Elford the butler, Peters the footman, Minnie Wade the maid. That's the lot."

Catterick put away his book and eyed Tolefree. He counted them up.

"Eight," said he. "You've detained out of that eight Elford the butler."

"Ah!" cried Catterick. "So you guess the theory? That half confirms it."

"Oh, no, Mr. Catterick," Tolefree expostulated. "That would be too dangerous. Mine was merely a shot into the brown. You'd not go so far as that on a mere theory, I'm sure. Serious thing to detain a man, even if you don't keep him long. You had something to go on. You spoke of evidence—"

"Yes – pretty good evidence, though not conclusive. Elford is a crook."

"You don't mean a professional crook?"

"No – but a crook, a sneak-thief. Caught red-handed – and by you."

Six

"Caught by me?"

Tolefree shook his head with a smile over the Inspector's enthusiasm. He really did appear to be enthusiastic. He literally rubbed his hands at Tolefree's astonishment.

"Yes, sir, – by you! But for you, Mr. Elford would have gone scot-free."

"Gross flattery, Mr. Catterick. I'd nothing to do with catching Elford. Entirely your work. You see, there was nothing in the world to show me that Elford was a crook, and I certainly had no idea of laying a trap for him."

"All the same, you trapped him."

This strange conversation was developing into a sparring match between Catterick and Tolefree, each trying to force on the other the credit of catching a crook. I read a scepticism in Tolefree: he was particularly anxious that Elford's detention should not be laid to his account. But he had not heard what Gillespie said to me over the snooker table. Gillespie had no doubt about the butler's crookedness. Perhaps Gillespie had coloured the Inspector's views.

"Yes, sir," the Inspector was saying, "you caught him red-handed without knowing it. You did it by preventing him from leaving the first floor. Mr. Gillespie backed you up. Not trusting Elford any more than a fox, he gave the warning to the footman as well. That settled Mr. Elford's hash. He couldn't get by with the footman on guard, and just because he couldn't get by even for the one little minute he wanted, he's now on his way to the Midwood police station."

The Inspector rubbed his hands again with obvious enjoyment of Mr. Elford's discomfiture.

"Now, I'll tell you what, Mr. Tolefree," he continued. "I haven't the least doubt Mr. Burnet brought you down here to discover Elford's peculations." (The Inspector liked that word.) "And after what's happened, Mr. Gillespie hasn't any doubt either."

"Yes?" Tolefree pricked up his ears.

"Yes, sir! But after he wrote his letter to you yesterday, he must have found some bit of evidence that made him act at once without waiting for you."

"That's curious," said Tolefree.

"But clear, I think. First, last evening he calls Mrs. Burnet away from a game of bridge."

"Oh? Was there a bridge party last night?"

"There was: Mrs. Burnet, Mr. Cossor, Mr. Gillespie and Mr. Denley. Now observe. Mrs. Burnet is called away by her husband, and she's in his study for a quarter of an hour. She comes back, looking annoyed, and calls off the game. The three men drop cards and go to the billiard room."

"Mrs. Burnet—" Tolefree interrupted; "has she recovered?"

"Yes. She's shaky, but lucid. She tells me her husband was in his study with masses of papers, apparently accounts. He wanted from her many details of household expenditure that she couldn't give him offhand. She suggested that it should all stand over till their guests had gone. He wouldn't hear of that – said it was essential to get things straightened out at once. She referred him to Elford, and after she'd told him all she could he dismissed her and sent for the butler. Elford was with him for an hour—"

"Where was Mrs. Burnet during that hour?"

"She returned to the drawing room and stayed there."

"Alone?"

The Inspector gave Tolefree a long look.

"I think so," said he. "Why do you ask that?"

"Because you haven't mentioned one of the party, Mr. Annesty."

"Oh, Annesty? He wasn't here last night. He came down from London this morning."

"Sorry," Tolefree apologised. "You were saying that Elford spent an hour with Mr. Burnet—"

"Yes, and then went back to the pantry looking like a thundercloud, with some papers which he locked up in his desk. This morning he was on the carpet again in the study. Peters, passing, heard very loud and angry words. Peters says he didn't stop to listen. Well —! No matter. Elford is in his pantry till lunch time with papers and books, and bites the nose off anyone who interrupts him. Now we have a situation, I think?"

The Inspector paused.

"Highly interesting," said Tolefree, "and at the end of it, I suppose, in the ordinary way Elford will lose his."

Catterick seemed to chew this over.

"I take your meaning to be that, in the ordinary way, a muddle of accounts due to peculation in the pantry means just plain dismissal?"

"Oh, I had no special meaning, Mr. Catterick. Don't let me interrupt you."

"Well, it was a bit more than that. I think Mr. Burnet was not the sort of man you could cheat and get away with it?"

He looked to me.

"Burnet," said I, "was the soul of generosity; but I imagine that if he was being done down he'd be implacable."

Catterick nodded

"Mr. Gillespie thought so too," he said. "The long and the short of it is that Elford's a crook, Mr. Burnet first suspected him, then found him out, and then told him what was coming to him. And now Mr. Burnet's dead. Look here."

Catterick drew out a folded sheet of foolscap, opened it, and gave it to Tolefree. He looked at it, pursed his lips and passed it on to me. I recognised Burnet's hand in the three or four lines written across the top of the sheet:

"*TO ELFORD.*

"*Unless you balance this account with all the necessary vouchers or a sufficient explanation, by this evening, I shall place the facts before the police.*

"*W.B.*"

Beneath this curt intimation was a debtor and creditor account, with figures which I did not stop to examine.

"I found that in Elford's desk," said Catterick, taking the paper from me. "If Mr. Tolefree had not thought of keeping everybody above stairs, there would have been no paper for me to find."

He folded and replaced it, and looked to Tolefree for some comment.

"It really seems as if we must allow Elford to be a crook," said Tolefree.

Apparently Tolefree had an acquaintance far closer than I could boast with the working of a policeman's mind. For, whereas Catterick seemed to me a rather self-satisfied and even ridiculous person, with his pat certainties about the noxious butler and his extremely dubious circumstantial evidence, Tolefree's first words when he had left us were,

"That's a pretty sound fellow! Shouldn't like to be a murderer trying to get away from Mr. Catterick."

"But, my dear Tolefree," said I, "surely – arresting a man on that evidence? Crossing the river before he gets there, isn't he?"

"Ah, but take particular notice that he's been careful not to arrest Elford. Detaining him for inquiries is a very different pair of shoes. You mark him: Catterick had a very definite idea in getting Elford out of the house. I'm curious about it. He's not finished yet."

Tolefree was right. Catterick had by no means finished. He did not finish till midnight had passed. And we stayed marooned in that silent drawing room all the time except for the moment or two when first Tolefree and then I strolled out into the hall, to find it just as silent and completely deserted but for the stolid policeman who kept guard on the door.

Meanwhile, as we afterwards learnt, Catterick had called for his Superintendent, who had come and approved and departed. Catterick had interviewed every person at Midwood, from Mrs. Burnet to the kitchen maid. He had taken them separately in Mrs. Burnet's boudoir, and made copious notes of all their statements; and before he looked into the drawing room to take leave of us, he had given a set of strict instructions which the policeman he left on duty was to see executed. He had sent for Elford's keys and locked the study. He had sworn everyone not to leave the house until he arrived again in the morning.

He took no statements from us and placed no embargo upon us; but he said it would be convenient if we remained at Midwood till next day.

No one had taken food, and no one seemed to have thought of food during the strain of the police inquiry. But when Catterick had gone off, Gillespie came and called us to the dining-room. The sight of the oval table laid for dinner and still undisturbed in that rich, dark room and the thought of the man who should have sat there as host gave me a nasty qualm. The contrast between one's fancy of old Burnet sitting proudly there with a lively company around him and old Burnet as he actually was in that dreadful room upstairs! I think it was only then that I truly realised the tragedy of Midwood.

Gillespie, pale and subdued, was making introductions to two men who stood by the fireplace, – Annesty, whom we had already met, and the secretary, Denley, who had looked into the billiard room for that brief moment.

A footman brought sandwiches, and Gillespie, busying himself about drinks, told the man to take something to Mr. Cossor in his room. For the first few minutes we stood about and talked under our breath as people do at a funeral. I noticed that Gillespie and Denley were on confidential terms; they had private things to say to each other. I noticed also that both Denley and Annesty were curious about Tolefree.

"Feeling better?" Tolefree put the question to Annesty.

"Lots. Afraid I made a bit of an ass of myself when I burst in on you in the billiard room. Couldn't help it. The shock was too much for me."

Annesty was, in fact, looking a different person now, in his country clothes, from the frightened and tousled object in a bath-robe who had collapsed in the billiard room.

"It must have been pretty bad," Tolefree agreed.

"It was particularly bad for me. I had special reason to be fond of Mr. Burnet. He'd just been very good to me. And this afternoon we were discussing a plan he had for adding to my gratitude. Then, within a few minutes to be called to see him again and to find – that!"

Annesty closed his eyes with a shudder.

"Better not talk of it, Annesty," Gillespie advised him. "We've all had about as much as we can stand."

"Yes, I know, Gillespie. But it's so awful. And now I can't get Elford out of my mind. I can't quite see it about Elford, can you? I was there when he looked into the room, you know. I'm convinced the fellow didn't know what he was going to see."

"Ah, of course," said Tolefree. "How does it strike you about Elford? What happened exactly?"

Annesty pulled out a chair and sat down.

"I think," said he, "I told you I'd only just left Mr. Burnet – time enough to get into the bath and no more – when Elford came up and asked me to call in at the study before I went down to dinner. I wasn't surprised. A point or two in the matter we were talking about had been left open. Well, Elford went down. He says he had got as far as the hall when he heard the shriek that startled Cossor and me."

"That seems likely to be true," said Gillespie, "because Alison's maid, who was just going up to dress her for dinner, met Elford in the hall, and they heard the shriek at that moment."

"It must be true," said Annesty, "because when Cossor and I got down to the corridor outside Mr. Burnet's room Elford was coming up the stairs with the maid behind him."

"Then Mrs. Burnet must have come out of her room to go to her husband's study just as Elford passed down from his visit to you. Did she see him?"

Gillespie answered Tolefree's question: Mrs. Burnet saw nobody while she walked the few steps from her door to Burnet's.

And having arrived at that point we began to look around for the basis of Catterick's theory, or what he said was his theory.

What was the theory?

Apparently that Elford had contrived to kill Burnet either on his way up to Annesty's room or on his way down. Annesty said he could not possibly have done it on the way down. There wasn't time. And as to the upward journey, Elford was supposed, at any rate, to be going with a message straight from Burnet. What did Elford say about that? When did he last see Burnet alive?

These questions brought out an essential fact. Elford said he had not seen Burnet since lunch time. All the afternoon he had been working on accounts in the butler's pantry. He fixed the time at 6.35 when Burnet rang through on the house telephone the first time and told him to find Annesty and give him a message. Gillespie had this from him in the excited talk that took place before the police came.

"Then," said Tolefree, "there was more than one message?"

"Yes – the first, at 6.35, was that Elford should find Annesty and say Burnet wished to see him."

Tolefree turned to Annesty.

"That's right. I didn't notice the time particularly. Mr. Burnet and I went up together from the drawing room to his study after tea and talked for an hour. I then left him and went to my room to look up some papers referring to our business. I was going through them when Elford came. I went down at once, taking the papers with me, and I suppose we talked about them for five minutes – perhaps a little longer. He said the time was going on and we couldn't finish them. I returned to my room, undressed and was just getting into the bath when Elford came the second time."

"In answer to another ring on the telephone?"

"Yes – there's no doubt about it. Peters answered the telephone and gave Elford the message which was that Mr. Annesty should be asked to call in at the study on his way down to dinner. Both Peters and Elford fix that time at ten minutes to seven by the clock on Elford's desk. Elford then decided that he couldn't do anything more to his accounts before dinner, and he stopped to lock everything up. That may have taken a minute or two. Then he went right up to Annesty."

Tolefree walked to the sideboard to put down his glass. He took a chair near Annesty.

"Let's get this straight," said he. "When you dashed into the billiard room to call Mr. Gillespie, it was seven almost exactly. I noticed it because Mr. Gillespie had looked at his watch a minute or two before and said it wasn't quite seven. So that, as far as I can make out, if Elford killed Mr. Burnet he must have done it in considerably less than no time."

"Ah!" Annesty exclaimed. "You agree with me?"

Tolefree nodded, and went on to tick off the points of his observation:

Burnet must have been murdered after 6.50 when he telephoned Elford and before 7 o'clock when Mrs. Burnet's scream was heard.

After getting the call Elford did not leave his room for a minute or two – say 6.52.

At the other end of the available time, as there must have been at least two or three minutes between Mrs. Burnet's alarm and

Annesty's arrival in the billiard room at 7 o'clock it must be assumed that she reached the study door not later than 6.57.

That gave Elford not more than five minutes to walk from his room to the second floor, bring Annesty out of his bath, give his message, and return to the hall.

"In what spare time he had," said Tolefree, sardonically, "he must have committed a violent and difficult murder so silently that at least four people who were within a few yards heard nothing of it. The most rapid and skilful murderer I ever heard of. Magical!"

He looked from one to other of us in turn and ended with a long gaze at Denley, who stood by Gillespie and had not so far said a word. The effect of Tolefree's look was remarkable. We all found ourselves staring hard at Denley. Only Tolefree and I in that group knew of his hurried visit to the billiard room in search of Gillespie. In this awkward moment I began to calculate the time of that apparition. It was a few minutes, perhaps two or three, before Annesty's. And Gillespie's, for whom Denley was looking, had returned immediately Denley left. My eyes shifted from Denley to Gillespie and met his. Our glance broke off almost before it was completed.

"Four people?"

Annesty was speaking. I suppose his question came with practically no interval between it and Tolefree's exclamation of "Magical!" But it seemed to me as if I had lived through an hour of horrible speculation and as if a chill had come upon the room.

"Yes – four at least," Tolefree answered. "There were you and Mr. Cossor; there was Mrs. Burnet; and there was Mr. Denley, was there not?"

"You were in your room, Jack?"

I felt a certain surprise on hearing Gillespie address the secretary by his Christian name.

"Yes, George – till the rushing about in the corridor brought me out."

"Then you didn't hear the scream, Mr. Denley?" Tolefree asked.

"No – it's queer, but I wasn't conscious of it. I happened to be typing. I expect the noise of the machine drowned it. My room's a little way off, round the corner in the west wing of the house. But I did immediately become aware of the running footsteps."

"Very likely – there'd be vibration, concussion," Tolefree assented. His look travelled round again and rested on Gillespie, who moved to the sideboard glass in hand, and turned yawning.

It was the signal for breaking up. We drifted out. In the hall, Denley said to Gillespie,

"George, – you haven't forgotten who's coming tomorrow? Will it be possible to send anyone to the station for her?"

"Damn!" said Gillespie. "I had, Jack. What a hell of a mess! I'll have to telephone Catterick first thing and get permission to send the car."

He saw us startled.

"I'd forgotten my sister Margaret's due tomorrow," he said, generally. "Nice thing for her!"

We murmured sympathy. Gillespie, Tolefree, Annesty and I went up the stairs together, and parted at the first floor corridor. Annesty went on left past Burnet's door. We two turned right and Gillespie took us to our adjoining bedrooms in the west wing.

"Sleep well," said Tolefree to me as Gillespie opened a door and switched on the light for him.

It was a most ironical piece of advice – and Tolefree knew it.

Seven

We ought, of course, to have gone to bed like two civilised Christians, and to sleep if we could after all these excitements. We should have done so had Tolefree been content to leave the uncloaking of Burnet's murderer to a highly efficient police organisation. He had said violent crime was not his pigeon.

But Tolefree was well aware of the irony of his salutation. He did not mean me to sleep well. Far from it. He deliberately designed to keep me awake two hours at least, and an indefinite further time; for an extraordinary project had grown in his mind in the last few minutes.

I turned into my bedroom, found it princely, with a beautiful fire burning, and prepared for a leisurely toilet. Some of the servants had evidently contrived to attend to their duties in spite of Mr. Catterick, for my kit was laid out in perfect order. As though, even when the most desperate strokes of mortal fate fell upon owners of great houses, the routine of great houses must by no means be disturbed. Though old Burnet was dead, his money still existed, and all this luxury meant old Burnet's money...

I had hardly kicked off my shoes when Tolefree came quickly and quietly into the room and said he would like to smoke a pipe with me.

I motioned him to the armchair by the fire and sat myself on the couch at the foot of the bed. He hoped I wasn't tired – too tired to worry out a thread or two of this tangle? Especially Burnet's purpose in sending for him and camouflaging him. Had I noticed that Burnet wrote the letter with his own hand, instead of dictating it to his secretary? Had I noticed that the secretary was on a very familiar footing with Gillespie? Well, whatever Burnet's purpose was, he meant nobody in the house to know anything of it or anything of Tolefree's identity. Catterick had a theory of that purpose – or he said he had. Catterick said Burnet called in Tolefree in order to trap a dishonest butler. Absurd!

I nodded to this. It did seem absurd.

Perfectly impossible, Tolefree thought. Burnet could do his own butler-trapping very well indeed – as he had shown. So there must have been something else, and it was something urgent – so urgent in fact that Tolefree had not arrived in time. Burnet's message came too late. The danger was already there. Whence had it crept on him? Not from Elford: murders were not committed because masters and butlers fell out about accounts.

Crept on him! Tolefree's phrase made me shiver.

It might have crept on him from the inside or the outside, he said.

"The outside?" I interrupted. "Surely—"

Oh, yes, Tolefree thought, that too was on the cards. He had been scouting round while I waited in the drawing room, and he had come to the conclusion that the outside must be considered a possibility, though it was difficult. There were narrow balconies along the front of the house – high, but under certain conditions attainable. That would have to be calculated.

But if from the inside, what a situation – as Catterick would say. Where, among all the people at Midwood who might have killed Burnet, would Catterick look for the murderer? And when was the murder done? Tolefree had theoretically reduced the time in which it could have been done to a specific five minutes. But Tolefree was puzzled by his own reconstruction. Not an impossible theory, it would have been utterly improbable but for the fact, established by two witnesses, that Burnet was alive at 6.50 when he telephoned the pantry, and that before seven o'clock he was unquestionably dead. Who in the house could have killed him?

Something Tolefree had said months before flashed into my mind: Show him four men, and he would guarantee to say which of them concealed a secret. I turned for a moment away from his ardent gaze. But then, Tolefree's proviso had been that the four men should be unaware of him. In this case, despite Burnet's precautions, everyone at Midwood had become aware of him.

Unspoken thoughts passed between us as we sat facing each other in that beautiful room. There was a chill in the air. Somewhere, within a little distance, in some such room as this, was the murderer of Burnet thinking his unspoken thoughts too?

"But look here, Farrar," said Tolefree, rising and looking down on me, "I didn't come in here to have an endless discussion. Something weighs hard on me. Catterick's as astute as they make the police. I'm surprised he's not thought of it."

"Thought of what?"

"Let's face up to the ugliest possibility. The man who killed Burnet may be in the house now. Catterick knows it. But he doesn't seem to have calculated that if that man is here he will take the first chance that offers of shifting any evidence that can tell against him."

"Evidence!" I exclaimed. "What sort of evidence are you thinking about?"

"I'm not. Only of evidence in general. There must be some. I can only guess *what*. But I do know *where*, Farrar! – that's the point."

"Where, then?"

"In Burnet's room."

I was startled. Catterick had locked up Burnet's room. Presumably he had examined it with a microscope. But looking into Tolefree's eyes I realised that here was more than a surmise. Tolefree knew something.

"I'm going to do a risky thing, Farrar," he said, as if with a sudden determination. "I've no right to do it. I can't drag you into it. But if you cared to take a chance—"

He paused.

I was just a bit too old and wary to be lured into the first adventure that offered. I stalled him off.

"What's the risky thing?" I asked.

"Oh, just an idea I want to test. I suppose you noticed nothing in Burnet's room that would suggest a risk to you? But, no – you looked all about and you didn't see it. I can't tell, of course, whether Catterick saw it. Perhaps. He may even have taken it away. But whether he has or hasn't I feel pretty sure someone else will try to get it. I'm going to try to find out who wants it."

"What is it?"

"A piece of paper – a scrap, a rag of paper. Look! – like this—"

Tolefree took a sheet of writing paper from the table under the window and tore a corner off it. He held up the corner.

"Just like this. You didn't see it?"

"No. But that's not surprising – not to notice a piece of paper in a man's study."

"But you observed that Burnet was a particularly tidy man?"

"He always was."

"Well, this was the only torn scrap to be seen. I had a careful look at it. I could even tell you what was on it. But that's neither here nor there for the moment. The curious thing was the place where it lay – between Burnet's right arm and his body. I think I know what it was. I may be right or wrong. We shall see. Are you game?"

"What – break into Burnet's room?"

I eyed him incredulously.

"Nothing so crude, Farrar. To discover who, if anybody, does break into Burnet's room – or tries to."

"Simply setting a watch, you mean?

"Just that."

Of course I was game for that. But it seemed to me we were bound to have our trouble for nothing. I put the obvious objection – that there was a policeman in the hall who would be bound to hear any noise made in breaking into the room. You didn't commit a burglary like that silently, and Tolefree's potential burglar must be fully aware of the danger. He looked hard at me.

"You forget how silently Burnet was killed," said he, "and if I'm not all at sea the potential burglar will be the murderer himself."

Tolefree was grave, and as he spoke the simple thing began to look risky.

Our doings in the next hour were appropriately furtive. Tolefree, putting his mind into that of the imaginary person he had conjured up, thought the house would first be allowed to go dead. Everyone would be given time to get to bed and to sleep. Towards two, he reckoned...

So we were to feign sleep. Lights out – silence. At half past one we were to mount guard. He left me now to go to his room and change from shoes into bedroom slippers. I switched off my light and followed him. We sat in his room in darkness, save for the little glow from the fire, not even enough to illuminate the dial of a watch. It was the difficulty of reckoning time and the need for consulting a watch that started our train of adventure. About twenty minutes, so far as I could guess, had passed. Tolefree fumbled in his suitcase and pulled out a light dressing-gown which he draped over the reading lamp on his table, intending to make sure of the time under the obscured light. He switched on – and nothing happened.

Tolefree suppressed an exclamation.

"See that?" he whispered. "I never thought of that! Try the switch by the door, Farrar."

But the lights were dead.

"It's time. Come on!"

He softly opened the door. The corridor outside was blacker than the room within.

"I'll go first. Keep your hand on my shoulder."

So we crept along to the staircase. All this part of the house was in utter darkness. Fortunately Tolefree, with this strange theory in his head, had been more observant than I as we came up, and had noted the turn from the wing where we were to have slept into the main corridor and the whereabouts of the staircase. I turned with him. I felt his shoulder dip, and I went down with him. After descending half a dozen steps we involuntarily stopped.

We heard a noise.

Noise was perhaps too strong. Our nerves were strung taut. But there was certainly a sound – not loud, but plain enough. It might have been the closing of a door: a kind of muffed thud. In the pitch darkness we could not judge its direction accurately. It seemed to come from below.

We waited a full minute, hardly breathing. That sound was not repeated. Nor did we hear any other. Tolefree suddenly moved on, keeping close to the wall, feeling for each step as he went. An extraordinary sensation that – creeping through absolute obscurity in a strange house. If Tolefree was right, somewhere else in that darkness someone else was creeping towards the same goal or had already reached it. And Tolefree appeared to be right – or what did the sudden failure of the lighting system betoken? But, again, could its failure have escaped the attention of the policeman at the door? Flights of speculation rushed through me at every stair. The descent seemed endless. Then Tolefree's shoulder rose.

We were in the first-floor corridor that ran past Burnet's room.

He paused a moment; then crawled slowly on. I half guessed and half saw the opening out of the corridor at the head of the great staircase. There was a current of air and a sense of dim light from below which only intensified the darkness where we walked. So that the lighting system had not been put out of action below stairs. Immediately, there came a touch of the ridiculous to ease the tension. The sound of snoring reached us faintly out of the silence: Catterick's sentry slept at his post.

We passed on, Tolefree measuring his stealthy paces. His hand came back and touched my arm; he stopped. We had reached Burnet's door. I felt him bend down, listening. There was nothing.

Nothing? – yes, something – an almost imperceptible squeak. My skin creamed. But it was Tolefree. He had moved. He was turning the handle of the door.

Then, surprisingly, he whispered the words, "It's open!" and in an instant we were inside Burnet's room. Grasping my shaking arm, he stopped immediately, I imagined him soundlessly closing the door. I held my breath. I could not hear Tolefree breathing. We were in the room of the dead, in Stygian darkness, and we did not know whether any other thing lived in that room but ourselves.

I was completely disorientated. Whereabouts lay old Burnet? ... I had no idea what Tolefree would do. Whatever he did must be an improvisation, because he had certainly not expected to find Burnet's room open. What he actually did was to say in a low voice (though it seemed to me, after all that strained silence, like a thunder-clap),

"Hands up!"

At the same moment he flashed a torch round the room. Two seconds were enough to show that no living being was there but ourselves. Tolefree strode across to the place where Burnet lay, and I followed him. The body had been set in order, the arms drawn to the side, and a sheet thrown over it. Burnet was as though in his shroud. Tolefree made the circle of light from his torch flit up and down the hidden shape. He touched nothing, but he pointed to me where at the right side the sheet was ruffled, pulled slightly off the ground.

"We're too late," he whispered, and turned away. Once he flashed the light upon Burnet's writing table. Then he sent the ray along the floor as if to point the way towards the door, and switched off.

"Go back just as quietly," said Tolefree, taking me by the arm.

He had paused by the door; he had silently turned the handle and pulled, when we were almost blinded by a blaze of light in the corridor, where every lamp leapt into being. It was fortunate that Burnet's blue carpet was a thick one, for I staggered back in fright as Tolefree pushed the door closed.

We heard a quick footstep outside. I felt the nervous jerk that Tolefree gave. But in an instant he had opened the door a crack and peered into the corridor.

"Come!" he called to me.

He dashed open the door, no longer trying for silence. We were outside. He pulled the door to with a bang and ran. For half an instant I saw a figure in a long robe at the west end of the corridor, but almost as I looked it had gone. Tolefree was after it, had reached the head of the staircase, when he pulled up in his tracks. The policeman was coming up the stairs three at a time.

"Hello!" he said, planting his big bulk in front of us. "What's the game?"

The rustic constable had transformed himself into a formidably menacing personality as he looked down on us.

"Don't know," said Tolefree. "We're all too late to find out. Didn't you hear the noise?"

"Noise? Of course I heard the noise. What are you doing down here?"

"I mean the noise a few minutes ago," said Tolefree, eyeing him coldly. "But you couldn't have heard it, or you'd have been up in time, constable. It's a pity."

Tolefree's tone brought down the worthy young man's temperature.

"There wasn't any noise but the banging and running I heard this minute—" he began.

"My good fellow," said Tolefree, "I should say no more about it. The noise was enough to bring me and Mr. Farrar down from the floor above – so, well, we'll forget it, don't you think? Better have a look round, hadn't you?"

"Yes, sir, naturally. But you haven't told me – I mean both you gentlemen are dressed, and it's rather late."

Tolefree glanced at his watch. "Quarter to two," said he. "Mr. Farrar and I were talking things over in my room when we heard the bumping about and came down to explore. Then a bang startled us. Somebody's playing tricks, constable. Up to you to find out who."

"Where was the bang from?" he asked.

"Here in the corridor somewhere, we think."

The constable walked past us towards Burnet's room. Tolefree detained me. We stood at the stair head and watched him. He passed Burnet's door with a glance and went on. I sighed and turned to Tolefree. He was staring hard at the closed door nearest to us on our right – Mrs. Burnet's, as I supposed.

"Queer nobody else has—"

Tolefree never finished his muttered sentence. An exclamation from the constable broke in. He was halfway down the corridor stooping over something on the ground. We hurried to him.

"Well, I'm damned!" said Tolefree under his breath.

The constable was pulling at the collar of a man who lay huddled on the floor. It was Peters, the footman.

Eight

Peters lay unconscious, but apparently not wounded. He was in pyjamas, with slippers on his feet. He had been carrying a box of matches, which had flown open and scattered its contents over the carpet.

The constable got down, pulled him over on his back, felt him. He looked up to us.

"Water," said he.

"Try back in your room, Farrar," said Tolefree. "I'll have a look this way."

Passing us, Tolefree strode on into the east wing. I ran back to my own room, found a carafe, and had returned to the constable before Tolefree arrived. I brought also a flask from my bag. The constable drenched the man's face with water and poured a spot of whisky between his teeth. He spluttered, opened his eyes, and said, "Hello!" – then scrambled to his feet and stood unsteadily. His eyes went to the door beside which he had fallen. His face paled, and he shrank back trembling.

At that moment Tolefree appeared.

"Can't find a bathroom—" he began; "but – oh, I see it's all right."

I mention these details because of their strange sequel. Small wonder, of course, that Peters stood shrinking and shivering: he wore only his night-clothes and he had been soused in cold water. But as he stared with goggling eyes at the door of Burnet's bedroom there was something more than sheer physical discomfort in his mien. It came out in the story he told us when we got him to his room. An astonishing but simple and straightforward story: he told it later on when Catterick put him through it, and he stuck to it through thick and thin.

Tolefree had said to the constable as they helped the man up the stairs that led to his quarters,

"Seems to have been no alarm in the house, notwithstanding all the row. Don't you think Mr. Gillespie had better be called?"

And it was I who, following Peter's directions, found Gillespie's room, not far from my own, and turned him out. Other ideas certainly occurred to me about what should also have been done immediately; but something in Tolefree's manner warned me to keep them to myself. So that none of those things had been done – or I thought not – when Peters, huddled in a blanket and sitting on the side of his bed, related his simple story to the four of us standing in front of him – the constable, puzzled and suspicious; Tolefree serious and very alert; myself excited and nervous; Gillespie in his dressing-gown, suddenly awakened, gaping and alarmed.

When the house went quiet shortly after midnight, so Peters said, as Elford was not there to give orders, he shut up downstairs, said good night to the constable in the hall and went to his room. Feeling excited and unable to sleep, he kept his light on and tried to read a book. He could not say exactly how long he read, but he thought it must have been twenty past one or thereabouts when his light went out. At first he thought the bulb had failed. He waggled the switch with no result, then turned over to go to sleep. But the thought suddenly struck him that a fuse might have blown or a wire fused. If the whole lighting system had gone wrong there might be trouble – perhaps fire. Anyhow, he could not rest. He jumped out of bed into his slippers, and tried a switch on the landing. It was dead. He went back for matches, and descended to the first floor. At that landing a door shut off the servants' stairway from the corridor. (This was the baize door which Tolefree had himself secured when he took charge after the discovery of Burnet's death.) Peters passed it and found the main part of the house also in darkness. He knew that on the wall of the corridor almost opposite Burnet's bedroom was a fuse-box through which ran the leads for that wing of the house –

"But not for the west wing?" Tolefree interjected.

No – not for the west wing. There was a corresponding box on the other side of the staircase for that. But at the head of the staircase itself was a master-switch for all the bedroom floors. If, thought Peters, a main fuse had not blown, someone might have accidentally knocked off the switch. What he did was to strike matches and endeavour to see the fuses. As he held the second match over his head and strained his eyes upwards he heard a door open, felt a draught of air, the light was blown out, and a voice said in his ear,

"Peters, what are you doing here?"

His knees gave under him and he knew nothing more till he saw the constable's face close to his and Tolefree and myself standing by.

"The voice? Did you know it?" Tolefree leaned towards him.

"Sir – as I'm a living man, I thought it was Mr. Burnet."

And that, on his quaint oath, was Peters's simple story. He had been frightened to death by what he thought to be the apparition of Burnet – though apparition is not quite the word, perhaps, for a ghost he never saw. Nothing could shake his certainty that as his light went out he heard those words – "Peters, what are you doing here?" He knew now that his imagination had betrayed him into fancying Mr. Burnet stood behind him. The constable's certainty that he had walked in his sleep did not shake him. Nor Mr. Gillespie's suggestion that he had suffered from a morbid feeling about the nearness of his master's dead body: on that he declared that at the moment he was not thinking at all about Mr. Burnet, but only about the fuses in the box above his head.

I waited for any comment Tolefree might make. He made none. Even when the constable went on to produce what to him was convincing proof that Peters was a somnambulist Tolefree held his peace, and I followed his example – though either of us could have disproved the constable's proof in three words. For he disposed of Peters's story thus,

"Must have been sleep-walking, Peters. The lights were never out, old man. You dreamt it all. So, turn in or you'll catch the hell of a cold, and my advice to you is – don't worry, and don't dream again."

He patted a bewildered Peters on the shoulder in fatherly style, and we went our ways. Much ado about nothing, said the constable to us, as we left him at the head of the grand staircase to resume his vigil by the door. If the lights had gone out he would have known it. What alarmed us must have been the bump Peters made when he collapsed.

Gillespie seemed to accept the explanation. Tolefree said nothing, even to me, except, "We've had enough for one night, Farrar. See you tomorrow."

Catterick was at Midwood before we met at breakfast on the Sunday morning, and had heard all about the disturbance in the small hours. He seemed to take remarkably little notice of the story he had heard from Peters – too little, as I thought, of the fact that so much disturbance had taken place without arousing his sentinel below. But, as Tolefree said, you couldn't be sure what was passing under the Inspector's grizzled thatch. He did not bother at all about us, but occupied the day in further examinations of all the people who had been above stairs when Burnet was murdered. Gillespie went off in a car to meet his sister. I should have gone home to London but for Catterick's insistence that everyone who was in the house on Saturday night might be wanted at the inquest which he had arranged for Monday.

Tolefree and I were thus left curiously to ourselves. Neither Cossor nor Annesty appeared, nor Denley; Mrs. Burnet was invisible. We understood that Catterick kept them all at his hand within call of Denley's office, where he was holding his investigation. Walking with Tolefree before lunch, through the park of Midwood and into the country beyond, I vaguely saw, in this brisk November morning, what a place it was that old Burnet had acquired; but only vaguely, for scenery could hardly get at my consciousness through Tolefree's exciting talk.

"Well, what about it, Farrar?" he said, as soon as we were clear of the house.

"I make nothing of it," I told him, "except that the constable's a fool and Catterick's not quite so smart as I thought."

"Don't be so certain about Catterick. I'm not."

"But he seems to accept the constable's silly notion."

"Seems is the word. And remember, Farrar, we haven't quite helped him, have we?"

That was true. For some reason unrevealed up to then, Tolefree had warned me to say nothing of our escapade. For all Catterick knew, we told the constable the whole truth. He merely understood that we were disturbed by a noise and were looking for its cause when the constable came upon us.

"Ticklish thing – butting in on a police inquiry," Tolefree said. "We've done no harm. So let's leave Catterick to run his own show. But I mean to discover why Burnet called me in. I think I'm entitled to that, don't you? And what's the odds that when I've found that out I'll be as close to the truth about Burnet's death as ever Catterick is likely to get?"

I thought the odds were narrow.

"Evens!" Tolefree exclaimed. "Dam' clever, that trick with the lights. And daring! – perhaps I'm glad we were five minutes too late. What do you think, Farrar?"

"You mean – we'd have been in danger?"

"Perhaps. Don't know. It was desperate going for him. If we'd caught him! But, even if he'd put us out, he couldn't have escaped. Here's a queer thing, Farrar! The man who murdered Burnet is only safe so long as he don't try to escape. See it? He's there – trapped! Let him wink an eyelid or move a foot and he gives himself away. That's old Catterick's game – detaining Elford. Just to induce the real man to make some move. They're a well-matched pair, old Catterick and the man that killed Burnet."

We walked in silence for a few minutes. There was one thing I had to ask Tolefree, and I put it to him now.

"You got out of Burnet's room in front of me, Tolefree. Did you recognise the man in the corridor?"

"Ah! – I wasn't sure if you saw him. Well — ?"

"Oh," said I, "quite impossible for me to recognise him. I caught sight of him perhaps for half a second, just as he flew round the corner. All I could actually see was a man in a dressing-gown. But you? – you had a longer look at him."

"An instant longer – but he was almost away when I opened the door. I'll answer your question, Farrar. I thought I knew him – but now I'm not sure. Something else happened—"

"It wasn't Gillespie?" I asked.

"No – if there's one thing I feel certain about it's – not Gillespie. I thought it was that secretary bird – what's he called? – Denley."

"Good Lord!"

"But as I told you, something happened, and I'm not sure. I couldn't swear to him. You didn't remark that I was rather a long time trying to find a glass of water?"

I had not remarked on it; but now I realised that he was – all the time it took me to go to my room and back, and, added to that, all the time it took the constable to bring Peters round.

"I was," said Tolefree. "In fact, I never looked for a glass of water at all. I wanted to make sure of something. I wanted to know whether anyone was awake in that wing of the house, Farrar – anybody up and dressed. I wanted to see the face of anyone I could find there. I did find something – very extraordinary, and I don't know what to make of it."

He hunched his shoulders.

"It's so extraordinary I can hardly believe it. Four bedrooms up there on the second floor of the east wing, exact replica of the place where we are in the west wing. Two of the rooms unoccupied. The other two – Cossor and Annesty. I looked into all of 'em. First an empty room – bed unmade. I flashed the torch around it. Next, a room like yours, with a fire just burning. I couldn't see anything by the firelight. I decided to use the torch. If I woke up anybody there was a good excuse – the trouble down below. I just flashed it across the bed: Annesty, curled up asleep. He didn't move. I slipped out. Next room to him – empty. Room across the corridor – fire dead, but warm. I flashed again. Corresponding room to mine. Nobody in it. Bed not touched. I switched on the light. On the writing table, a pouch of papers and some documents lying there. On the floor, Cossor's suitcase and travelling trunk – marked 'J.H.C.' – beside his walking shoes. But nowhere any Cossor. I switched off and came down. So now!"

"Good heaven, Tolefree! You don't think—"

I pulled up in the road to stare at him.

"I think a devil of a lot, Farrar – but so far, my dear fellow, thinking's got me nowhere."

Nine

Cossor! But it was so grotesque that I stood there in the road gaping at Tolefree as though he had taken leave of his senses.

Cossor – the high and mighty, the famous King's Counsel, ornament of the Bar, whose only business with murderers was to get them hanged. Cossor!

"It's unbelievable, Tolefree," I said.

"What is?"

"That Cossor—"

I stuttered – that Cossor should be anywhere but in his bed asleep at that time of night – at any rate that Cossor had been about when any of those things happened and had not disclosed himself.

"You don't doubt my word – and I don't doubt my eyes," declared Tolefree. "All I say is that while you were down there bringing Peters round Cossor was not in his room or anywhere in that wing of the house. That's all I say. But it raises the very devil of a question! Could it have been Cossor who did the scared rabbit act along the corridor? Cossor or the secretary? Till that's settled... you see?"

But the idea that Cossor could possibly be anything else than a pattern of propriety – and a rather starched propriety at that – it was grotesque. Cossor acting the scared rabbit! But Tolefree stuck to his text: Cossor's room was empty. Why? And, Cossor not being in his room, where would Cossor be at half past one in the morning? Could I answer that?

I put up theories to have them knocked down one after the other.

"He might have been working on those papers when the light failed and have gone to explore," I ventured.

That, said Tolefree, might be a very good explanation of Cossor, or of Denley either – but for that scamper along the corridor, and but for the fact that neither of them turned up afterwards. And what about Peters?

"Either of them might very well have challenged and frightened Peters," said I, "seeing him sneaking about with matches—"

Tolefree shook his head. If either of them had challenged Peters innocently, and frightened Peters into a fit, would he have left Peters there unconscious? Besides, I must have forgotten that someone had certainly been in Burnet's room. The unlocked door proved that.

"I suppose you don't suggest," he said, "that we only dreamed we went into Burnet's room?"

"No – of course I don't, Tolefree."

"Well, then, what d'you make of this? I played early bird this morning, and here's my worm: someone had locked that door! Some time in the night – afterwards."

"Then, old Catterick—" I exclaimed. "Catterick will never know anybody had visited the room – unless you tell him."

"Can't say, Farrar. Old Catterick keeps his own counsel. He may or he mayn't see the two or three things we saw – or at any rate I saw. But let's stick to Cossor. Try to imagine what happened in the few minutes before and after the lights went out. Somebody must have crept quietly to the master switch at the head of the stairs and switched off. Now! He's got the darkness he wants. For a few uncertain minutes. He can't be disturbed till someone switches on the lights again. But that may happen soon. So he hurries. A key to Burnet's room. He's there. He looks for what he wants. He either finds it or he doesn't: I don't know. But the search takes him just the time it took us to get half-way down the stairs – no longer. You remember the thud we heard? Peters falling. Then he gets rattled. He hides to make sure whether anyone has heard. Probably round a corner of the corridor. So he doesn't see us or know anything of us. At least, I think he doesn't. But when he steals back to lock the door, then he either hears us in Burnet's room or sees our light. He gets the wind up. The question is: was it he who switched on the lights and ran for it?"

I followed Tolefree's argument closely.

"Why should he switch on the lights?" I objected.

"Ah – now you have me. It's exactly what I can't understand, Farrar, why the lights were secretly switched on. Do you think by any chance the man who did it wanted to see who we were?"

"By gosh! And if he did see—"

"As he very well may have done when that blunder-headed policeman held us up—"

"By gosh, yes!"

"And if he did see us, I'm up against a tougher job than if he didn't – that's all. But one thing's got me beat beyond all the rest. Has it struck you? That policeman galumphing upstairs like a mad elephant and shouting challenges at us, and the banging of the door, and the running – did you notice that all the uproar disturbed nobody?"

The point had not occurred to me.

"If Cossor was anywhere near," said I, "and if you're right in suspecting that Cossor... well, you wouldn't expect him to show up? Or Denley either if it was Denley we saw running. Would you?"

"No – but it brings them jolly well into the picture, doesn't it? Denley's room, next to his office, is on that floor, just under ours. He must be one of the Seven Sleepers if the row didn't wake him. But that's not what I mean. Did you realise that we weren't five yards from Mrs. Burnet's room?"

"But – good Lord! Tolefree – you don't suggest that she—"

"Suggesting nothing," he answered shortly. "Just remarking. That Mrs. Burnet was five yards away when we all started to wake the dead, and her maid in the room next to her. So you will observe that, if we rule out Gillespie and Annesty, who were in bed asleep at some distance in opposite directions, there were four people within earshot. Cossor – wherever Cossor was, he was wide awake. Denley – close by. Mrs. Burnet and her maid – closer still. And yet, not one of 'em—"

Tolefree shrugged himself.

"That's the strangest thing in the whole performance, and it causes you to think hard."

It did. But the thoughts were too fantastic to reconcile with any probable truth. I walked silently by Tolefree's side for some minutes, picturing the sequence he had conjured up. A possibility occurred to me in a flash.

"Tolefree!" I exclaimed.

"Brain storm?" He smiled.

"Maybe. Look here! – we're searching for a murderer, aren't we? We don't want to play about with Mrs. Burnet or her maid. They couldn't—"

"Couldn't have done that beastly job? Of course not. What about it?"

"Or Cossor either. A man like that! Why, Tolefree, it's an outrage to think of him – like that."

"Hm – well?"

"Or Denley – he don't seem to me to be the type."

"Nor to me. But then – unfortunately, you know, there's a corpse. You can't dismiss the corpse, can you? What's the great idea?"

"Elford—"

"My dear Farrar! Elford was safe in the lock-up. Whoever burgled Burnet's room last night, it wasn't Elford."

"Naturally not. But Peters – he was Elford's understudy, next in the hierarchy, so to speak. If Peters was in Elford's confidence, or under Elford's thumb, couldn't you imagine—"

It was now Tolefree's turn to stop and stare.

"You could," I insisted. "It's feasible. Suppose Peters was in league with Elford. I don't know how. But he might be. Suppose it. He's had plenty of time to fix up a plan with Elford to get into the room at night and take whatever Elford wanted. They'd been together on guard, but they couldn't go into the room then. It would have been dangerous – too many people about. But at night, when it was all quiet—"

"Peters has got to be a mighty smart chap to bring this off. But go on."

"Well – I don't know, Tolefree. He knows the house blind-fold, of course. He can steal down unheard in his slippers and switch off the lights. Then all the rest follows as you say."

"Until Mr. Peters hears the ghost of Burnet whispering in his ear and goes off to bye-bye on the carpet? My dear Farrar—" Tolefree expostulated.

"Not at all. Until Cossor, disturbed at his work by the failure of the light, goes out to see what's the matter, and comes upon Peters lighting matches in the corridor and says, 'Peters, what are you doing here?' And, Peters's nerves not being equal to the strain, he conks out."

Tolefree walked on, cogitating.

"The brainstorm's only a ripple after all," said he. "Why should Peters light matches to look at a fuse-box when he knew very well why the lights were off – having switched them off himself? He did carry matches, you know. Why should he even carry matches?"

"If he hadn't a torch – and he hadn't – he must have wanted light for a moment or so in Burnet's study, mustn't he?"

"Hm – yes. But why did he light one in the corridor when his dearest wish was that no one should know he was there?"

"Don't know. But he did. Suppose he heard Cossor's footstep and was – well, just afraid of the dark?"

"Aren't we supposing him to be the kind of bold and dare-devil flunky who can steal in the dark into a room with a corpse to do a bit of burgling?"

"Certainly there's that, Tolefree. But nerves are queer – you never know when even a footman's nerves will give out."

"True; you don't." Tolefree smiled. "We won't turn on the ironical tap, will we, Farrar? I've got two or, let me see, three difficulties about this hunch of yours. Two of them mechanical. I don't know how you get rid of Cossor after he's frightened Peters into fits. Where is he?"

"Don't you think he may have heard us? Suppose he was fumbling about in the dark there with Peters when we came along? Even the tiny noise we made opening Burnet's door—"

"Ah – well, perhaps. But if Cossor is on the square and merely looking for a reason for the failure of lights, won't the discovery that people are prowling about there in the dark make him raise an alarm first thing?"

I could find no answer to this.

"Second mechanical difficulty – if Peters got into Burnet's room he must have had a key. What became of it?"

"It might very well have fallen anywhere unnoticed."

"You think so? Well, Farrar, the third difficulty is psychological. I don't think Peters capable of this, and nothing will make me think so. I admit your brainwave brings in a new idea or two – but I can't fit Peters into them. I've got a light on the affair that you don't possess. Here it is. Let's stand in this gateway."

One of the crucial bits of evidence in the Midwood affair will always be associated in my mind with a landscape – the misty, November scene from a five-barred gate looking across the meadows towards the grey mass of trees by Burnet's place. Tolefree leaned against the gate, took his notebook and pencil, and made a hasty drawing. He passed the book to me. This is what he had drawn:

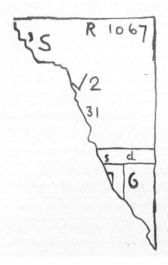

"I told you I knew what was on the corner of paper on the floor by Burnet's body. I memorised that, Farrar. Not much to remember. Not much to go on. But that's what Peters wanted, or Elford wanted, if you are right. Now why should Peters or Elford want that?"

"What is it?"

"You see what it is – the corner of a bill."

I handed the notebook back to him.

"Aren't you putting rather a lot on that?" I asked. "A mere scrap – perhaps a bit of a tradesman's account – one of those things Burnet had been considering with Elford in the morning—"

"Maybe. But I think not. If you were right, the scrap would probably still be there – on the floor or in the wastepaper basket. If I'm right, either Catterick has taken it and sees in it what I see. Or it was taken by the person who went there last night. You see what we've got to believe – if I'm right? That scrap is important for what's not on it. The sheet from which it was torn – that's the thing. I think that sheet was an hotel bill. I think Burnet held it in his hand just before he was killed, that the rest of it was grabbed away from him, and that he dropped the scrap as he fell."

"An hotel bill! What makes you think it was an hotel bill?"

"It just looked like that. Good, smooth, creamlaid paper. Narrow-spaced blue lines. Red-ruling for cash. Fine quality printing. Series numbering. Automatic cash entry. The evidence of the lettering itself. An hotel, somewhere in the W2 postal district which keeps its accounts with an automatic printer. It's perfectly simple. Give me a directory and a taxi and I guarantee to discover it in one morning."

"But an hotel bill, Tolefree! Why should Burnet be killed for an hotel bill?"

"Don't know, Farrar. But I can imagine several reasons. Can't you think of reasons why persons would not like to have other persons in possession of their hotel bills?"

"You mean that this wasn't Burnet's own hotel bill, but—"

I checked at the horrible suggestion that Tolefree conjured up.

"Don't know that I mean anything in particular," said he; "but Burnet must have had a reason for asking me down to Midwood, mustn't he? What I've been wondering is whether he wanted to show me *that*."

Ten

It was a horrible suggestion.

So loathsome that I conceived a momentary distaste for Tolefree who had put it into my head. After the first stare of horror and surprise had passed between us, we turned to walk back in silence.

Old Burnet come to this! Old Burnet the victim of a beastly intrigue – calling in a detective to pry into an intrigue – about to violate his own sanctity – killed because he had suspected an intrigue! A pretty ending this to old Burnet's belated romance and his sudden translation from a busy, happy, simple City life into the queer hybrid world of Midwood. The place seemed sinister now – as if itself had leered while it trapped this alien upstart. What business had old Burnet to be living in a costly palace with an extravagant queen, entertaining costly eminences like Cossor, patronising costly artists like Annesty, suffering costly and inefficient butlers like Elford? – old Burnet who knew all about ships and trade but nothing about society or art, who had made a big fortune by careful management of the things he knew with the help of a staff that worked like a perfect machine?

A pretty ending.

I looked askance at Tolefree. He had built up the foundation for this theory so diabolically, pretending it was but a theory, and leaving no way of escape from it. Insinuating things into my mind one after the other, and leading up to the beastly solution of which he seemed so confident. Cossor; Mrs. Burnet; that silent corridor; the door that stayed shut while we made noise to wake the dead – all confirming the thing that was at the back of his mind. Other things began to worm into my memory. The obvious deflation of Burnet's hopes and dreams during the last year or two. His sort of wistful comeback. What I had thought to be merely disillusionment with a new way of life, a nostalgia for the old one. Did it all mean this – as Tolefree hinted without putting it into words – that Burnet was being betrayed and knew it, and had set a trap for his betrayer – too late?

The grey day seemed greyer and colder. I put only one question to Tolefree while we made our way back through the park.

"Are you going to put this up to Catterick, Tolefree?"

"Not now," said he. "Perhaps not at all. There's a lot to fill in, isn't there? I want to meet Cossor. And Mrs. Burnet. I want to explore the secretary's mind. And as soon as Catterick releases us, I'm going to find that hotel. Then I'll decide what to tell him – if anything."

Catterick seemed pretty satisfied with himself. We found when we reached Midwood that he had given complete liberty to everyone, finished his investigations for the time and gone away. He did not care what anybody did or where anybody went so long as all who were in the house on Saturday evening attended at three o'clock the next afternoon for the inquest. Gillespie and Annesty were together in the hall. Cossor had departed. He was engaged in a case in the King's Bench on Monday morning and had arranged with Catterick that if the coroner thought his evidence necessary he should be advised in time to motor down. Catterick, with the deference due to his eminence, promised that he should not be needlessly disturbed. He thought, so Gillespie said, that so far as the discovery of the body was concerned Annesty's evidence might be enough.

Tolefree, with a significant glance to me, began his secret inquisition at once.

"Mr. Cossor an old friend of Mr. Burnet?" he asked, taking the cigarette that Annesty offered him.

"Not very," Gillespie said. "Cossor is a cousin of Alison's. That's how."

"Ah, yes, I see. Mrs. Burnet was a Miss Cossor?"

"No," said I; "a Miss Orton, wasn't it?"

"Yes – distaff connection with Cossor. They did say, years ago—"

Gillespie stopped. Tolefree made no sign of curiosity. The rest were silent. Gillespie had to fill the blank somehow.

"I ought not to be chopping gossip. But it was said that years ago people thought of a match between Alison and Cossor."

"Oh, gossip—" Tolefree shrugged, as though he would pass the topic.

"More than gossip, Gillespie," young Annesty put in. "No secret about it. Your uncle told me himself."

"The devil he did?" exclaimed Gillespie. "He never told me anything about it."

"Well, I was saying how I admired Cossor and often went to hear him in court, because he's just the perfect stage counsel, and one couldn't have a better model. And then he mentioned that Cossor was Mrs. Burnet's cousin and might have been her husband but for some fuss in the family – objection to marriage of cousins, or something."

The topic passed. Tolefree, except for his first question, took no part in the talk, and seemed indifferent. But I could almost see through his coat to that page of his notebook where he had written the few words remembered from a scrap of paper, and I shuddered as I glanced up the grand staircase towards that silent corridor.

A small dinner party followed a dull day. Gillespie and Denley went off to see Miss Gillespie in the quarters they had found for her in the village. We yawned through the meal with Annesty and lounged in the drawing room afterwards.

"Coming for a breather before bedtime, Farrar?"

Tolefree threw down the paper he was reading and stretched himself. I got up.

"You care for a turn, Mr. Annesty?" Tolefree asked.

Annesty looked up out of his book, and smiled a refusal from the depths of his armchair.

"Nothing so spartan for me," he said. "If you don't mind? November nights in the country—" (he pretended to shiver) "well, this'll do for me till I can persuade myself upstairs."

We left him.

"Not sorry he didn't come," said Tolefree, as we moved along the terrace. "Had to ask him. But now's our chance – no Cossor, no Catterick. Only you and me and a ladder. Take me?"

"Hanged if I do," I answered. "What ladder? And why a ladder?"

"What ladder? A light, handy one belonging to the gardener. I located it when I was doing a prowl this afternoon. Why a ladder? My dear Farrar – you must have noticed that it's impossible to get up to that balcony without a ladder, but quite easy if you've got one."

Such was the prelude to one of the most bizarre of all our adventures at Midwood. Tolefree had a "hunch," so he called it, that Catterick could have given no more than a superficial look at the balcony outside Burnet's study and its relation to other balconies on that wall of the house, and he now proposed to discover whether it had anything to tell us about the crime. When he left me in the drawing room on the Saturday night waiting for Catterick, he made as close an inspection as the light allowed of the south front, and the idea occurred to him that the balcony might count for something. That afternoon he had studied the question at leisure. Eight windows pierced the wall on the first floor. Counting from the West, left to right, they were (1) window of the maid's room; (2) window of Mrs. Burnet's bedroom; (3 and 4) windows of Mrs. Burnet's boudoir; (5 and 6) windows of Burnet's study; (7) window of Burnet's bedroom; (8) window of Burnet's dressing-room. In the corridor on the inner side of these rooms were only four doors because the maid's room intercommunicated with Mrs. Burnet's, and Burnet's study with his bedroom.

Outside eight windows were four narrow balconies of stone with rather graceful rails and copings. Each joined two windows and extended a little distance on either side of them. Thus there was a balcony outside Mrs. Burnet's two rooms, a second in front of her boudoir, a third outside Burnet's study, and a fourth before the windows of his bedroom and dressing-room. All overhung the terrace along the south side of the house.

These dispositions had been vaguely in my mind. Now, as we walked the terrace talking in low tones, Tolefree made them clear, and unfolded the idea that had come to him. At first I deduced from his talk of ladders and ease of access that he was speculating about an attack on Burnet by someone who reached his room that way; and there was a sense of relief in the thought. But he soon brought me back to realities. How the thing could be explained, he pointed out, if the man who killed Burnet was an agile fellow able to take a four-foot stride! He had measured off the space that separated the balconies. There was exactly four feet between the copings of the two central ones. It was, he said with a grisly humour, as if the architect had designed the place for convenience in the killing of Burnet!

I began the kind of protest I had made in the morning: Horrible... grotesque... unbelievable...

Tolefree became impatient.

"All right, Farrar," said he, "if it's not true we won't believe it. But why the deuce do you balk at trying to discover the truth? Even if the man who killed Burnet is an eminent K.C., or any other sort of surprising and unprecedented murderer, we've got to face up to it, haven't we? I should like your help in this job; but if you don't care about it I'll go on and do it myself."

Five minutes afterwards I was carrying one end of a short ladder which we found hanging on a wall of the kitchen garden, and presently helping Tolefree to raise it against the balcony outside Burnet's study.

The house was dark and silent. In the cloudy night we could just see the mass of the stonework above us. I could hardly make out Tolefree's form as he went up. My job was to keep watch and give warning if need arose. I stood holding the ladder by a rung and steadying it with one foot at the bottom. There was not much danger of a surprise, for the servants were away on the other side of the house, Gillespie and Denley had not returned, and Annesty was either still deep in his armchair or gone to bed. The only persons in our neighbourhood, Mrs. Burnet and her maid, were not likely to be aroused by any little noise we made. Still, the remote possibility of a surprise kept me on wires...

Tolefree had climbed over the parapet. I could not see him, and he moved so silently that I heard nothing. Till his signal came – a little excited "Hist!" I saw a glow for a moment against the window; it disappeared. "Hist! Coming down," said Tolefree in a whisper. The next instant he had slid down. "Quick! Get the ladder away. Drop it here. Lie doggo!" This in my ear. We lowered it to the ground. "This way!" he whispered. "Not a sound!" – and he pulled me a few steps to the left. We stood against the wall of the house under the balcony of the boudoir.

There was a click, as of a latch above us. A whispered word followed immediately.

"Ned!—"

I held my breath.

"Is that you, Ned?"

Silence, a sigh, another click, and the noise of a bolt pushed home.

Tolefree kept a grip on my arm for what seemed an age after the shooting of the bolt, my heart drumming hard all the time. At last he whispered, "Now – quietly!" We stole the few paces to the spot where we had dropped the ladder, took it back to its place, and found our way silently to the hall door.

In a tremble of consternation, I wanted to go straight up to my room. Tolefree said in a whisper that Annesty would think it strange if we did not say good night. He walked into the drawing room and I stood at the door. Annesty looked up from his book with a yawn and a smile.

"What's it like outside?" said he. "Had any adventures? You look scared, Mr. Farrar."

His smile had changed to a stare of surprise. Tolefree said something about coming into a blaze of light out of pitch-darkness and threw him a goodnight. Then we both turned away.

I went into Tolefree's room with him. He fished a flask out of his bag and gave me a nip of whisky.

"Well?" he said. "What about it now? A rumpus like the Day of Judgment in the corridor at two in the morning won't disturb the lady's slumbers, but let a mouse step on the gravel outside and she's there asking for Ned! What about it, Farrar?"

Eleven

ON Monday morning, thirty-six hours after Burnet's death, Tolefree put what seemed a staggeringly impertinent question to Gillespie. It was a lovely morning, gilded by a burst of rare November sunshine. As we strolled on the terrace for the first cigarette after breakfast, I was admiring the loveliness of the lawn, across which two wide-spreading cedars cast long shadows. Tolefree's words brought my eyes round to him in indignant astonishment.

"Of course," he was saying to Gillespie, "we shan't know the details of your uncle's will till after he's buried; but do you happen to know, Mr. Gillespie, whether he's made you his heir?"

A cool youth! The question took him off his guard for a moment. He paused in his walk and stared hard at Tolefree. Then he said, very deliberately,

"If you think me a possible runner for the murder stakes, Mr. Tolefree, you can cut it out. Nothing doing. You've only got to wait for the funeral and then you'll know what my uncle's done with his money."

Tolefree took the rebuff just as coolly. He stood facing the young man gazing straight into his eyes, and made no rejoinder for a perceptible second or two. Then he said,

"*Cave!* Later on... Here's Mr. Annesty."

Annesty had come round the corner of the house and approached us.

"Good morning, Gillespie," said he, nodding to us all. "Have you asked Mr. Tolefree?"

"No," Gillespie answered, shortly. "Mr. Tolefree's been asking me."

The newcomer sensed some strain in the air. He raised his eyebrows as his glance passed between us. He turned to me with some remark about the morning and we walked on in an uneasy bunch. Tolefree rescued the peace.

"My questions were idle pastimes, Mr. Annesty," said he. "But yours – was there anything — ?"

"What d'you think, Gillespie? Shall I put it to him?"

"As you please. If you want his advice—"

Gillespie almost shrugged, as if to suggest that his opinion at that moment of Tolefree's advice about anything was low.

Annesty, apparently suffering some discomfort, took a few paces in silence. His clean-cut, expressive face was puzzled. At last he said,

"Well, I've got to have somebody's advice. Perhaps you'll all three help. I was asking Gillespie last night about the evidence at the inquest – how far one ought to go – I mean by way of volunteering information."

"Why," said Tolefree, "only one piece of advice is wanted there. If it's information with any bearing on the death of Mr. Burnet, you're bound to produce it. You'll be sworn to tell the whole truth, you know."

"Naturally. Though I've never yet given evidence in a court, one understands in a general way. Only it's not quite so simple as that. There's a thing that doesn't seem to me to have any bearing on the crime, and still I don't know whether I ought to mention it. If I don't and it comes out afterwards, people will say, 'What an extraordinary thing for a man like Burnet to do!' And they'll want to know why I said nothing of it."

"Extraordinary thing?" Tolefree echoed.

"Yes: I suppose it must look an extraordinary thing. I'll tell you. I think I said last night I seemed to have been the last person who spoke to Mr. Burnet, and that we were then discussing a favour he was doing for me."

"By the way," Tolefree interrupted, "had you known Mr. Burnet long?"

"About six months – perhaps more. Yes, it was in the Spring I met him; let me see, April..."

Annesty stopped and looked at Gillespie.

"Think I should go on, Gillespie?" he asked.

"Don't see how you can avoid it now."

Gillespie's face was a cloud.

"It's this that makes it so difficult, Mr. Tolefree," said Annesty. "When I told Gillespie last night, I was astonished to find that he knew nothing about it – or anybody else in the family. I first met Mr. Burnet one night at supper at the Wigwam—"

"Wigwam?" Tolefree looked startled. "Rather notorious night club, wasn't it?"

"It became so. But anyhow 'twas pretty popular among people in our crowd before they closed it down, and you know how all sorts get attracted to such a joint. So, as far as I was concerned, it was no surprise to find a man like Mr. Burnet there. I just blew in that night, sat down next to a fellow I knew, and took no special notice of anyone till I got into talking with Mr. Burnet across the table and found him interested in what I'd been saying about a production scheme—"

"Production?" said Tolefree.

"Yes – a rather new idea in revue I had on my mind."

"Old Burnet!" I exclaimed. "Interested in a revue? Why—"

"Well – there you are," said Annesty. "You're startled past belief, and so was Gillespie. From your point of view it was an extraordinary thing."

"Was he — ?" I began, and checked the question for very shame. A miserable memory had come to me.

"Was he sozzled, do you mean? Why – no, Mr. Farrar. Hardly even exhilarated – just interested. I don't mean specially in me

– I'm not such a jackass as that. No – in the milieu. It was new to him, obviously – and stimulating."

That nasty recollection, of a night in the Spring when Burnet turned up late at my rooms in Manchester Square, recorded my sole experience of anything irregular in Burnet's conduct. But Annesty's tale showed that it was not an isolated affair. Annesty had been keeping something back, but when he resumed the tale he rushed ahead.

"Anyhow," said he, "Mr. Burnet was a man who liked to have his own way. And having got his teeth into this he made me undertake to see him about it later on. So one thing led to another. I had a notion of negotiating for a season at the Odeon. He encouraged me to put feelers round on that. I couldn't get far without money. Then, three weeks ago, he astonished me by offering to advance a thousand pounds for preliminary expenses – of course on the understanding that it was a debt to him against a possible success."

"Good Lord!" cried Tolefree. "You've taken me out of my depth, Mr. Annesty. You'd no knowledge of any such Burnet as this, Farrar?"

"A thousand pounds!" I exclaimed. "Why, I knew Burnet for an open-handed giver – but—"

"Quite so," said Annesty quietly. "You see my difficulty, don't you? I never asked him for a thousand pounds. Shouldn't have had the cheek." He smiled. "He insisted on knowing how much it would cost to bring things to a head before the New Year, and I just threw out a figure at a guess. There wasn't a more astonished man in London than this one when he quietly said he'd provide the money and told me to get on with it. Now – ought I to drag all this out?"

Tolefree did not answer at once. We had paced the terrace from end to end before he said,

"This isn't all, of course, Mr. Annesty."

"No – I'm sorry to say it isn't."

"Your interviews with Mr. Burnet took place in London, I suppose?"

"Yes, at his office."

"And you met Mr. Gillespie there?"

"Yes – once. He called in Gillespie to introduce us."

"That was when he arranged about the advance for expenses?"

"Yes, the very day. He called in Gillespie, and he said a curious thing – you remember, Gillespie?"

"Quite well," said Gillespie. "He said, 'This is Mr. Annesty. I want you to know him. You'll probably see more of him."

"And no doubt," Tolefree went on, "you were invited down to Midwood for this weekend to have the rest of the story made known to you – I mean, why Mr. Burnet, who'd never had anything to do with theatres in his life, was now prepared to risk the large sums of money which he probably would have risked if he'd lived."

Annesty assented.

"And was that what you talked about on Saturday afternoon?"

"It was."

Tolefree waited. Annesty walked on, brow pursed, silent.

"Have you told Mr. Gillespie what you haven't told us now?"

"Yes – Gillespie knows the whole thing."

He evidently meant to say no more except at Gillespie's bidding, and Gillespie was in a black mood.

"You perceive that any advice I could give would be useless unless I knew the whole story," said Tolefree.

"Get it all off your chest, Annesty." Gillespie jerked out the permission. "You've gone too far to keep anything back."

"Well then – Saturday afternoon we had a curious talk. He hemmed and hawed a lot and wasn't at ease. Something he couldn't quite get out. But he managed to let me know that his support was conditional. There was a lady. He was interested in her. She was one of the young talents that had never had a chance. And so on. You know the sort of thing. Or if you don't I do. So he was to nominate the leading lady. That was the meaning of it all."

Gillespie, both hands plunged into his pockets, walked along beside me frowning at the ground. I imagine I was gaping with mouth wide open. Tolefree seemed to be absorbing every syllable and tone.

"And you?" he said.

"Well, that's where I break off," said Annesty. "I told him I'd have to think about it."

"Because you knew the lady?"

Annesty turned quickly to him.

"Why, no!" he exclaimed. "Because I didn't know the lady and he wouldn't mention her name until I'd given him what he wanted. That was the whole thing. It was why I left him when I did. And I haven't the slightest doubt that when he sent for me he'd made up his mind to tell me who it was. That's how I figure it out. He'd thought it over and persuaded himself that it was only reasonable I should know what I was promising. Well – that was all. You know what happened."

"But," said Tolefree, "although he didn't tell you, Mr. Annesty, you had no doubt who the lady was?"

"What makes you think that? No – I hadn't the faintest."

"Strange! – you in the profession. A rich man, night clubs, stage-doors, all that sort of thing. One would have thought it must be common gossip."

"No, sir. I saw Mr. Burnet at a night club only that once. I never heard of him at a stage door. Until Saturday he was to me just a capitalist with an idea that he'd like a new sort of flutter."

"Flutter! Old Burnet have a flutter?" I almost laughed at the incongruous picture.

"Well, there you are! Exactly what I thought," said Annesty. "Even now, you can hardly believe it. And the question I want answered is whether I ought to trot all this out at the inquest."

"Just one moment." Tolefree stepped along musing. "Mr. Burnet was with a lady when you saw him at the Wigwam?"

"Any particular lady? No. There was a mob. I can't even recall who they were. Anybody. You see, the thing made no impression on me then, except that Mr. Burnet himself was keen or seemed keen on my idea – and that was remarkable enough!" he said, with a little laugh. "People aren't usually keen on my ideas. I could hardly believe I was awake when, going out, he made an appointment for me in the City and gave me his office address."

"I don't know what you mean to say, Tolefree." Gillespie stopped and we stood round him. "But I don't see what all this has to do with my uncle's death, and I can't believe it's necessary to drag – to soil – to wash dirty linen in public. Uncle Wellington is dead and whatever it meant, all this is dead with him. Why resurrect it?"

There was pain in Gillespie's voice and eyes. He had been fond of Burnet.

"You've said it exactly, Mr. Gillespie," Tolefree replied. "All that matters to coroner or police is to find who killed Mr. Burnet, and as he certainly wasn't killed by an anonymous lady in whom he had an interest – which may, by the way, have been perfectly clean and legitimate – if Mr. Annesty will take my advice, these episodes will be known to none except us four."

It was not what I had expected Tolefree to say. But I shared in the relief which the two young men sighed.

"Thanks," said Gillespie.

"That straightens it out," said Annesty.

But Tolefree had not quite done. He remarked to Annesty that Catterick was "pretty cute." Had Annesty given him any hint which might suggest questions on his relations with Burnet?

Only, said Annesty, to this extent: that he had naturally mentioned Burnet's generosity to him, and that they were talking over theatrical business during the afternoon. But Catterick was all for the details of what happened on Saturday afternoon – talked round and round it, especially as to everybody's whereabouts and as to whom he saw at any given moment. Worried times and positions over and over again. Made notes of everything.

"I've no business to ask," said Tolefree. "But was he particularly curious about anyone person?"

"Yes, he was."

All of us looked hard at him when he said those three words and stopped.

"You don't care to say whom?"

Annesty made an impatient little gesture.

"I don't suppose it matters."

"It was Denley."

"Denley!"

Both Tolefree and I echoed him in the same instant. Gillespie laughed out.

"Jack Denley? He's worrying about Jack Denley?"

"Why, the man's a born fool."

"I daresay, Gillespie. But that's what he did. When had I seen Denley? Where was Denley? When did he come on the scene? And where did he come from? Over and over again. Couldn't help noticing it."

Tolefree whistled. We turned into the house.

Twelve

"Incredible? I should never have expected to hear a man who'd lived long in the City use the word. Nothing's incredible. Anything can be true."

It was Tolefree's answer to my repeated complaint that I was being required to believe the unbelievable about Burnet.

He had asked for ten minutes alone with me and Gillespie before lunch. We were sitting on a divan at the end of the billiard room. And having delivered himself of this generality, Tolefree got up and stood facing Gillespie.

"You and I have to come to an understanding," said he. "You got very peeved with me this morning. If you're going to stay peeved, goodbye! The murder of your uncle interests me no longer."

"Peeved is inadequate," said Gillespie. "I was damned angry. Who wouldn't be?"

"Who would? If you'd thought half a tick – but you rushed to the conclusion that I was a beastly Paul Pry asking insolent questions out of his sneaking curiosity. Why the devil should I be curious about you?"

"All the same it was a rotten question to ask under the circumstances," Gillespie protested.

"That's not a bit clever of you, Mr. Gillespie. If I'd been ass enough to suspect what you thought I suspected, is it likely I should have given myself away so simply? I didn't want to know a darned thing about whether you were to become the head of the house and his representative. Are you? Because a great deal hangs on the answer to that."

"Well, I can't see what it's got to do with anybody; but, if you must know, I think he probably made me his heir, with a provision for Alison. He'd spoken about it twice lately when we were discussing business. But I never gave it a serious thought. Why should I? Uncle Wellington seemed good for years. All this was far away in the future."

"But you're not your uncle. He probably wasn't the man to take chances, eh, Farrar?"

"Long-headed—" I began.

"Of course, or he wouldn't have had this—" Tolefree waved his hand around. "Now, Mr. Gillespie, here's the reason of my beastly curiosity: are you prepared, if you become the master of Midwood, to hand on to me the commission your uncle intended to give me?"

Gillespie raised astonished eyebrows.

"If not," Tolefree continued, "I leave after the inquest is over. I can't hang about Midwood and perhaps get into collision with the police unless I've some authority."

"But," Gillespie exclaimed, "I don't even know what the commission was. How can anyone know?"

"Not in detail. But we do know that he wanted my help in a difficult affair, that he asked me to join this weekend party incognito so that no one in the house should suspect a private detective – and don't we therefore know that the difficult affair must have had some relation to this party? Annesty has fallen by accident on a secret in your uncle's life. That may have something or nothing to do with the inquiry I was to make. It may also have something or nothing to do with the murder. But I'm keen to know what was at the back of his mind. I'm inclined to think it may be important for you. Anyhow, you'd like to keep his name as clean as possible? Of course. Then do you feel inclined to call it a deal?"

Gillespie sat for a few moments frowning at the floor.

"The police—" he said.

"Yes, the police – they'll worm their way to some sort of truth about this, but it'll be a long job. I don't want to cut across the police. I shall probably help them. But there are people who have to be considered – you, Mrs. Burnet for example. Skeletons in the cupboard—"

"All right," said Gillespie, looking up suddenly. "I suppose you've some idea – or plan?"

"Idea? – yes, several ideas. Plan? – I'll tell you what I propose if you answer me one more insolent question."

Tolefree smiled over his own epithet.

"I suppose Catterick has asked it already. Whatever you told him, tell me the honest-to-god truth, Mr Gillespie, and all the truth. Where did you go, and what did you do on Saturday evening when you left Farrar in the billiard room? Every minute of the time."

I expected another wrathful explosion. Instead of blowing off, however, Gillespie looked Tolefree straight in the eye, and they stayed thus posed for several seconds. At last, Gillespie said,

"Catterick did ask me the question. What I told him was that I went to telephone my sister, who was coming here on Sunday, to make arrangements about her train and fetching her from the station."

"Yes? And that was only part of the truth, wasn't it?"

"Actually it wasn't the truth at all, Tolefree. I did in fact put in a call to my sister – she's teaching at a school in London. But that wasn't what I meant to do when I left Farrar. I went to speak to Denley."

"Ah! And what happened?"

Tolefree, leaning against the table, pulled a ball out of the pocket and sent it spinning round. Gillespie watched it to a standstill before he answered.

"Can I trust you? Can I?"

He leaned forward with his chin in his hands, gazing at Tolefree.

"If you can't, don't employ me. We finish now. It's for you to decide."

"By God how I'd like to trust somebody!"

Gillespie's voice trailed down to a whisper.

"I thought it was like that, Mr. Gillespie," said Tolefree, quietly.

"See here, Tolefree!" Gillespie seemed to shake himself into a decision. He got up and took Tolefree by the lapel of his coat. "See here I – I'm putting the happiness of three people in your hands. If you betray it—"

He sagged at Tolefree's exclamation of anger.

"Sorry, Tolefree," said he, dropping back on the divan. "Take no notice of that. I ought not to have said it. You've seen there's something amiss. I'll tell you the whole story."

Tolefree reached for the ball and sent it spinning again.

"When I was in the middle of the first game with Farrar," said Gillespie, "I remembered that I'd promised to see Denley before dinner about sending a message to Margaret. For God's sake stop fidgeting with that ball!"

Tolefree came and sat between us.

"You're nervy," he said. "I understand. Take it quietly. I can guess a good deal."

"Well – I went up to Denley's office and he wasn't there. As I came out again, and turned the corner into the main corridor I saw him creeping along between Uncle Wellington's door and Alison's—"

"Creeping?"

"Well, sort of stalking, up against the wall. I was so startled that I stopped on the corner. He got to Alison's door and put his ear against it. Then he looked up and saw me. I walked along to him and said, 'What the hell's the matter with you, Jack? What about phoning Margaret?' He stood with his back to the door looking like nothing on earth, and said would I

phone Margaret as he had a lot to do before dinner? Then he
pushed off, leaving me staring. I thought first he'd gone batty.
Then I remembered he'd had a bit of a turn-up with Uncle
Wellington in the morning – some row about Elford's accounts,
and I guessed Uncle Wellington had been reading the Riot Act
to him and knocked him off his perch So I went down and tried
to get through to Margaret. I waited a few minutes, gave it up,
and came back here to Farrar – and found you. That's the whole
dam' thing."

"Not so very awful after all," said Tolefree.

Gillespie, who was literally sweating over the story, cried out
in a tone of relief and surprise,

"You don't think it is?"

"Well – you've been letting your imagination go, haven't you?
Never said a word about it to Denley since, I expect? Afraid of
– well, just afraid?"

"Damned if I knew what to think! But you—"

"Just tell me a few things. Why should Denley be concerned
about a telephone message to your sister?"

"Got a pash on her – and she on him. As good as engaged."

"Ah! – and Mr. Burnet? He knew? He approved? Or not? He
was rather fond of Miss Gillespie, wasn't he?"

"More than fond. He was a second father to her. She could
twiddle him round her finger. He liked Denley too. He was
quite pleased about it."

Tolefree smiled, and said it was as he had thought: Gillespie
had let his imagination run riot. He made a little disquisition
on *post hoc ergo propter hoc*. Gillespie, he said, was suffering from
what he called reflected fancy.

It astonished me for a minute or so to hear Tolefree meandering on in this fashion – until I saw the effect of the sermon on
Gillespie; it was like a bromide. His excitement calmed down,
and his brow cleared.

"Well," said Tolefree, "here's my proposal. Sort of pact –
the three of us in a triple alliance to get to the bottom of this

business. You, Gillespie, give me your authority to take any step of which all three of us approve in order to discover your uncle's purpose when he wrote that letter to me. You and Farrar become my colleagues in the job. We're to help and not hinder the police but at the same time we're to save the memory of Mr. Burnet from any needless stain. How does it strike you?"

"I'm on!" Gillespie cried.

Tolefree looked at me.

"Don't quite see where I come in, Tolefree," said I.

"As Burnet's best friend."

"Yes, but that's a rather vague and unofficial capacity."

"No matter. I want you – for a reason. Don't you see the remarkable thing about this murder – a most extraordinary thing — ?"

Tolefree paused, looking at us in turn.

"What?"

"That we were the only three people in Midwood on Saturday night, barring the servants in the kitchen, who could not possibly have done it."

Gillespie and I gaped at him.

"Yes! Think it out. Anybody else in Midwood except us, who'd wanted to murder Burnet and had the necessary strength and cunning, could have done it. But not either of us. Farrar, you were in the billiard room here all the time. I was brought here from the front door, so to speak. Gillespie was here except during the few moments when he went to inquire about the telephone message to his sister. Everyone else but the servants – and that excludes Elford, remember – was in a position to have done it. And, believe me, everyone else is under suspicion. Old Catterick has seen that from the first. He'd sized it all up before he came to us in the drawing room, Farrar. You recollect? – he made no stipulations to us. He even recited to us the names of the people he had to account for. And now we're under no sort of embargo – free to do what we please. I've a pretty clear notion of what we ought to do. I think we can do it. Are we all game?"

Thus originated the pact which, in the end, brought about the solution of the problem of Burnet's death. That astute policeman, Catterick, saw three parts of the way into it, but no more; and the reason why Catterick, with all the strength of an excellent police organisation behind him, could get no further was that he did not possess Tolefree's faculty of deduction from a physiognomy. I had no doubt that when he had sat for an hour at the inquest that afternoon, looking steadily all the time at the faces of the people who, as he said, were more or less under suspicion, Tolefree had made up his mind. The rest was merely a drive for evidence to confirm his judgment.

But this is anticipating.

The interest of Tolefree's achievement lay in the processes by which he sifted a mass of surmise until he had left nothing but a tiny body of indisputable fact.

The first step in our virtuous conspiracy was to take Gillespie entirely into our confidence – tell him the story of our two nights' adventures, make him aware of the existence of that scrap of paper and its contents which Tolefree had memorised.

The story gave Gillespie the horrors. But he was a courageous fellow. Though more than one person in whom he was interested was going to get hurt, he flinched at nothing that might help to reveal his uncle's murderer.

"The surgeon's knife is merciful – sometimes," said Tolefree. "Let's cut for the tumour Annesty's found. Your uncle had a secret unknown either to you or to Farrar. We've got to uncover it – and quickly, before Catterick sees through it."

But Catterick, I reminded him, was in the dark: he knew nothing of the scrap of paper.

Tolefree was not so sure about that. He had been thinking it out.

"When you consider what must have happened before they laid out Burnet under that shroud – I think you must allow for the chance that the scrap's in Catterick's pocket-book. He may not see in it what I see. But on the other hand he may. Anyhow, I'm taking no risks."

"How do you see it?" Gillespie asked.

"As a corner torn off an hotel bill. The question is – whose bill? It may be Burnet's. It may be another person's. I expect to discover tomorrow. But let's suppose it to be Burnet's. If you can throw any light on it, Gillespie, we shall save time. I put a lot on it because I feel certain that was what Burnet was going to show me. Do you know where Burnet ordinarily stayed in London? And how often? I mean since he's had Midwood, and recently?"

"No. I'd no idea he was ever away from Midwood much. He'd been at the office a little more during the last year, but I always understood he just went to and fro: came up in the morning, lunched at his City club, and went home in the evening."

"Don't know any hotel he ever used?"

"Never heard him mention one. It's a beastly notion, Tolefree, this—"

Gillespie made a wry face over it.

"I know. But we face up to everything, we three, don't we? And here's another turn of the knife. Suppose this was not Burnet's bill, but someone else's? Mrs. Burnet's — ?"

"By God!" Gillespie exclaimed. "I'll not believe it. Alison—"

"Go slow, young man," said Tolefree. "I'm not asking you to believe anything. But we must hypothesise. If it were Mrs. Burnet's, and for any reason in the world Burnet either wanted it himself or desired to keep it out of another person's hands – that would fit, you know."

"Beastliness..." Gillespie muttered.

Tolefree hardly noticed the interruption.

"It would fit," he repeated. "We can't ignore it. Mrs. Burnet's part in this must be examined. You're friendly with her?"

"I like her. I think she's a nice woman."

"I should judge from what Farrar tells me that she's charming. But also that lately there had been a certain – what shall I say? – cooling? – between her and Burnet?"

Gillespie agreed, grudgingly at first – then, under what seemed to be pressure of strong feeling, burst out,

"Oh, the whole thing's a damned tragedy – hopeless!"

He got up and stood in front of us, tousling his hair in his agitation.

"Frightful!" he said. "You two fellows can have no idea. You heard what Annesty said this morning? About Uncle Wellington's remark to him – that there'd been a chance of a match between Alison and Ned Cossor? Well, that was so. It didn't come off – I don't know the exact reason. That's neither here nor there. But you can guess that on Alison's side it wasn't exactly a love-match with Uncle Wellington. And then – well, there's Midwood, and all this tomfoolery. And Uncle Wellington, after little more than a year of it, feels like a fish out of water. The first glamour is over. Then you can see what an ill-sorted pair they are. Don't suppose they'd two ideas in common. But Uncle Wellington, all the same, was a gentleman, and Alison's a lady. I believe in her. Anyhow, Tolefree, what's all this leading up to?"

Gillespie ran his hand through his hair again and looked desperately unhappy.

"My dear Gillespie – it leads up to nothing except an attempt to get at the truth. Remember, I'm not drawing conclusions. I'm only trying to get at facts. One of the facts I must get is the ownership of that hotel bill. Think of it as a mere detached fact, and tell me whether you know where Mrs. Burnet stays when she goes to London."

"I don't know," said Gillespie, shortly. "If I did – what use would that be? If there was anything fishy about an hotel bill, that wouldn't be the hotel."

"Of course not, but tomorrow I shall know the date of this particular bill. You see that if Mrs. Burnet wasn't in London on that date—"

"Hateful! Oh, how dam'd hateful it is!"

"What d'you mean? That would prove that she couldn't be concerned," said Tolefree.

"It's all hateful – I mean, nosing around like a lot of Peepin' Toms—"

It was at this point that Tolefree brought out the story of our vigil under the balcony.

"Well," said he, "it's not a pleasant job, I admit. But you'll remember, Gillespie, that there's a corpse upstairs which has got to be explained. It's very necessary to find out whether Mrs. Burnet could possibly have been mixed up in any way with the document that was torn from your uncle's hand just before he died. And I'll tell you why... Sit down. Take it calmly."

Seated by his side I was watching Gillespie's hands while Tolefree described the scene on the Terrace on Sunday night. I saw them tremble and then clench. When Tolefree reached the point where we heard Mrs. Burnet calling for "Ned" he leapt to his feet.

"Oh, my God!" he cried out. "What a horror!" And then, "I'll not believe it, Tolefree!"

Tolefree shrugged his shoulders.

"I don't mean that I doubt what you say. But I'll not believe what you suggest. I just won't! Alison's not that. She's a good woman... She is..."

His voice faded away.

"You go too fast," said Tolefree, quietly. "Why assume anything on so narrow a basis? I'm not asking you to believe more than the plain evidence of our eyes and ears; I don't want you to draw any inferences. None. Simply to recognise that, having come by some of the facts, we ought to come by all."

"I know." Gillespie's voice was hoarse. "But it knocks me over – the very thought of a possibility. Alison – and Ned Cossor! It's impossible! There must be some explanation..."

It hit Gillespie hard. He appealed to Tolefree with a sort of desperation.

"Of course there's an explanation. But we've got to reckon with this: it may even be the horror you dread. Human nature's unaccountable, Gillespie. And now, I'm sorry – but I'm bound to tell you something else. I haven't mentioned it yet, even to Farrar. I wanted to be sure of my ground with you first..."

Tolefree's tone was ominous. He went on after the pause,

"On the balcony outside Burnet's study, there's a depression in the lead covering of the floor. Just a couple of square feet – very slight, but enough for the accumulation of rain water. The rain water washes down dust. The dust becomes mud: you know the sort of deposit. When I looked at that last night, I saw a fresh, sharp footprint, toe pointing towards the window."

I exclaimed inarticulately.

"Unhappily for the man who made it, he wore an easily recognisable boot. It was, in fact, a brogue shoe. It was soled with a patent composition in a well-known pattern. That foot-print may go a long way towards hanging somebody – or saving somebody from the hangman."

"Hell!" said Gillespie.

Tolefree gave him a long look and waited. But he said no more.

"Exactly," said Tolefree.

Thirteen

As Tolefree and I went into the hall after luncheon, a crowd of men clattered through to the door. The coroner and his jury had been up to view old Burnet's body where it now lay in his bedroom. They had also inspected the corridor and the study. They were now on their way to the Midwood village institute, where the Coroner's Court would sit.

Catterick acted as whipper-in of the procession. Tolefree said to him as he passed,

"Shall you want us as witnesses this afternoon?"

"Probably not, Mr. Tolefree. But, I'd like a word with you in private now. Come in here, will you?"

They went into the little telephone room. Tolefree threw a word at me over his shoulder: "See you at the Institute at three, Farrar." I passed out to the terrace, descended to the gardens, and lit a cigarette. At the end of the lawn I found an attractive grass walk, with what I think used to be called "ornamental borders" – at any rate a profusion of plants and a surprising number of blooms for the time of the year. It was closed in on both sides by a close-grown and smooth-clipped hedge of cypresses, seven feet high: two vivid green walls. Tightly mown turf edged with splashes of colour in the sun, protected from the wind – an inviting place for a saunter. This little paradise had been old Burnet's. It had been coloured and shaped and clipped to its exquisite perfection with old Burnet's money. Yet I doubted whether old Burnet ever seemed to "belong" – whether he ever looked at the water in the little stone pond where aquatic plants were growing with as much pleasure as even I felt, standing on the brink and watching the reflection of my cigarette smoke drifting across it as in a mirror.

It was while I lazed there speculating about Burnet's malaise in all this rural pomp that I became unwittingly and unwillingly an eavesdropper. There were voices on the other side of the hedge – a woman's and a man's. They had been murmurs. Then the woman's voice sounded very low but clear:

"It's rotten! How are you going to explain it?"

"I'm not. I shall say nothing about it."

"But if they ask you?"

"Leave me to find a way out."

"But you say George saw you!"

"Well – George didn't seem to make anything of it. I don't think he even noticed a thing – and he's not said a word to me since."

All this in a breathless way that took me off my guard. I realised that I was doing involuntarily what I would not willingly have done. I considered how to make my presence known.

"If I were you" – the woman's voice after a pause – "I'd make a clean breast of it."

"I can't, Meg."

"Jack! Why? Jack – I'm afraid... Jack! what's that? Somebody..."

A puff of the breeze had taken a whiff of my cigarette smoke over the hedge. It was more than time for me to move. I made noises: I whistled, cleared my throat. I set off briskly to the end of the walk, whistling while I went. I turned, where the hedges finished, into a gravelled path and walked back, overtaking Denley and a girl who were slowly moving towards the house.

He introduced me to Miss Gillespie. I said some sententious banalities about the lovely day being incongruous to the melancholy of the occasion. She looked at me much as she might have regarded a relic out of the Ark. I raised my hat and went on.

Margaret Gillespie was a fine replica of her brother on a smaller scale and in a more decorative style. She had his fair hair, his grey eyes, his complexion, his alertness and grace of movement – all refined and feminised. She was rather tall and very self-possessed. I thought that if this girl was afraid of anything it was not for herself. Nothing finicky here. No airs. I did not wonder that old Burnet had taken to such a niece.

About Denley, of whom so far I had seen very little, there was something a little alien to me. Possibly only because he seemed untidy. A young fellow who wore nondescript clothes and wore them anyhow, a soft collar, hair unkempt, so that he could shake it over or back from his forehead, a shambling way with him, was not my vision of the ideal private secretary – though in truth I could not have said why personal spick-and-spanness in my mind connoted business efficiency. Of course, I was conscious all the time of Gillespie's strange account of what he saw in the corridor.

But the confidence I had now surprised must be respected. Whatever bearing it might have on the thing Tolefree was digging out, no one but myself should know of it.

What a banal setting for a poignant scene was that institute hall where presently I saw Miss Gillespie seated among the little knot of villagers! Stark bareness hung with fusty maps and villainous prints, small billiard-table pushed into a corner, pitchpine bookcase with dusty glass front and ragged books higgledy-piggledy, stove with an iron pipe piercing the wall.

Amid these surroundings a grim drama was played. For here sat Tolefree at my side, scrutinising faces, weighing words, eliminating this and reserving that, patiently making or confirming his conclusions. The witnesses, undergoing their ordeal at the hands of the coroner, passed unconsciously through a far severer ordeal in the mind of this mild-looking man who sat motionless on a bench watching them.

The coroner, a Dr. Fleming, a middle-aged, business-like person, probed every story just as deeply as Catterick wished and no deeper. Catterick himself asked no questions. He had obviously primed the coroner: the inquest on this day was to be a fishing inquiry which would give no hint of any theory Catterick had formed.

Without waste of time or words, the coroner plunged into the middle of his business. He told his jury they were called to discover the cause of the death of Wellington Burnet, who had been found in his study on Saturday evening with fatal injuries to his head. The question for them to determine was how the injuries were inflicted and by whom. The person who first saw Burnet after his death was Mrs. Burnet, and he would call her at once.

Mrs. Burnet entered the room in a dead silence, and was shown to a chair at the coroner's right hand.

"Alison Burnet, of Midwood, aged 31, widow of Wellington Burnet."

The coroner was writing.

She looked steadily in front of her, as though she saw nothing. A handsome, patrician-looking woman, dark, proud, a singular mixture of haughtiness and intensity in her face. I seemed to be seeing her for the first time.

"Take the book, Mrs. Burnet..."

"...the whole truth and nothing but the truth."

It was a rather husky voice of good quality. She spoke distinctly. And she proceeded neither to tell the whole truth nor to confine herself to the truth.

"When did you last see Mr. Burnet alive?" the coroner began.

"Between five and six o'clock on Saturday afternoon. I can't say exactly – possibly it was half past five."

"And where?"

"In the drawing room. We had taken tea. He left with Mr. Annesty to go to his study."

"You had a house party, of whom Mr. Annesty was one?"

"Yes."

"Between half past five and a quarter to seven, where were you, Mrs. Burnet?"

"In my boudoir."

"That is a room on the same floor as Mr. Burnet's study, is it not?"

"The adjoining room."

"Yes. The jury have seen the house and will understand. At what time did you leave your boudoir?"

"About five minutes to seven. I had rung for my maid to come and dress me for dinner—"

"The maid is Minnie Wade? Yes? Where was she then?"

"I thought she was in her room, which communicates with mine; but she was not. I rang my bell."

"And I suppose that bell sounds in the servants' hall? Well – then—"

"I went to my husband's study to see whether he had finished his business. I knocked. There was no answer. The door was not locked. I went in—"

Mrs. Burnet faltered. The coroner waited.

"I could see no one, and I walked towards the door of his dressing-room. Then I caught sight of him lying on the floor with a stain of blood on his forehead. I suppose I must have cried out. I don't know. I bent down and spoke, I touched him. I felt his pulse. Then I knew he was dead. I rushed out of the room. I remember reaching the doorway, and I remember nothing else till I found myself in my own room and Dr. Jacquelin there."

The coroner wrote on for a few seconds.

"Now, Mrs. Burnet," he said, "supposing, as seems likely, that Mr. Burnet was alive at ten minutes to seven, and when you discovered him at something after five minutes to seven – I gather it must have been before seven o'clock?"

"Yes, certainly before seven."

"Well, supposing those two times, Mr. Burnet must have died a violent death in the room next to you between ten and five

minutes to seven. He must have received a heavy blow and taken
a heavy fall. Did you hear anything?"

"Nothing whatever."

"You were awake – not dozing?"

"Sitting before the fire reading."

"One gets absorbed in a book. Perhaps — ?"

"I cannot say there might not have been a noise. Simply, I did
not hear it."

"You were alone in the room?"

"Quite alone."

"'I was quite alone in the room,'" the coroner repeated slowly
as he wrote the words. "Now, Mrs. Burnet, I want you to pay
particular attention to this question: when you went into the
study and discovered your husband lying on the floor, did you
notice anything either in his hand or lying near him?"

I felt the jerk that came to Tolefree's nerves. Catterick! –
he knew all about the scrap of paper, and he had thought of
something which escaped both me and Tolefree – that the first
person who saw Burnet after his death being Mrs. Burnet, she
might not only have seen the scrap of paper, but might be the
person in possession of the rest of it. And yet, if Catterick had
suspected that Mrs. Burnet was concealing this, would he have
put her on her guard by forcing the question on her in public?

These two or three ideas flashed in and out of my consciousness in the instant between question and answer. If Mrs. Burnet
was hiding an essential fact, what an actress! She turned her head
slightly towards the coroner and raised her eyebrows.

"No – nothing whatever," said she.

He wrote the answer.

"You saw that Mr. Burnet had been felled by a terrific blow.
Was there in the room to your knowledge any weapon or object
with which it could have been inflicted?"

"You mean—" she seemed puzzled. "You mean did I see anything there which looked as if it might have been used?"

"Well – as to that?"

"I saw nothing at all."

"Then I will ask you whether you knew of anything that had customarily been in the room, which could have inflicted such a blow, and was not there when you went in."

Mrs. Burnet frowned over this.

"I can think of no such thing," she replied. "And I don't think anything was missing. At least I noticed nothing out of place. Of course I wasn't looking for anything unusual. I was there only a moment or two."

The coroner bent over his foolscap, but wrote nothing.

"Did you," he resumed, "observe whether the windows of the study were open or closed?"

"No. But closed, I should imagine. Mr. Burnet usually closed the windows and drew the curtains when his lights were lit. The people who examined the room afterwards would be able to tell you that, wouldn't they?"

"Yes, of course, Mrs. Burnet. But it is important to know what was the state of things before anyone entered the room, and immediately after your husband's death. However, you naturally made no close observation of anything except Mr. Burnet himself. The jury will quite understand that. Now I believe there are balconies outside the windows on that front of the house?"

"Yes – four of them."

"In fact, I have here a plan which shows how they are arranged. Will you tell us whether they are often used?"

"Hardly ever. Certainly not at this time of the year. I should doubt whether anyone has been on them for months – unless it were servants cleaning the windows."

"I see. But can you tell us whether, if any person had been on the balcony outside Mr. Burnet's room that evening you would have been aware of it?"

Again a spasmodic start from Tolefree, doubtless perceptible only to me, who was sitting close to him. Catterick was certainly a close old fellow, and missed very little. But Mrs. Burnet stood the examination about the balconies without even a flicker of the eyelid.

"Unless the person had been on the balcony outside my room," she was saying, "I could not have known of his presence. Even then—"

"Yes – and even then?"

"What I mean is that a person might have been there without my knowledge – except for this, that there is no other access to the balconies than through the rooms. To have reached my husband's balcony anyone would have had to go through his study."

The coroner peered at the plan on the table, and nodded.

"And if anyone had passed through your room in order to get to your balcony – it could not have been unknown to you?"

"Naturally not."

"You might have gone to your bedroom at some time, and a person might have passed through while you were out of the boudoir?"

"If I had gone to my bedroom – but I did not. I was in the boudoir all the time."

"It had rained on Saturday morning, but cleared up in the afternoon, had it not?"

This seemingly irrelevant question provoked Mrs. Burnet's first gesture of surprise.

"Why?" she asked. "I hardly remember. Yes, I believe you are right."

"Supposing your husband to have been killed by a blow from some heavy instrument between ten minutes to seven and five minutes to seven on Saturday evening, Mrs. Burnet, I need hardly ask the question, but I put it as a matter of form – do you know who killed him?"

"No, I do not."

"Do you know of any reason why any person should want to kill him?"

"No reason whatever."

"You know of no one with whom he had quarrelled recently?"

"No one – unless you can call his anger against Elford a quarrel."

"We shall hear about Elford. No, I do not mean that sort of dispute. You were not conscious that he had an enemy?"

"Certainly not."

"Or that he felt strong enmity towards anyone?"

"I never heard him express even strong dislike of anyone."

"Your own relations with Mr. Burnet were, I believe, of the friendliest and most affectionate kind?"

"Quite."

"There was no cause of difference between you?"

"None."

"And as to finance, no difficulty of any sort?"

"I don't quite follow," said Mrs. Burnet.

"The one answer no doubt covers both questions. But as a matter of form again I will put it that Mr. Burnet never raised any questions with you as to allowances or expenditure?"

"Absolutely not. He was the soul of generosity. The only matter of that kind he ever discussed with me was during the last day or two – some muddled accounts of Elford, the butler."

"Ah, yes – we shall get all that. Well, Mrs. Burnet, I will recapitulate for the benefit of the jury the points of your evidence. You say that at the time when the death of Mr. Burnet must have taken place, you were in the room next to him, that you were alone, and had been there alone for nearly an hour and a half; that you heard nothing amiss in the next room; that you went to see whether he had finished his business and found him dead on the floor; that you noticed nothing unusual in the room – in its arrangements, I mean – and that you saw nothing in Mr. Burnet's hand or lying near him; that no one could have got on to your balcony without your knowledge; that your husband had no enemies, and you have no idea who killed him or why anyone should want to kill him; and that your own relations with him were clear and affectionate. Are there any other points you think you would like to make?"

She shook her head.

"Then, if no member of the jury wants to ask a question" – he paused – "I will read over your deposition. Stay – there is just one thing. The lighting of your husband's study. I think the jury observed a floodlight in the ceiling and two lamps on his writing table. Were these the only means of illumination?"

She frowned, as if trying to picture the room.

"I think so," she said.

"Nothing else in case of a failure of the electric light. No lamp or anything?"

"I cannot remember that there was anything else. The electric light has never failed that I know of."

"Thank you. Then, Alison Burnet, you say you are 31 and reside at Midwood, and you depose as follows..."

In five minutes Mrs. Burnet had signed her deposition and Catterick had moved back her chair for her and given her a place at the side of the room. People coughed and shuffled their feet after a long period of constrained silence.

Three other witnesses went through quickly. First Dr. Jacquelin, with his business-like account of his examination of Burnet's body. He said Burnet had been killed by a terrific blow with some heavy thing, a blunt thing, since it had not made a severe wound. It had cracked Burnet's skull like an eggshell. Burnet could by no possibility have inflicted such an injury on himself.

"I will ask you a question, Dr. Jacquelin, which does not bear on your professional observations, but may be of some importance. When you examined the body, was there anything held in the hand?"

"Nothing."

"Quite sure of that?"

"Perfectly."

"And you saw nothing on the floor near the body?"

"What sort of thing?" asked Jacquelin, bluntly.

"Anything whatever that he could have held in his hand."

The doctor reflected a moment.

"No. I recall nothing. So far as I remember, the floor was quite clear. Of course, I wasn't looking for anything except the injuries."

"Naturally. Well, thank you, doctor."

Elford came next. A subdued and fearful Elford. He told his story straightforwardly enough. He was examined first in great detail about the telephone messages from Burnet and their times. His testimony was consistent and could not be shaken. Burnet was alive at ten minutes to seven when he telephoned the message to be taken to Annesty. At five minutes to seven he was dead. Elford was called upon to explain the system of internal telephones. It had no connection with the public system. The house was wired in six rooms. There was a telephone in Mr. Burnet's study, another in Mrs. Burnet's boudoir, one in Mr. Denley's office, one in Elford's pantry, one in the servants' hall, and one in the billiard room. It was on this wire that Mr. Burnet's messages had reached him.

Elford's martyrdom came at the end.

"Now, Elford," said the coroner, "I'm going to put some questions to you which you can answer if you like, but I must tell you that you are not bound to commit yourself in any way." Then followed a long examination on his discussions with Burnet about accounts. Elford's distress grew until he was pale and perspiring under the torture. He admitted that his accounts were in confusion. He admitted that there were discrepancies which he could not explain to Mr. Burnet, and that Mr. Burnet was very angry about it. He did not deny that Mr. Burnet had threatened that if he had not squared up certain accounts by Saturday evening the police would be called in.

"Had you squared them by Saturday evening?" the coroner asked.

"I was at them all the afternoon. No, I had not finished. I couldn't finish. The muddle was too big."

"Now, Elford – answer or not, as you like. Did you go into Mr. Burnet's room on your way up to Mr. Annesty?"

"On my solemn oath, no, sir."

"Did you go into that room on the way down after you left Mr. Annesty?"

"I swear to God I didn't, sir."

The coroner looked him in the eye during a quivering second or two.

"What shoes were you wearing that afternoon, Elford?"

"Shoes?" The question surprised him. "The same shoes I'm wearing now. I should have changed before dinner-time."

"Just let the jury look at the soles of your shoes, Elford."

There was a touch of grim comedy as Elford slid back the chair and lifted his feet to display first one sole to the gaping and mystified jury and then the other. Elford's shoes were unexceptionable: plain black shoes, with smooth soles.

But Catterick! Tolefree stole a glance at me. There was not much that Catterick missed.

Fourteen

To few other persons in that room could the excitement of these passages in the low steady voices of coroner and witnesses have been so tense as to Tolefree and me. Not even to old Catterick. For we knew more than Catterick – perhaps more than anyone else except the actual murderer of Burnet. We knew that some time during that afternoon the man who killed Burnet would sit in the chair by the coroner's side and tell whatever lies he had invented.

Tolefree had sat like a graven image, his gaze concentrated on the occupant of the witness-chair, without a motion except those two little nervous starts when the evidence showed how far Catterick had penetrated the fog. I felt sure that when the thing was over and we left the hall, Tolefree would have made up his mind in his own method. He would know who had killed Burnet. The rest would be a quick search for facts to confirm his hypothesis.

When Elford, looking extremely sorry for himself, had signed his depositions and gone his way, Annesty was called in.

He gave us a little glance of recognition as he took his place and the oath was administered to him. Horace Annesty, 28, of 115, Carlyle Mansions, Maida Vale, actor. Annesty had nothing to say of which we were not fully aware, and he refrained from saying the things which we had agreed to keep to ourselves. He described his friendship with Burnet, whom he had met at a London Club. Burnet had expressed interest in a theatrical enterprise of Annesty's, and had been exceedingly kind to him. He took him to his office in the City and introduced him to his nephew, Mr. Gillespie. He subscribed handsomely to the preliminary expenses of the production Annesty had in hand, and in all sorts of ways displayed friendliness and generosity. This all culminated in the invitation to join the house party at Midwood.

"We have heard from Mrs. Burnet," said the coroner, "that Mr. Burnet was the soul of generosity. His subscription to your project – was it large?"

"Substantial," said Annesty. "It was a thousand pounds. But that wasn't all. He was prepared to go much further. In fact, that is what we were talking about on Saturday afternoon."

"Ah, well, – let us come to Saturday afternoon. We have been told that after tea Mr. Burnet took you off to his study. That was about half past five—"

The coroner went minutely into all the movements of that hour and a half between the breaking up of the drawing room party and the discovery of Burnet's body. Catterick, whose echo he was, plainly wished to establish beyond a doubt that Burnet was killed in the five minutes to which the other witnesses had reduced the time-problem. The examination on this point therefore concentrated upon the hour at which Annesty left Burnet alive, after his second visit to the study. He could not fix it by clock or watch, but only by the fact that he had returned to his room and was in his bath when Elford's knock came.

It was noticeable that Catterick, as shown by the direction of the coroner's questions, was chiefly concerned about what Annesty saw in the corridor when he rushed down in answer to Mrs. Burnet's cry. The examination became very close and deliberate. The coroner, referring to a sheaf of notes, posed his questions slowly and wrote the answers carefully.

"How long after Elford left you did you hear the cry?"

"Almost immediately. I should think less than a minute," said Annesty. "In fact, I had just sat down and kicked off my slippers. Then I got into them again and rushed to the door to listen."

"How far should you think Elford could have got by the time you heard the cry?"

"He seems to have got as far as the hall, for he was coming up the stairs just as we ran to Mr. Burnet's door."

"If he was in the hall at the time of the cry, he would not have had time to visit Mr. Burnet's room on his way down? You see the importance of this? Only through you, Mr. Annesty, can we get at it."

"Yes, I see. There would have been no time for Elford to go into Mr. Burnet's room. It is quite impossible that he should have done so."

"That is on the way down?"

"Yes, on the way down."

"As to what he might have done on the way up, you can, of course, say nothing?"

"Naturally, nothing at all."

The coroner paused, wrote, referred.

"You used the word *we* just now. That refers to you and — ?"

"Mr. Cossor."

"Will you say how you and Mr. Cossor came to be together?"

"We met just outside the door of my room. He seemed to be listening for a repetition of the cry, or for some other sound – just as I was."

"Was Mr. Cossor's room near yours?"

"Yes, two rooms away on the opposite side of the passage."

"Did you see Mr. Cossor come out of the room?"

"No. When I opened my door he was there, in the passage."

"And you could not tell whether he had come from his own room or from anywhere else?"

Annesty appeared to try to squeeze some meaning out of this. He cocked his eyebrows to the coroner.

"Of my own knowledge, no," said he. "But there was no doubt he did come from his own room. He told me the cry had disturbed him."

"Then you had some talk with him about it?"

"Hardly talk – just a flying word or two as we listened. Then we heard running footsteps and both flew down to the first floor. Just as we reached the door and saw Mrs. Burnet lying on the floor, Elford rushed from the top of the staircase with the maid behind him."

"Which was in front as you came into that corridor – you or Mr. Cossor?"

"Mr. Cossor was actually in front, but we were practically together."

"Did you see any person other than Elford and the maid before you stopped to attend to Mrs. Burnet? Was there anybody in the corridor, or anywhere visible?"

"No one."

"You saw nothing of Mr. – er—" the coroner consulted his notes – "Mr. Denley?"

"No. Certainly not before we stopped at the door. Afterwards, I can hardly say whom I saw or what. Elford looked into the room and saw Mr. Burnet stretched out there. I went to his side and found he was dead. And then I thought of nothing but running for Mr. Gillespie. Elford told me he was in the billiard room and I went there."

The coroner seemed loth to let Annesty go. It looked as though Catterick had hoped to extract something from this witness and was disappointed. The questions came back to the point as to whether Annesty was bound to have seen or could have seen anyone who happened to be in the corridor, and the point of Cossor's exact whereabouts when the cry was heard. But Annesty could say no more than he had said. He left the chair.

"Call Edward Cossor."

I shivered as the coroner spoke to the constable at the door, and Tolefree turned a momentary look on me. As for him, he betrayed no agitation, only an intense concentration on the scene.

I found myself reflecting, with a little unreasoning surprise as the Court awaited Cossor's entry, that I hardly knew him by sight. He had loomed as the largest figure and the most mysterious in all our discussions. He had been in the background of Mrs. Burnet's life, and perhaps of Burnet's death, during all the hours since Tolefree's revelation to me on Sunday morning; but in physical fact I had seen him for only a few minutes immediately after my arrival at Midwood.

Now there he was, coming in – tall, grave, dignified, the fine-drawn figure familiar to all readers of the newspapers, keen, cool, clean, alert, bowing slightly to the coroner, and taking the seat the constable indicated, with no more notice for the rest of that little excited world than if it did not exist.

It was almost amusing. The coroner and the jury regarded him with a very obvious respect, amounting to awe. Tolefree and I were perhaps the only persons in the room who would be able to judge whether Cossor was fulfilling his oath or lying like a gas meter.

He really was formidable in that company, and he carried off the Olympian pose perfectly. His dark eyes were sophisticated and bold. His thinly pencilled eyebrows, his thin straight nose and his thin lips gave him an almost ascetic expression. But he was hard as nails – that brown complexion and his quick muscular movements showed me an athlete in the pink of condition. Comparing with dear old Burnet, I could not deny that Cossor was as completely in Mrs. Burnet's world as Burnet was completely out of it.

How was Catterick, who sat looking like the Sphinx, going to get over the inferiority complex that had possessed the Court? Get over it he must if he intended to pursue the same line with Cossor that he had taken with Mrs. Burnet.

At first, it seemed, Catterick was going to let Cossor have his own way. But presently it became a game of diamond-cut-diamond between these two.

The preliminaries being over, the coroner said,

"You have a great deal of experience of procedure, Mr. Cossor. Perhaps it would be convenient if you would tell us what you think to be relevant to the inquiry, beginning with the last time you saw Mr. Burnet alive?"

"I last saw him alive in the drawing room at Midwood at about half past five on Saturday afternoon. I then went to my room to work. Just before seven, I was disturbed by a loud shriek and went out to the passage to listen. There also came Mr. Annesty, whose room was near. He was in a dressing gown. He spoke about the sound which he too had heard. Then we both heard hurried footsteps below and rushed down…"

The rest of Cossor's statement did not differ at all from Annesty's.

I saw Catterick push a paper under the coroner's eyes. The coroner wrote for a few moments after Cossor had finished speaking. He took up Catterick's paper.

"Thank you, Mr. Cossor, for a most lucid account of the affair." He had not complimented anyone else on his lucidity, though Annesty had been every bit as clear, and a little more expansive. "So far as it goes, it is quite plain. There are, however, one or two questions about which you may be able to help us."

Cossor inclined his head.

"You have known Mr. Burnet – how long?"

"Since his marriage."

"That, I believe, was some three years ago. But I understand you had known Mrs. Burnet much longer?"

"Naturally. She is my cousin. I have known her nearly all her life."

"So that it is to be presumed that but for your relationship to Mrs. Burnet, there would have been no acquaintance with Mr. Burnet?"

"Probably not."

"But you were on terms of friendship with him?"

"In a general way, yes. Hardly on terms of confidence."

"So that if Mr. Burnet had in his life either at Midwood or elsewhere any enemy who might seek to do him injury, you would not be likely to know of it?"

"No. I never discussed any personal matters with him. In fact, I knew of no enmity in his life."

"And Mrs. Burnet has never mentioned the subject to you – never expressed any apprehensions about her husband?"

"None whatever."

"If, Mr. Cossor, it happened that Mr. Burnet had within the last few days of his life, taken a step which suggests that he did apprehend some trouble, you would have no knowledge of it?"

"I had no such knowledge."

"You have been often at Midwood?"

"Several times – quite lately only."

"Within, say — ?"

"The last year."

"Not in the earlier time of the marriage, then?"

"No, not until the last year."

"And in your observation, the relations between Mr. and Mrs. Burnet were friendly and affectionate?"

"Perfectly normal."

"Nothing that you saw disturbed them?"

"Nothing whatever."

"You had, I believe, at some prior time made a proposal of marriage to Mrs. Burnet, who was then Miss Orton?"

The question gave Cossor a jolt. He shot a lightning glance at Catterick.

"I had. But I do not see where these questions are tending," he said.

The coroner looked uncomfortable. He possibly did not know himself. But he stuck to his book of words.

"Coroners have a wide license, as you know," he said. "But leave unanswered any question which you think unjustifiable. I will pass from that. I want to make quite sure about the events which happened between the breaking up of the party in the drawing room and the discovery of Mr. Burnet's body. You went immediately to your room when you left the drawing room. Had Mr. Burnet then left?"

"Yes, he was first away with Mr. Annesty."

"And who were left in the drawing room when you went?"

"Several people. Mrs. Burnet, Mr. Gillespie, I think one of the guests, and perhaps Mr. Denley."

"You went straight to your room?"

"As far as I can remember, yes."

"Had no conversation on the way?"

"I think not. Nothing fixes a conversation in my mind."

I felt that little movement in Tolefree again. Catterick had made a point which we had missed.

"If the maid says she passed you and Mrs. Burnet in conversation outside the door of Mrs. Burnet's boudoir, is she correct or mistaken?"

Cossor took a moment to consider this.

"I cannot be positive. It is possible we met in the corridor and spoke. I cannot remember."

The coroner studied Catterick's paper.

"Mrs. Burnet was almost the last to leave the drawing room. She must have been some minutes behind you."

"I have no recollection that will help you."

"Then we will leave that. You were in your room from about half past five until you were disturbed by the shriek at five minutes to seven. You were not outside the house at all that evening?"

"No."

"In no sense were you outside the house?"

"I don't quite follow," said Cossor, with a show of impatience for the first time. "Can one be outside the house in more senses than one?"

"I expect I express myself awkwardly," said the coroner, slowly. "However, you were not outside the house. Now we have it on the doctor's authority that Mr. Burnet must have been killed by a blow of very great force. This could not have been done without noise. You did not, at any time between half past five and five minutes to seven, hear an unusual noise?"

"Certainly not. The first noise I heard was the shriek which brought me out of my room."

"During your stay at Midwood have you noticed anything which would suggest to you an explanation of the death of Mr. Burnet? I ask you that, Mr. Cossor, because no one is better qualified than you to assess the value of evidence."

"I have noticed nothing," said Cossor, with emphasis, "and if I had noticed anything I should have communicated it at once to the police."

Catterick did not fall down dead when Cossor flung this very pointed remark at him; instead he sat looking the stolid lump of unintelligence which he certainly was not.

The duel had ended. The coroner was at the end of his book of words. He read over Cossor's evidence, and Cossor joined the other witnesses.

The rest of the inquiry, until the very end, was anticlimax. They called the maid and Denley. The coroner paid some attention to Denley. He had evidently been asked to be curious about Denley's whereabouts in the critical minutes. Denley declared that he was in his office typing, and that he had heard nothing, not even Mrs. Burnet's scream. He had been surprised on coming into the corridor to see Elford and Peters hanging about outside Mr. Burnet's room, and it was from them that he learned what had happened. He had not left his room until then, and consequently had seen no one in the corridor about the time when the murder was supposed to have been committed.

Like Cossor, and like Mrs. Burnet, he lied well and convincingly. I wondered whether perhaps he had been better advised to make a clean breast of it, as Miss Gillespie suggested.

Gillespie himself was not called. The coroner said he might be wanted at an adjourned hearing, but the last witness for the present would be Inspector Catterick.

Catterick had sprung more than one surprise that afternoon, but this was the greatest of them – that he should himself go into the box at so early a stage of the inquiry. Tolefree whispered to me, "Watch him carefully."

Catterick's object soon became apparent to us. He was there to lay out just as much information as he wished to be known to everyone concerned and to try a psychological experiment. Watching him carefully, as Tolefree desired, I observed first that he shifted his place at the table and did not speak from the witness chair. He faced the form on which they all except Cossor sat. He placed in front of him on the table a small suitcase.

Then, without any leading from the coroner, he occupied a few minutes in stating the result of his inquiries, or what he said was their result, in the course of which he revealed nothing that had not been said three or four times already. Having completed this story, he rather patently waited for a cue from the coroner.

"Now, I need hardly ask, Mr. Catterick, whether you made a minute examination of the room in which the body was found?"

"I went over it very closely."

"And did you there find anything which would throw any light on the crime?"

"Unfortunately, nothing at all."

"Under the circumstances – seeing that the killing was done apparently within less than five minutes of its discovery – you would have expected to find more traces, would you not? With regard to the instrument, whatever it was, that felled Mr. Burnet, it must have been something big and heavy, and, one would suppose, difficult to spirit away so completely?"

"Certainly I expected to find some indications."

"But there were none?"

"None at all."

"Are you satisfied that between the time when Mrs Burnet screamed and the time when you saw the room nothing had been removed from it?"

"Of course it is impossible to be certain, but I am satisfied – yes. The only persons who had access to the room have satisfied me."

"So that whoever killed Mr. Burnet took away with him the instrument that killed him?"

"Probably."

"Now, what do you say about the probability that the weapon was taken into the room of deliberate purpose or found in the room and used so to speak on a momentary impulse?"

"I should assume the latter," said Catterick. He paused, and his eye ran along the row of witnesses. "It seems to me that if a person had gone into the room resolved upon murder, some other weapon would have been used – I mean a weapon acting in a different way."

"Yes? So your conclusion is that the blow was probably struck with something that the striker found in the room?"

"I think so."

"I asked Mrs. Burnet whether she could think of any object which was customarily in the room and was missing after the murder. She could not. But you heard her say that in such a moment she did not look particularly, which is quite reasonable."

He had not, however, put the question to Elford, who would be far more likely to know. The outlines of Catterick's stratagem took shape, but at this point nobody could have guessed at its extraordinary ingenuity.

"Quite reasonable," said he. "I should not expect anyone to notice such a matter in the circumstances."

"But have you made any inquiries yourself?"

"Naturally I have. One thing which I have cause to believe was in the room when Mr. Burnet entered it for the last time was not there when I examined it three hours after."

"What was it?"

"This was it!" said Catterick, who had been fingering the latch of the suit-case and flipping the spring up and down. He now stood, flung open the cover and took out a tall, heavy, richly chased silver candlestick, and with a rapid gesture, lifted it as though he would bring it crashing down on the coroner's head. But his eyes were on the row of witnesses. It all passed in an instant. There was a gasp of astonishment from the jury and immediately he had placed the candlestick on the table before the coroner and taken his seat again.

"You will doubtless bring evidence to prove that it was in the study before the murder?"

"Yes," said Catterick. And he added, without a blush, "Strictly speaking that evidence should have been called first. But you asked me the question. The man who cleaned the silver on Saturday morning and put the candlestick in its usual position on Mr. Burnet's desk can be called."

"Perhaps you can tell us the circumstances in which it has now been found?"

"Yes, it was restored to the study and found there."

"When did you find it?"

"On Sunday morning. It had been placed there during Saturday night."

Catterick's eyes were wandering up and down the row of witnesses.

"That is strange," said the coroner. "You had a police guard there on Saturday night?"

"Yes – in the hall. I am making some investigations into the question of the guard on Saturday night, and no doubt I shall have some evidence to bring at your next sitting."

"Then we will not go into that now." The coroner regarded the candlestick. "I suppose," he said, "the gentlemen of the jury should not handle that? You would wish to preserve any fingerprints it may bear?"

"Unfortunately," Catterick replied, "there are no fingerprints. But I should be glad if the candlestick remained untouched. There is an excellent reason. It has been perfectly cleaned, and since cleaning it has been handled only with gloves or cloths."

"Cleaned?" The coroner raised his eyebrows. "Does that really signify anything? You said the servant had cleaned it on Saturday morning."

"Yes. But I have had it tested chemically. The last cleaning was done with soap and water. The servant who cleaned it on Saturday had used a patent silver polish."

Again Catterick's eyes were flickering up and down that bench against the wall.

"And is that candlestick a weapon with which the blow could have been struck?"

"It weighs seven pounds," said Catterick. "It is eighteen inches long. It has a heavy base. I think it could have struck the blow. But that is only a lay opinion. I think it did strike the blow, but I cannot prove it – yet."

Fifteen

The coroner having given his order for burial they put Burnet underground next morning in the solemn churchyard of Mid-wood.

Hardly till his coffin disappeared behind the mound of earth, straining the muscles of the shirt-sleeved men who held the straps, did I fully realise that old Burnet was veritably and unquestionably dead, and that I should see him no more. It was a melancholy business, that funeral, with its lugubrious sounds and its more lugubrious silences, in the still air of a misty morning, and amid the drip, drip, drip of moisture from bare branches.

No public announcement had been given out. Only the Midwood party and a few villagers stood round the grave, with one grey-headed figure I knew very well – Kitson, the junior partner in Burnet's firm of solicitors – and just one stray news-paper man who had stayed on in Midwood for the resumption of the inquest.

It rather surprised me to find Mrs. Burnet there at the head of the mourners: so often the ladies of a stricken family leave this last ritual to their men. But there she was, Gillespie on one side of her and his sister on the other. She looked pale and sorrowful, but brave.

"A good breed!" Tolefree whispered in my ear as we stood with Annesty and Denley watching the trio go to the edge of the grave and look down.

Only Cossor of all the house party was missing that day.

We walked back through the park, Tolefree and Denley ahead, Annesty and I following. It was the first time the actor and I had been tête-à-tête.

"I'd wanted to talk to you, Mr. Farrar," said he. "You were Mr. Burnet's oldest friend, weren't you?"

"Yes," said I; "probably few people have known him longer."

But for a time this introduction led to nothing. We walked side by side in silence. Annesty shivered.

"Are you sensitive to exterior impressions?" he asked. "This thing's getting on my nerves – today more than ever. All this gloom. Did you notice poor Mrs. Burnet's eyes just now? How she bore it all – except with her tragic eyes?"

"She's having a trying time." I could find no other platitude to say.

"Yes. It's that – the greatness of her trouble – makes it hardly decent to talk of one's own little affairs. But do you suppose the coroner will finish the inquest tomorrow?"

He had adjourned it for two days so as to avoid a sitting on the day of the funeral.

"Either that or take a long adjournment," I thought.

"Then we may be clear by Thursday?"

"In all probability."

"I've got to find someone to take Mr. Burnet's place quickly now, you see, or my scheme breaks down. And it's going to be hard, Mr. Farrar."

For a moment I had a little nervous apprehension lest he was going to ask me to pick up his scheme where Burnet's death had left it. But I was wrong. That was not why he wanted to talk to me. He had indeed some difficulty in getting at the subject.

"I'll have to try the usual people," he went on. "Anyhow Mr. Burnet made it a bit easier. He enabled me to get the thing into shape. If he'd lived... I wonder."

He pulled up and glanced at me as though speculating on the possible answer to a question.

"You as a life-long friend of Mr. Burnet... that woman..."

He stuck there.

"What woman?" I exclaimed, staring.

"The woman whose name he was going to tell me when... I wonder... You never heard anything that would be a hint?"

"Certainly not," said I. "Burnet's life, so far as I know was perfectly clear of all that sort of thing."

"Yes? Well, it's a mystery. It's all mystery from beginning to end. Extraordinary performance at the inquest, I thought, didn't you? I heard the coroner did funny things – like making the butler fellow show the sole of his shoe? Did you see that?"

"Yes, he did."

"Didn't that strike you as being curious? I thought it the queerest thing—"

As an isolated fact it was undoubtedly queer enough. But I did not take Annesty into my confidence.

"He'd just asked Elford whether he was out of the house on Saturday evening," said I.

"Well – that was what made it so queer," Annesty persisted. "Because everyone knew that the police rushed Elford out of the house themselves to the police station. And there were other curiosities, didn't you think? – the way he handled Mr. Cossor?"

I did not want to discuss the evidence with Annesty. He could know nothing, as we knew it, of the cloud that hung over Cossor, and he was not in our triple pact. I passed it off with the observation that the police had their own ways of coming by evidence, got him back to his own business and kept him there.

Peters met us in the hall with the request that we would make ourselves at home in any part of the house except the drawing room for the next hour. In that room the family had assembled for the reading of Burnet's will, the document that played so notable a part in the wild doings of the next few days.

It was when Tolefree, Gillespie and I met in Tolefree's room in the afternoon that its significance began to appear. Gillespie told us in general terms the main provisions of the will. As he expected, it was a late will, made only three months ago. Burnet had created a Trust (joining me and his lawyer, Kitson, as trustees) for the purpose of paying Mrs. Burnet an income of five thousand a year. Having set aside capital sufficient for this purpose, he made several legacies. He left five thousand each to Margaret Gillespie and John Denley, and a further five thousand in trust for their children if they should marry. He provided for old members of his staff in London in proportion to their salaries and length of service. To me he bequeathed any object of art at Midwood which I might choose as a memento of our long friendship. Then, with one exception, he left the whole of the remainder of his estate to George Gillespie, his nephew, expressing the hope that he would continue to control the London business himself or, if he wished to retire from it, consult me about its future.

Burnet thus disposed of a fortune running into nearly a quarter of a million, according to the estimate his lawyer had given to Gillespie.

The exception was made in a clause which, so far as Gillespie could remember ran like this:

"I give and bequeath to Thomas Yonge, of Adams House, Bishopsgate, in the City of London, the sum of £500 sterling, to be paid by my executors in lawful money of England, within fourteen days of my death, the said money to be expended by the said Thomas Yonge at his discretion in accordance with his instructions from time to time received from me."

It was a trivial legacy compared with the rest. It would have excited no special interest but for the unusual terms of the clause. But these, combined with the revelation Annesty had made of an unsuspected phase of Burnet's life, aroused our curiosity.

"A woman, of course," said Tolefree.

"*The* woman," said I.

"So I fear," said Gillespie.

Who was the said Thomas Yonge? Gillespie had no idea. But Tolefree and I knew Thomas Yonge very well. He was a solicitor in quite a large way of commercial business in the City. The only remarkable fact about the transaction was that Burnet's solicitors, who did everything for him, were Menzies, Warren and Kitson, the well-known firm in Lincoln's Inn: it was Kitson who came down to Midwood and read the will and took luncheon with us afterwards. Burnet had evidently employed Yonge on special business which had no relation either to the affairs of his firm in London or to those of his private estate at Midwood.

We hammered all this out. Then Gillespie said,

"Do you put a lot on this woman – if she exists, Tolefree?"

"I don't know how much I put on her," Tolefree replied. "Can't link her up. On the whole, it doesn't look to me as if your uncle had any such woman in mind when he asked me to come down to Midwood. He could hardly want to consult me on – well, on any such topic as that, could he? All the same, it's rather important to find her."

"I should think this Yonge—" Gillespie began.

"But I shouldn't," Tolefree interrupted. "And you wouldn't if you knew Mr. Yonge. An oyster is loquacious compared with Tom Yonge. What say, Farrar?"

"I've known far more expansive people," said I.

Tolefree took a step across the room and back to his seat on the edge of the bed.

"Look here, Mr. Gillespie," said he. "If you know anything about this woman—"

"But I don't!"

"Or if you know anybody who does know anything of her – what about that?"

Gillespie gazed in surprise.

"How did you discover – ?"

"I didn't discover at all," Tolefree broke in on his question. "You aren't used to concealing your thoughts, that's all. You do know in some indirect way about this woman. And our agreement, you know, is no concealment among us three."

Gillespie drummed a foot on the carpet and looked troubled.

"I'd no idea of concealment in that sense," he said. "But I did want to keep her out of it."

Tolefree gave a long low whistle.

"Like that?" he said, and paused. "But you can't, you know, Gillespie."

"What the devil do you mean by 'like that'?" cried Gillespie, flushing deep. "You don't think I—"

"Perhaps you'd better say explicitly exactly what you want me to think," said Tolefree.

"I told you I knew nothing about the woman. But Margaret does know something of her, and I wanted to keep Margaret out of the beastly business. What's wrong with that?"

He got up from his chair and looked down angrily on Tolefree.

"Sorry, Gillespie. But if you'd been explicit – However, that's where the wind sits, is it? And I suppose that if your sister knows something, Mr. Denley knows it too?"

"I'm sure I can't tell you."

Gillespie was offended. Tolefree remained cool.

"But you can tell us what Miss Margaret knows," said he.

"That shows you don't know her. I can't tell you. And now I doubt whether she'll tell you or anybody else."

Tolefree walked to the window and looked out into the misty landscape.

"I'd like to see Miss Gillespie," said he, turning to us. "Would she object?"

"I guess not. I wouldn't be surprised if she was rather anxious to weigh you up. I'll fetch her if you like. You'll find her a tough handful."

"Yes?" said Tolefree, with a fleeting grin. If you'd be so good—"

He spent the minutes of Gillespie's absence in contemplation of Midwood Park. Only once he threw a sentence over his shoulder to me.

"We shall get there, Farrar."

But not, I thought, if he antagonised Miss Gillespie. I had not forgotten the scene in the green alley and the look that young woman gave me.

Nor had she forgotten me.

When she came into the room with Gillespie, she nodded a casual how-de-do before her brother introduced her to Tolefree. I watched them, fascinated, the fearless girl and the man of wiles. Tolefree plunged at once.

"Very good of you to come, Miss Gillespie," said he. "Has your brother told you why we troubled you?"

"No," said she, "but I can guess."

"Ah – well, that eases things."

"You think so? I rather think not."

Tolefree pulled a chair into place for her. "No?" said he. "Perhaps you would say what your guess is."

"But I wouldn't. Not a word, Mr. Tolefree. Not a solitary word!"

She looked from him about the room and rested her look on me for a moment.

"You know who I am, and why I'm here?"

"Yes," she replied. "You're a private detective, and you're fishing for information."

"And you don't approve?"

"That depends where you fish," said Miss Gillespie. "And on the tackle you use."

Upon this her eyes came back to me, and I saw with discomfort that they were hostile. Tolefree followed her every movement.

"You think you've reason to complain that I've been fishing unfairly?" he asked.

"I hate eavesdropping!"

Tolefree flashed a glance between us.

"So do I," said he. "And I assure you, Miss Gillespie, that I've done none."

"That's a – prevarication," she declared. "If you haven't done it yourself, someone's done it for you. Same thing."

Tolefree threw up his hands.

"I assure you – no," said he. "Some misunderstanding."

"Misunderstanding my grandmother!" said Miss Gillespie. "I challenge Mr. Farrar, there, to say whether he didn't listen to a private conversation yesterday."

For the first time Tolefree looked, or pretended, annoyance.

"Farrar!" he ejaculated.

"Miss Gillespie is mistaken," I said. "I listened to no conversation."

"More prevarication. If you didn't listen, you overheard."

The blazing of her grey eyes and the contempt of her delightful snub nose made me feel more than ever like an objectionable insect out of the Ark. Tolefree looked questioningly at me.

"Sorry if Miss Gillespie doubts my word," said I. "If I overheard anything I immediately forgot what it was, and I shall never remember it."

Tolefree and Gillespie stared at me.

"Never," I repeated.

"Margaret!" said Gillespie, "you must believe Farrar."

Her answer was surprising for a girl. She rose and held out her hand to me.

"Stop!" said Tolefree. "If this is a pact to hide anything, Gillespie, I throw in my hand. You can't monkey about with a case like this. Either perfect confidence, or we part company here and now. Miss Gillespie, you're a young woman of sense. If your private conversation which Farrar heard – I assume by accident – was personal, well and good. If it had anything to do with the death of Mr. Burnet, I'm not going to be a party to hiding it. Good heavens! Think of it! – Farrar! – have you taken leave of your wits? Gillespie! – you know this won't go."

"I know nothing," said Gillespie.

"Have you told your sister of our undertaking?"

"Of course not."

"Very well. But I think," said Tolefree, "she should be told. Then we should possibly hear less about secrecy. Miss Gillespie – I believe you were fond of your uncle and he was devoted to you. Someone murdered him in this house on Saturday evening. You see in this room the only persons in the house at the time who could not possibly have been his murderers."

Watching the girl as Tolefree spoke I saw her face pale and her lips compress.

"They are leagued together, these three men," Tolefree went on, "to discover the truth of what happened that night. They think they may have to explore a long way before they find the real clue to the truth. They think you know something of it. And one of them, at any rate, thinks that it's your solemn duty to help them and that you ought to let nothing put you off that duty."

She was a bit rattled by Tolefree's vehemence: he did talk very emphatically. But she was game.

"If that's all, George," said she, "I think I'll be going."

"I told you, Tolefree," said Gillespie.

"Yes, you did. And now I'll tell Miss Gillespie, since she asks for it. This: that I haven't yet put Mr. Denley through the third degree, and that it's coming to him if she can't ward it off."

"You're a gentlemanly person," said she quietly. "Good afternoon."

"One moment, Miss Gillespie. You might tell Mr. Denley what's coming to him – or a part of it. You might ask him to prepare a plausible explanation of his strange conduct in the corridor just before seven o'clock on Saturday evening. He'll need it."

The effect on the girl of this brutality was devastating. She was striding out; she had the door handle in her hand. She stopped as if she had been stunned and turned to look at us all. Every particle of colour had left her face. She put her hand to her side and leaned against the door.

"Tolefree!" cried Gillespie. "You've no right to bully her. That was a dam'd awful thing to say."

The girl recovered herself in a moment.

"George," she said. "Come away. You don't shine in a company of cads and liars. Mr. Farrar, I'm glad I didn't shake hands with you."

"Don't misunderstand me, Miss Gillespie." Tolefree spoke quite coolly. "Farrar—"

"Mr. Farrar said five minutes ago that he did not remember anything he overheard, and by inference that he'd said nothing to anyone about it."

"Farrar," Tolefree pursued, "has never even hinted that he had seen you, heard you, or spoken to you. You misunderstand me and you misjudge Farrar. I said a brutal thing to you deliberately. If I had not said it you would not still be in the room. I apologise. Please be seated again and listen to reason. Gillespie, persuade her! You know how urgent it is."

But she needed no persuasion. Something in Tolefree's manner had altered her mind. She walked back to her chair and fixed her look intently upon him.

"Make yourself easy about Mr. Denley," said he. "We know he's concealing some knowledge of what happened just before seven o'clock on Saturday. I think him foolish, but I'm not his judge. I may find it necessary to squeeze the facts out of him, though I can almost guess what they are. I don't want you to say a word about Mr. Denley. But you have some information on a totally different matter which may be of the utmost importance to me. If you give it freely, you risk nothing and endanger nobody of any consequence to yourself."

"If that's true, why couldn't you have said it to begin with? Why all that beating about the bush?"

Tolefree screwed his face into a little grimace.

"I hope you'll know me a little better," said he. "Then you'll understand my failings. One of 'em is a taste for seeing how people react to violent sensations. No – don't!" He checked a threatened outburst. "I'm well aware of my insolence. Your brother's already told me all about that. As a matter of fact, if you reflect you'll see that I hadn't much chance of going straight to a rather delicate point. You weren't exactly – shall I say effusive? – were you? Now, Miss Gillespie, you're a modern girl, and you won't mind if I talk in plain terms. On the surface of things there's no visible motive for the killing of your uncle, whoever did it. But you know the saw: look for the woman."

Her eyebrows contracted into a frown, and she sat up stiffy.

"Farrar here had known Burnet intimately for many years. He never saw anything fishy in Burnet's conduct, and believed that Mrs. Burnet was the only woman in his life. But it has come to our knowledge that there was another woman. To discover that woman and all about her association with Burnet – that's what we want. You can help us."

"Not much, I fear." She looked at her brother, standing by. "George, I haven't even let on to you about this. It doesn't seem decent. Dear old Uncle Wellington—"

"I felt like that, Margaret," said Gillespie. "But if Tolefree thinks it important, better get it out."

It came out, in jerks, with promptings from Tolefree. A common little story – a thing that had been best hidden and forgotten but for any light it might shed on the event of Saturday night.

The girl held a post as teacher of French in one of the business schools in Tottenham Court Road. She kept house for her brother at Highgate. She took two evening classes a week, in an

Institute at Blackfriars and on those two evenings rode down in the tube to Charing Cross and changed into the Circle train. One evening in June she was in an end seat of the train going home, buried deep in a book, when she heard a familiar voice and looked up. Burnet sat in the seat in front of her, talking to a woman. When she saw the woman she buried herself in the book again. They had apparently got into the train at The Temple. They did not see her. She slipped out at Charing Cross unnoticed. It was unpleasant to see Uncle Wellington in that way, and she did not wish him to know she had seen him.

And then? Tolefree encouraged her.

And then, twice more, a little later.

"Did they get in at The Temple again?" asked Tolefree, eagerly.

Yes. The first time they were further off in the train, and she had no difficulty in concealing herself. But the third time, Burnet saw her. He made no sign of recognition. Afterwards, to her surprise and embarrassment, he spoke to her about it – one day when she had called at his office for Gillespie. She paused, and looked Tolefree straight in the eye.

"Need I talk of that?"

"It would be well to repeat exactly what Burnet said, Miss Gillespie."

"He said very little. It wasn't what he said. It was the trouble and shame in his face. He said, 'I must tell you, my dear, that when you saw me in the train the other evening I was with a person to whom I couldn't introduce you. And a person I should like you to forget.' That was all."

Tolefree sat silent, cogitating. No one spoke for several seconds. Then Tolefree twisted his lips to a smile.

"I know you hate eavesdropping, Miss Gillespie. But I beg you earnestly to say what you overheard of the talk between Burnet and this woman."

"Nothing – that is, nothing material."

"But anything! Anything at all, material or not. The woman's name – or the name he called her?"

"No name was mentioned. She was a fairly vulgar woman—"

"I understand," said Tolefree. "But was any other name mentioned – person, place, anything?"

"There was a name. It meant nothing to me, but I remember it because it was curious. They talked about the Wigwam."

"Ah!" we exclaimed all together. The girl looked startled.

"Does that mean something to you?"

"Yes," said Tolefree. "We'll tell you later on. But think hard, Miss Gillespie. Nothing else in the talk that you could fasten on to? No name, say, of an hotel? No indication where they were going? Station? Anything!"

"I heard nothing of that."

"No destination, then. But of anything of any other person, place – anything?"

"No person to identify. There was something about a man. I remember that because it brought out the woman's vulgarity. About a man, she said, who wasn't a patch on Uncle Wellington – something like that, you know – in a sort of leering way."

"Ah," said Tolefree, with a look at me, "not easy to identify, as you say, Miss Gillespie. The woman – you saw enough of her to describe her?"

"Yes, I think. Enough to recognise her the second and third time. A bold-looking woman, with yellow hair and a rich complexion. Well-dressed – I mean fashionably. Rather overdressed. Slim, about middle-height, not so tall as I am. Age, I should say thirtyish."

Tolefree listened and nodded, as though composing a mental picture from her words.

"And your uncle? How did he react to her?"

"Hard to say. He didn't talk much. He seemed to treat her with a rather quaint courtesy. Not familiar. But you know his style – he never could be familiar."

"Didn't squeak with joy when she compared the other fellow so unfavourably with him?"

"No," said Miss Gillespie, with a frown.

"Ah, well," Tolefree rose, "you've given me something important to chew over. I'm deeply obliged. I apologise again for my brutality."

"But all this—" said Miss Gillespie. "It can't possibly have anything to do with Uncle – with anything that happened here on Saturday?"

"Nevertheless you will find that it has everything to do with what happened on Saturday," said Tolefree. And he repeated, "Everything!"

Sixteen

As I hung about on the platform of the Temple Underground Station that night at half past ten, waiting for the three or four passengers who had alighted with me from the train to reach the top of the steps, and when the last of them had gone, dashed up myself, through the barrier and round the corner into Norfolk Street, keeping in sight a hurrying figure, I thought of Tolefree's exclamation, "Everything!"

If Tolefree was right, I might be on the brink of old Burnet's secret.

It had happened thus.

At dinner there were only Gillespie, Denley, Annesty, Tolefree and myself with Mrs. Burnet. We felt awkward with Mrs. Burnet. She made no sign of regarding us as the intruders we were, it is true, and our relations with Gillespie were vaguely understood. But she gave us an uncomfortable sensation of her wonderment about what we all meant. Neither Annesty nor Tolefree nor I meant anything in particular to her; we were Burnet's friends. My two companions knew her not at all and I had hardly seen her since the wedding. We were relieved when she left us. Then we could talk about the subject that monopolised our minds. At least a part of it, for in the presence of Denley the discovery we had made through Miss Gillespie was not mentioned.

But what began as talk soon developed into a monologue. When Tolefree started putting all the facts together in a sort of considered statement, we subsided into listeners.

"Catterick thinks," he said, "he's certain to get his man in a day or two. He's extraordinarily astute. I'm not sure he won't bring it off. He reckons he's talking all the time to that man – in everything he says or does. He'll rely on breaking him down – on forcing out of him some little sign that will give him away. The man's got to have iron nerves to stand it. Did you notice the play-acting with the candlestick yesterday? It was very clever."

"You mean that gesture when he raised it above his head, Tolefree?"

"Yes."

"It struck me as rather melodramatic," said Annesty.

"And me," Gillespie added.

"But if Burnet was killed with that thing, and if the man who killed him was looking on while Catterick performed, and Catterick was scanning all the faces among which his might be, don't you think—"

"But, Tolefree!" cried Annesty, "that means that the man was there among – do you mean among the witnesses?"

"I don't mean anything, my dear fellow; but that's what Catterick means – that this man was somewhere in that room."

"Good God!"

Annesty looked round the table.

"That's a facer," said he.

Tolefree smiled. "We're not all here, you know, Annesty."

I did not catch any purpose in the turn Tolefree had given to the talk – until I saw Denley look at his watch, say a word to Gillespie, and go out of the room. Within a minute, Tolefree had broken up the party. He got me alone in the hall when Gillespie and Annesty had strolled along to the billiard room.

"You're for it, Farrar!" he whispered. "See Denley? Fidgeting with his watch for the last half hour? Going off in a hurry? Get after him. Watch him. I guess the 9.10 train from Midwood. You can just do it. If he's not at the station, come back. If he goes, don't let him out of your sight, but don't let him see you. I'd love to do it myself, but there are other fish to fry. I'll explain to Gillespie. Now off with you!"

Tolefree, unusually excited, communicated some of his excitement to me. Otherwise I should have thought twice.

As it was, I found myself presently hurrying through the park and on to the station. There was at first no need for concealment, because the night was very dark, and no figure could have been recognised even a yard away. Only when I came within range of the station lights did I take precautions. I reconnoitered the platform from the road bridge at the London end. Tolefree had guessed right. Denley was there. He stood in the doorway of the Booking Office under a lamp. No concealment about his journey, wherever he intended to go.

I did not approach the station entrance till the lights of the train were in sight. Then I waited for Denley and the only other passenger to take their seats before passing through with the return half of my ticket and diving into the nearest compartment.

I watched the platforms at each of the two stopping stations. Denley did not leave the train. We ran into Charing Cross at ten minutes after ten. He had no suspicion of being dogged. I might have kept close on his heels without fear, for he went ahead like a man with a vigorous purpose. Out of the station. Down Villiers Street at a smart walk. Into the Underground. Into the first train going east.

Then I realised, with a thrill of distaste, that I was sitting in a corner of a Circle train just as Miss Gillespie had sat, and travelling over the same mile of line in the reverse direction. And Tolefree's "Everything to do with it!" rang in my ears.

I might indeed be on the brink of Burnet's secret. But how could I face Miss Gillespie again? Who could have dreamed – certainly not she! – that her lover would lead me there?

Up Norfolk Street, into the noisy Strand, along the pavement to the east, past the Law Courts, into Fleet Street, jolting and pushing and always keeping that hurrying figure in view.

Only just in time I dodged into a doorway. Denley had stopped before a low arch. He pulled a bell handle. From where I stood I could hear the old-time clangour. And then I knew what I was up against. Denley was going into The Temple. Unauthorised people with no business to state were not allowed in The Temple at night. Here in the middle of roaring London, with the printing presses screaming all round, and a hectic life going on late into the small hours, was an area of monastic calm, as close-tiled as a medieval city after curfew!

The gate groaned open, Denley passed in, the gate groaned closed again.

I had lost him. Unless indeed there was one off-chance. I badgered my brains for a name. It came.

The bell clanged again. The gate opened.

"To see Mr. Richards in Temple Gardens," said I.

"Straight down, sir," said the porter.

The gate closed behind me. Quick footsteps on the flags in front, some distance ahead now: mine were quicker behind. He turned left, and I ran. When I reached the corner his footsteps were rousing the echoes of Elm Court. I let him pass through. I ran again. Through Fig Tree Court I trailed him, round the narrow path by the Temple Church, and into the great open space beyond. Then I was safe. He hurried across the gravelled way, making straight for the middle door of Paper Buildings.

A minute later I was striking a match to read the names painted on the wall. And immediately I knew.

For I read,

"First floor left: Mr. Edward Cossor, K.C."

Denley and Cossor... In Cossor's chambers at that time of night? An appointment, certainly – or almost certainly... Cossor hardly lived in his chambers.

The burnt match dropped from my hand. I moved on east-ward.

The Temple at night is a goodly and pleasant place for people on their lawful occasions. Such as the few sparse people who strolled to and fro by the railings overlooking the lawns, gener-ally two-by-two in low converse, the end of a cigar occasionally glowing. But not a good place for a furtive watcher like me – an inexperienced, self-conscious, amateurish watcher, imagining that every passer-by suspected his business. And having been suspiciously regarded by two of them, I took a sudden and doubtless a rash decision.

I returned to Paper Buildings, walked straight in at the entry where Denley had disappeared, and climbed quietly to the sec-ond landing. I had argued thus:

If Cossor does not live here, he has come to his chambers tonight to meet Denley. When their interview ends, he will probably leave. They may leave together. It is unlikely that there will be any traffic on the stairs at such an hour. I can wait unobserved and unsuspected on the floor above till Denley goes. Then I can follow him – or both if they go together.

A dim electric bulb burned on each landing. I stole past Cos-sor's chambers. He had sported his oak: a double door closed him and Denley in. I dared to find the switch and put out the light on the second landing. Then I could lean over the banister and watch and listen.

That was how the fantastic thing occurred. I had stayed there motionless and silent for probably a quarter of an hour, waiting for the sound of an opening door. A quarter of an hour of absolute silence. Then suddenly a burst of sound came – angry voices. Cossor's door had been flung wide and two figures had flitted out. I could not see them clearly, for I drew back instinc-tively and the door flung wide was in the way; but one of them was a woman, and she had a shrill voice.

"A pretty pair of rascals you are! You can dam' well get out of the soup yourselves. I'm not helping you!"

"Kindly moderate your language and your voice!"

It was said in Cossor's coldest tones, and the woman's retort seemed pat.

"You've got the guts of an iceberg, Ned Cossor! But you needn't try anything on me. I'm not having any, see? Don't know what happened down there – but I can imagine. Don't think I can't read the papers, do you? He was a funny old mutt, but I guess he was a better man than any of you lot. And I'm not having any – see?"

"Good night," said Cossor. "You can find your way out."

"And good night to you, Mr. Cossor."

There were quick steps down the stone stairs.

"She's a tiger!"

That was Denley. I could see neither of them now. The open oak barred my view. Their voices dimmed.

I was in a quandary. Tolefree had said, "Watch Denley – don't lose him." But I knew that Tolefree also wanted, perhaps even more eagerly, some information about that woman. I was making up my mind to disobey orders and follow her when the voices below became plain again. Denley was coming out.

"She's angry with you, sir. Perhaps I can get better luck alone. I'll try. You said about halfway up, didn't you?"

"Yes, on the left. I shall see you tomorrow. I'm motoring down to Midwood."

"Very well. Good night."

Denley was going. He would escape me. I dared not stir before Cossor's door closed. Then I had to steal down the stairs. When I reached the pavement, Denley was out of sight. I hurried towards Middle Temple Lane. When I turned out of the archway into the lane, Denley stood at the porter's lodge a hundred yards away waiting for the gate to be opened. I had to linger till he had gone and the porter had returned to his lodge before I could venture near. Then my luck, which had held so good, ran out. The porter, who would make some remarks about the weather, and unfortunately remembered that I had asked for Mr. Richards in Temple Gardens, asked whether I had seen Mr. Richards, who, he said, had only just passed in, and I was explaining to him my regret at having missed Mr. Richards, when a quick footstep came to a halt beside me.

Cossor was there!

He peered at me in the light from the lodge.

"Why! – Mr. Farrar, isn't it?" he said.

"How-de-do?" I contrived to stammer it out. "I've just been down to see Richards in Temple Gardens – and missed him."

Cossor looked into my eyes as he might look into those of a lying witness in the box.

"How curious!" he said. He held my eyes for an uncomfortable moment. Then he said, slowly, "Very curious! I've just had a visit from Denley. He's only this moment left. Wonder you didn't see him."

"Mr. Denley's the last who went out, sir," the porter remarked, jingling his keys.

"Ah. Well, good night," said Cossor as we passed through the gate. A crawling taxi stopped. Cossor got into it. I was left on the pavement of Fleet Street, all hope gone of picking up the tracks either of Denley or of the woman.

My début as a sleuth was a failure. I had lost the trail. Worse: I had put the quarry wise to the pursuit. For Cossor knew as certainly as if I had told him that the visit to Richards was a fake.

Seventeen

Catterick exploded two bombshells when the coroner resumed his inquest.

He gave an entirely new turn to the case by disclosing the reason why Elford had been asked to show the jury the sole of his shoe: the police had found a footprint outside Burnet's window – a strongly marked print of a particular kind. He insisted upon two aspects of this discovery – the time at which the print was presumably made and the character of the impression. He had worked it out exactly in the same terms as Tolefree. Whoever stepped on the balcony must have been there after the rain of Saturday morning and while the little depression in the stonework was wet. And, whoever it was, the person was neither a resident of Midwood nor a visitor, for no such shoes could be found belonging to either.

Up to this point the inference from Catterick's presentation of the evidence had been that the police attributed the murder to a person who had reached Burnet's room from the corridor, and as the number of persons who could do that was limited, the chase had seemed close. It must now be admitted that the murder might have been done by a person who approached Burnet's study from the outside.

Was there any evidence beyond the footprint to support the theory that the murder might have been the work of an outsider, the coroner asked? Yes, Catterick said, there was. He described the position of the balcony. He gave measurements.

Then he dropped his second bomb. The police, he said, had found unquestionable signs of an ascent to the balcony by means of a ladder – the faint marks of its feet on the terrace, and the distinct scraping of its sides on the coping of the balcony. They believed they had discovered the ladder itself – a ladder used by the gardeners and kept hung on a wall of the kitchen garden. Footprints, too confused to be possible of identification, showed that two men had moved the ladder, and that recently. The gardeners themselves had not touched it for more than a month.

While this portentous evidence was being given, Tolefree sat looking at Catterick like a graven image. I controlled my features as nearly as possible to the same stolidity, and looking at Cossor I saw the like expression on his face.

Catterick had shifted the whole bias.

His tacit theory involved two men at least in the crime, and by moving the approach from the inside to the outside of the house he had increased the number of potential murderers almost to infinity.

He did make some attempt to reduce the category. He had Mrs. Burnet recalled and questioned again as to her knowledge of any personal enemies or enmities in Burnet's life. She knew of none. Gillespie was also placed in the box: he could throw no light on the question. The servants were put in to say whether they had noticed any strangers about the grounds either on Saturday or previously. Naturally they had no information to give. By that time (and it was well into the evening) the coroner had gone as far into the case as he could reach. He announced that he proposed to adjourn the inquest without a date, and to call the jury together when there was anything more to tell them. The witnesses were released, and the Midwood house party broke up next day.

That night, however, all the persons who had been present on the Saturday when Burnet was killed were in the house at dinner. I found myself, with a certain embarrassment, sitting opposite Cossor. How admirable was his nerve! When Mrs. Burnet and Miss Gillespie had withdrawn and we burst into talk about the inquest, he, who had hardly so much as noticed our existence before, took the lead and brought all his skill to bear on a statement of the case just as if we were a court and he a prosecutor.

Three of us knew much and suspected more. Denley knew many things that perhaps we did not know. Cossor was aware that I had been trailing a clue in the Temple the night before, and perhaps guessed that I had discovered the visit paid to him by the woman who treated his dignity with such scant ceremony. But Cossor ignored all this. If he was conscious of the atmosphere of duelling that seemed to surround him and Tolefree he gave no sign of it.

"Catterick must have had some purpose in keeping that footprint up his sleeve till the last moment," said Tolefree.

"Undoubtedly. It's quite plain." Cossor fingered a cigarette. "Catterick is playing a game. Catterick is possessed by a fixed idea. It's manifestly wrong, but he's the type which never lets go of his idea. He has found a set of circumstances which will fit a theory – or nearly fit it. They may fit twenty other theories. But this one is his beloved child. He will never desert it."

"You can see into his theory?" said Annesty, in a tone of hero-worship. His histrionic admiration of Cossor shone in his face.

"Why, of course. So can you all. What can be clearer? Catterick believes that one of us murdered Burnet."

"Good God!" Annesty exclaimed. "That's what you said the other day, Tolefree—" Tolefree nodded. "But where do the footprint and the ladder come in?"

Tolefree shrugged his shoulders.

"All that," said Cossor, "is a blind. All that is for the benefit of the public. All that is meant to put the real criminal off his guard. Catterick will watch for what he thinks is a false step by one of us and then pounce. Don't you agree?"

He addressed the question to Tolefree.

"Certainly," said Tolefree.

"Well – that's Catterick's child – the theory that someone in the house has taken advantage of an extraordinary set of circumstances to do this murder so cleverly that not a single flaw can be found in his alibi. I don't know what put it into his head – unless it was you!"

"I!" Tolefree exclaimed.

"I mean your presence here and the reason for it. Burnet brought you down as a private detective to join the party for some special and urgent reason. Catterick deduced from that a fear in Burnet's mind – a fear of someone in the party. He has not reflected that if Burnet really had any fear or intuition of danger it may have referred just as logically to a danger from the outside."

"I was going to say," Tolefree remarked, "that nothing in Mr. Burnet's letter to me suggested any such fear at all. He wanted to consult me on a difficult matter, he said. It might have been any matter – business, or what not. Business inquiries have always been my mark."

Tolefree was a capital actor. He said all this as though he had never seen a ladder or heard a woman's whisper.

"Well – that's as likely a guess as any," said Cossor, reflectively. "You see, coincidence has been too much for Catterick. It nearly always is, in my experience. At any rate it's the first and apparent coincidence that they fasten on, rather than the subtle and less visible coincidences that may lie behind. So Catterick's great discovery is a bluff."

"But you don't doubt he made it? He didn't invent it?" Annesty asked.

"Oh, he made it, unquestionably. But that's exactly what I mean by the subtle coincidence which he misses. Isn't it quite evident that the ladder and the footmark do point to the truth – that Burnet was murdered by someone who got through the window and attacked him and escaped by the same way?"

"Ah! – you think that?"

It was Tolefree who spoke: we all had the air of hanging on Cossor's words.

"I think there can be no question about it. Every other thesis falls to pieces. Between the time when Burnet rang down to the butler's pantry his message for Mr. Annesty and the discovery of his body by Mrs. Burnet there were five minutes. His assailant could have stepped into the room while Burnet stood with the telephone in his hand, the thing could have been done there and then, and the murderer out again in two minutes."

Tolefree pushed a wine glass over the tablecloth, describing imaginary patterns.

"Yes," he said. "That might be. But a ladder and an attack in this fashion – it means premeditation."

"Of course. It was a thorough-paced killing, wasn't it?"

"Very. But that presupposes that the killer would come armed—"

"Naturally."

"And with something more conventional than the silver candlestick with which he actually did the job."

"You mean the candlestick with which Catterick says he did the job," said Cossor, quietly.

"I see. You don't believe in Catterick's candlestick?"

"Do you?"

Tolefree considered the question.

"I've rather accepted Catterick's account of it," he said. "But I suppose you would put very little on the servant's story of the movement of the candlestick?"

"I should think it's a thing about which a forgetful servant might prevaricate, to put it no higher than that. But I base myself rather on the times that cannot be shaken, on the impossibilities of Catterick's theory, and on the strong possibilities of the opposite theory. I think that would be found right beyond all cavil – if the police would get at the possibilities rather than the impossibilities. But you won't shake a man like Catterick, and the longer he chases the shadow the further away will the substance be. Isn't that where you come in?"

"I?" Tolefree lied solemnly. "Oh, I've no *locus standi* at all now. Burnet's commission to me ended with his death. I shall never know what it was."

After dinner there was a conventional half hour in Mrs. Burnet's drawing room. There the topic of the crime was taboo. Some subtle influence had been at work which made this the least constrained and most natural gathering since Saturday afternoon. I suppose it was mainly the withdrawal of the police guard and the sense of relief which followed; but the thought came to me that we were all recovering from the death of Burnet. It is not very flattering to human complacency to realise how unimportant a man becomes when he is dead. Gillespie was the most decent young fellow in the world. His new overlordship of all that had been Burnet's did not betray him into any display of arrogance. But there was a nameless change in his position, and a trifling difference in the way he held it. He took the deference naturally and modestly.

I caught his sister's glance now and again. It expressed no friendliness to me, but she seemed to be reading my very thoughts when Gillespie gave an order to Denley and Denley left the room to carry it out.

The party broke up about ten o'clock. Cossor was driving to London early in the morning, and had offered Annesty a lift. He did not extend the invitation to us, though Tolefree had proclaimed our intention to return to town. The two went off to bed as soon as Mrs. Burnet had retired. Later on, Denley and Miss Gillespie melted away. Gillespie excused himself while he went to have a word with Mrs. Burnet. Tolefree and I were left in the room. Elford came in and attended to the fastening of the windows for the night; we drew up chairs to the fire, and he held a laughing court-martial on me for my failure in London.

Not that it was an absolute failure, or that I could have done anything better once I had gone up to the second landing. That was the mistake. By waiting below I could have traced Denley to his goal. However, a little patience would get us there, said Tolefree, and that was a job to be done without Gillespie's knowledge, for he would not stand for any spying on his future brother-in-law.

"But depend on it, Farrar, that shrill young woman is the key of the enigma."

"Old Burnet—" I could hardly believe this of old Burnet even now.

"Yes, I know. Queer... I wonder what Cossor was driving at tonight?" he exclaimed, suddenly switching away from the subject.

"His theory of the balcony and the window?" said I.

"Theory! Good Lord, Farrar – Cossor's no fool, and he knows I'm no fool. He's right enough about Catterick's bluff. Catterick is simply laying false scents. But why does Cossor take up that hobby as well?"

"You mean he's putting up a double bluff? Trying to bluff us?"

"I can't quite see through him. The key of the enigma is the shrill woman – not so? She links Burnet and Cossor and Denley—"

Tolefree shivered and frowned. He was sitting in a chair on the right of the fireplace. I was on the left, facing him. He dropped his voice to a whisper.

"Talk on," he said, "about anything. Don't turn. I'm going to move. Talk on without stopping. Pretend to talk to me. Now!"

I babbled something about the train we were going to catch in the morning. Tolefree rose. He said aloud,

"I'm in a draught here. I'll move over there." And as he passed my chair he muttered, "Somebody listening: window's been pushed open. Carry on. Talk away."

I continued to maunder of trains, departures and arrivals, how long it would take to get to the station, how glad I should be to get back to my office – while Tolefree stole away to the door and silently passed out of the room. The few following minutes were unbelievably ridiculous. I nodded to space. I made disjointed remarks to a non-existent Tolefree. I acted as best I could, and thought how asinine I should look if Gillespie suddenly came back and found me spouting to the universe. But all the time there was an uncanny sense of a presence – pure suggestion, for I should never have thought of it but for Tolefree's discovery. I felt, or imagined I felt, the draught from the window, but I dared not look round.

The astonishing end of my vigil came in perhaps three or four minutes. I jumped as a scuffle of feet along the terrace outside broke silence, and was immediately followed by an explosion and the crash of glass. With mouth agape I saw an oval mirror over the fireplace crack and star and a large piece of it fall.

Then I ran – not to the window through which the shot had come, but to the door, and into the hall. No one was there, but I heard a stir above stairs and a door opening, and voices.

The hall door was ajar. I looked out into a black night and called, "Tolefree!" Tolefree did not answer. Shaking with fright, fearing what I might find there, I went round to the terrace. The light from the drawing room windows made three patches of light on it. Peering as I went I covered its whole length. No one was there. I ran back to the hall just as Gillespie came down the stairs two at a time.

"What's up? What was the noise, Farrar?" he cried.

And while I told him what had happened, the hall became full of people. Cossor, Mrs. Burnet, Annesty, Elford, and the servants.

"Elford," said Gillespie, "bring lights. Who's got a torch? You have – good. We must look for Mr. Tolefree."

"Better be careful about lights, Gillespie," said Cossor. "They make good targets."

Somehow we spread into the grounds and over the lawns. I found myself with Cossor, groping about under the wall of the terrace.

"You couldn't tell which way the footsteps went?" said he.

"Impossible. I only just heard the rush and then the shot."

"If it smashed the mirror it must have been fired at the window – probably as Tolefree went by. We'll find him that way. There's a desperado somewhere, Mr. Farrar, eh? What about Catterick's theory now?"

I had no stomach for discussing theories just then. I was full of apprehension for Tolefree.

"Tolefree must be all right," said Cossor. "If he was hit we'd have found him in the line of fire—"

And as he spoke a cry was raised ahead of us. Gillespie and Annesty with Elford had gone straight along the terrace and down towards the kitchen gardens. There, not far from the scene of our larceny of a ladder, they stumbled over Tolefree. Elford's torch revealed him, lying on his face and hands in the path. Gillespie had just turned him over as we came up. All our fears were immediately quelled when Tolefree gasped and opened his eyes. In two moments he was scrambling to his feet.

"Who did that?"

The question came with such a burst of anti-climax that we laughed with relief. Tolefree took out his handkerchief and wiped his face. It was gravel-rashed on the right side. He soon recovered from his grogginess.

"He got away, I suppose?"

"What happened, Tolefree?"

"Were you hit?"

He told his story while he stood wiping his face and brushing down his clothes.

He had crept along the terrace, saw a man with his ear to the window, but unfortunately crunched a stone before he was within five yards. The man bolted and Tolefree after him. He heard the shot as he leapt down the terrace steps. Just before he reached the wall of the kitchen garden, the man pulled up dead and kicked as Tolefree ran into him. With his wind knocked out Tolefree took a purler and saw stars – and nothing more till Elford's torch was shining in his eyes.

"Then the shot wasn't fired by the watcher at the window?" said Cossor.

"Impossible," said Tolefree.

"So there are two of them, as I thought. Douse the light, Elford."

Blackness settled round us again as we strained our eyes instinctively into the lawns and the park. Someone suggested that we might as well move in.

"Listen!" said Tolefree.

The sound of footsteps came to us along the drive that swept round the lawns towards the hall door. We waited in absolute silence till they were quite close. Then,

"Hands up!" cried Tolefree. "Put the light on him, Elford."

The beam wavered round and settled on the figures of Denley and Miss Gillespie.

"What the devil do you mean? Is this a practical joke, George?" said Denley, furiously.

"No, Jack. Come inside and we'll tell you all about it."

Eighteen

Margaret Gillespie's half-term holiday was over. She travelled to London with Tolefree and me next morning.

A queer journey, that. In the back of all our minds was the scene of the night before when she and Denley had leaped into view out of the darkness as the beam of Elford's torch hit them. And afterwards the curious, embarrassed wait in the drawing room, with the splintered mirror looking down on us, while Catterick was informed and got into his clothes and his car and brought two constables to the house. And, with Catterick there, the examination of Denley and the girl about their movements after dinner, their walk in the park, and their whereabouts when the shot was fired. They had a perfectly rational reply to everything. Miss Gillespie was leaving in the morning. They had taken a stroll through the grounds when the dinner party broke up – about half past nine. They walked down the main drive to the village, and along the public road to the gate by which Tolefree and I had returned on Sunday morning. In Midwood Park they met no one. Along the road one villager going homewards, who called good night. Returning, no one. They were half a mile from the house when they heard the shot, a faint sound. The little breeze blew behind them. They thought nothing of it: poachers probably. Not till they were near the house, just before our light blinded them, did they notice anything unusual. Then, at the further end of the kitchen-garden wall, they walked into a man who stood with his back to them – or almost walked into him. A shadow appeared a few feet in front of them, and the man swung round with an exclamation and darted away.

"Which way did he go?" Catterick had asked eagerly.

"Towards the garden wall: he jumped off the drive on to the turf and vanished."

"You heard him exclaim something?"

"A mere ejaculation," said Denley.

"But his voice — ?"

"Not easy to identify a voice—" Denley stopped with a jerk.

We had been grouped round these two in the middle of the room – Gillespie, Cossor, Catterick, Tolefree and myself, with Elford and the servants in the background.

Denley was staring over my head towards the door. Catterick swung around. Peters, the footman, stood there. He was in mufti, held a hat in his hand; had apparently just entered. In an instant everyone had turned to stare at him.

Catterick stepped out of the group and his heavy hand fell on Peters's arm.

"Where have you been, Peters?"

The man shook off Catterick's hand with a motion of annoyance.

"Outside, looking round," said he.

Catterick turned to Elford.

"This man's not in livery. What does it mean?"

"Only that this was Peters's evening off, Mr. Catterick."

"So you spend your evening off outside looking round, eh?" Catterick snapped at him.

"I do nothing of the sort," Peters replied. "I've been looking round for the last half hour or so."

"Ah – well, perhaps you'll tell us what you found? Where were you at a quarter past ten?"

Catterick had fixed upon a quarter past ten as approximately the time when the shot was fired.

"Coming up the drive from the village," said Peters.

"Ah!" Catterick spoke with an air of calculation. "Ten o'clock closing time at the Midwood Arms. How far to the house – half a mile? You must have been within sight of the house at a quarter past."

"I was," said Peters. "And within hearing, too—"

"Yes – within hearing."

"And you saw nothing and heard nothing!"

"I didn't say so," Peters answered coolly.

Catterick sprang on him.

"Then why have you only just turned up? Why didn't you come and say at once what you saw and heard? Get it all out, Peters, or you're for it, my man!"

"You haven't given me much chance of getting it out, have you?"

Which, we realised, was perfectly true. I saw Tolefree's spreading smile.

"You're a cool customer," said Catterick. "Just tell me exactly what you did and what you saw and heard, from the time you left the Midwood Arms. I'll confirm with the Midwood Arms later on."

"I think not," said Peters. "You've imagined the Midwood Arms yourself. I've not been near the place."

"Oh, oh?" said Catterick, while Tolefree's smile broadened. "Then you'll have to give a further account of yourself. If you weren't at the inn, where did you spend the evening, Mr. Peters?"

"I don't know that you've got a right to ask me that, have you?"

Catterick gazed at him wrathfully.

"No, I haven't, you hair-splitting, logic-chopping son of a sea-lawyer! But I'll tell you this – I can pretty soon get a right to ask you anything. So cough it up, Mr. Peters."

The inspector's deplorable lapse from politeness had no effect at all on Peters. He looked down his nose; he was every inch the supercilious footman of Gillespie's despite.

"I paid a visit in Midwood village," said he. "I left at ten o'clock. I returned to the house. When I came round the corner of the lawn, I saw the drawing room windows lit up, and in front of the middle window a man was standing. He was in a funny attitude – half peeping and half listening. I thought it queer."

Now we were all silent, in a semi-circle, with our eyes on Peters.

"He was very still, except for the slight movement of his head."

"Who was it?" Catterick barked.

"At that distance I couldn't have recognised him if I had known him."

It was a curious way of putting the case. Catterick seemed to consider it for a moment.

"Well – then?" he said.

"Then I saw another man stooping along the Terrace from the direction of the main door – at least I saw him pass the first window. He'd hardly got past when the first man seemed to hear him and bolted, with the second one after him, and at the same instant there was a shot and a smashing of glass."

"And," said Catterick, "you were a disinterested spectator of all this, just standing there looking on?"

He did not knock Peters off his perch.

"The whole thing lasted not more than half a minute," said Peters.

"I wonder," Tolefree asked quietly, "whether Peters saw the shot as well as heard it?"

"Yes, sir, I did."

"Where did it come from?"

"The flash was under the cedar nearest to the Terrace."

"That's revolver range, isn't it?" Tolefree turned to Gillespie.

"Yes – about thirty or forty feet," said Gillespie.

"You weren't standing under the cedar yourself by any chance?" Catterick was in a temper.

"Not at the moment," Peters replied, with another look down his nose. "But I was thirty seconds afterwards, and I was just too late to nab him. He heard or saw me, and he ran for it – got away in the dark down by the kitchen garden. I've been prowling around there ever since, but he's got clear. I had one fright, when Mr. Denley and Miss Gillespie came up the eastern drive."

"Ah!"

That was a chorus.

"Why did you bolt from them Catterick snapped. "And you must have seen the party searching for Mr. Tolefree. Where were you then?"

"I didn't bolt. I was watching. I got out of their way. I thought I'd seen something that wanted explaining. I wanted to go on watching. That's all."

Catterick sniffed.

"Watching what? Don't be so dam' mysterious!"

"I thought I'd seen which way the man went. And if he went that way, he couldn't get out again except by going into the house. And as he wouldn't be likely to do that, I thought I was bound to get him."

"How d'you mean – couldn't get out again?"

"I thought he'd slipped down by the wall of the garden to-wards the stable yard. If he did, he couldn't get out without either going through the house or coming back to the corner where I stood."

Catterick made a contemptuous noise in his throat.

"And you mean to tell me," he said, "that you stood there on sentry within a few yards of all these people while they were picking up Mr. Tolefree, and never called their attention?"

"Yes, I mean that."

"You're the most unconvincing liar I ever met!" exclaimed Catterick. "Either you knew this man, or you've rigged up a cock-and-bull yarn because you yourself—"

"Pardon me," Tolefree said. "There might be an explanation. If you would ask Peters—"

"Ask him yourself." Catterick shrugged his shoulders, glaring at Tolefree.

"There were a few minutes between the rush and the shot and the time when you saw the torchlight coming along the terrace, Peters, weren't there?"

"Yes, sir. Quite three or four minutes."

"Where were you all that time?"

"Just about where Mr. Denley and Miss Gillespie saw me – under the trees at the end of the drive."

"Watching what?"

"The corner of the garden wall. If he came back to get away, he'd have had either to cross the open where you were or to keep close to the wall and come round that corner, and I'd have caught him. Supposing I was right and he'd gone down that way, he was in a blind alley – the house one side, the garden wall the other and the stable yard at the end. If I'd left the corner for one minute, he could have slipped through, and that was the only way."

Tolefree nodded to that.

"It was very dark, wasn't it?"

"Yes, sir – and the torchlight you were showing made it darker all round."

Tolefree looked apologetically towards Catterick. "There were one or two other points—"

"Go on," said Catterick.

"Well, Peters – a delicate question. Had you any suspicion about this man? I mean, did you give even a wild guess at him?"

"No, sir – it was too dark. People were just shadows. I could only guess at Mr. Denley and Miss Gillespie, though they were close to me."

"About the shot. You were the only man who saw it. Should you think it was fired at the man who was watching at the window, or at me?"

"I don't think it was fired at you, sir."

There was a gasp of surprise. I, and apparently all the others, had supposed the attack was on Tolefree. Catterick pish-tushed.

"How the deuce could you tell that? They couldn't have been three yards apart, running, in the dark!"

"Of course I couldn't tell it," Peters snorted. "I said I think it was fired at the other man. It came just as he ran, and it smashed the third window over there. It must have missed him by inches. If it had been fired at Mr. Tolefree it would have gone through the middle window. At least that's how it strikes me."

The rest of the catechism of Peters added nothing to knowledge. But the whole episode piled a new complication on Catterick's problem and ours.

The servants had gone. Catterick had telephoned the station with some instructions. Cossor and Annesty had once more departed to their rooms. Denley and Miss Gillespie also. The Inspector and the three of us, Tolefree, Gillespie and I, were left to make what we could of the puzzle. The admirable police officer had been badly rattled: we could not doubt that. He had fresh evidence to reinforce his bluff about some unknown villainy outside the Midwood house party – if bluff it was. But he was not happy about it.

"It looks as if you'll have to search for a solution outside the walls of Midwood after all, Mr. Catterick," Gillespie said.

"Well? Have I ever said the solution was inside?" Catterick frowned at us all. "That perishin' footman knows a lot more than he's said. I'll squeeze it out of him! I never believed his yarn about Saturday night. I'll give him somnambulism!"

Tolefree broke in on his growling.

"Suppose, Mr. Catterick, we took a light and had a look under the cedar?"

"All right; but we shan't find much."

"I think," said Tolefree, "if we do that, it'll be fair to tell all the others and give them a chance to come along."

Catterick looked startled.

"Why in God's name have all that crowd?"

Tolefree put out his hand and touched the Inspector's arm.

"Think a moment," said he. "Won't it be fair – and, shall I say, wise?"

Catterick screwed up his blue eyes without answering at once.

"I see," he said slowly. "Well – that's an idea. Very well."

Gillespie was asked to tell Cossor, Annesty and Denley that we proposed to examine the spot where the shot was fired, and to suggest that they might like to be present.

Shortly seven of us were crossing the lawn and approaching the cedar with a torchlight flickering over the ground in front. Turf was soft and wet in November, the bare space under the cedar branches, as Tolefree expected, covered with mud which took the slightest impress of a foot. We stood on the edge of this space, peering as the torchlight flitted over it. The silent inspection lasted for some moments. Gillespie carried the torch.

"Light up the ground near the trunk, Mr. Gillespie," said Catterick.

There, where the roots sprang out of the ground, was a confusion of footmarks. For the rest, the story of the night was printed as plainly as in type. Someone with a neat, smooth shoe had approached the tree from the lawn under the terrace and walked deep under the shadow of the branches. His footprints entered the ring of confusion near the bole. He had left with a longer stride. Two of his prints carried him away at right angles to the line of approach. Crossing his marks came a deep heavy imprint which went straight across the bare space without touching the muddle in the middle.

"So," said Tolefree, "Peters told the truth."

"Looks that way," Catterick admitted. "The fellow came in here, walking lightly. He went out there running, and Peters after him."

Tolefree bent down, while Gillespie directed his light on the nearest print, and measured it with a little steel rule.

"Eight inches over all," he said, and measured his own shoe for comparison. "A lightish man with a small foot. Very good shoes, I should say. Mr. Denley, – you're a lightweight. Put your foot alongside and let's guess what sort of figure he had."

Tolefree's daring absurdity made me catch my breath. His object was so clear and his pretext so ridiculous: as if the comparison of a boot with a footprint would enable him to guess at the figure of a man! But Denley without a word immediately advanced his foot into the circle of torchlight. It was clad in a neat evening shoe. Alongside the print it seemed the same length, but was certainly broader. Then, as if by an infection, we all in turn compared our feet with the print – my number nine huge by contrast, Gillespie's bigger still, Cossor's longer and more pointed, Annesty's black walking shoe clumsy.

"A smaller man than any of us, by the look of it," said Tolefree. "Well, Mr. Catterick, it hasn't got much more to tell us, I think, but it confirms Peters. I suppose you'll take a cast?"

"The morning will do," said Catterick.

But in the morning, before Catterick could take a cast, every mark on the ground had been scuffled out. Tolefree and I took a look at the cedar before breakfast, to test Peters's speculation about the direction of the shot. It could undoubtedly have been fired from that spot, pierced the third window and smashed the mirror. It was then that we saw the work of obliteration done some time during the night after our visit. Tolefree wagged his head over it.

"Not surprised, are you, Farrar?"

But I was.

"I'm not," said he. "I rather fancied it would happen. But it was too late. It'll help to hang a man in the due efflux of time."

This was the pabulum I chewed over during that queer journey to London, when not one of us mentioned it or said a word of Burnet's tragedy, but Tolefree devoted himself to the entertainment of Margaret Gillespie with small talk while I sat behind my newspaper and thought.

Between London Bridge and Cannon Street, Tolefree said to her,

"Is there a telephone at your school?"

"Yes. Why?"

"Give me the number. I may want to ring you up. Here's mine. You may want to ring me. In any case, if we don't get in touch before, will you dine with me and Mr. Farrar tomorrow night?"

"I have lessons from seven to nine."

"Ah – in the City?"

"Yes, at St. Bride's."

"Better still," said Tolefree. "Supper at a quarter past. We'll meet you outside the Institute at nine. If I produce Mr. Denley at the same time you won't mind? I don't promise, but I may."

"Oh?" she said, with her eyebrows up. "Very well, – thanks."

She left us at Cannon Street for the Underground railway. Tolefree went to his office and I to mine. My head clerk waited till I had shed coat and hat before he came in with a pile of correspondence.

"A telephone message for you, sir – to ring Mr. Cossor in Paper Buildings as soon as you arrived."

I seized his bundle and threw it on the table.

"Get me through at once, and don't let anyone butt in," I said.

Cossor's voice came immediately after the ring.

"That you, Mr. Farrar? Can we meet today? I'm in court from two to four. After that?"

"Any time," I told him.

"Say four-thirty at your office? Good. You're on confidential terms with Tolefree, aren't you? Very well. I'll tell you when we meet."

"Would you like Tolefree to be here?"

"Good Lord! Not for worlds! A private conversation, and not a word about it to anyone beforehand. Four-thirty, then?"

Nineteen

At three o'clock, Tolefree and I sat ante-chambered in a tiny waiting room on the fifth floor of a Bishopsgate Street office building.

Tolefree had walked into my place after lunch in a state of elation for him.

"Found her!" he cried.

"Her?"

"The shrill woman – the key of the enigma. Miss Poppy de la Valle, if you please. What think of that?"

"Nothing," said I. "Never heard of her."

"Nor I. But isn't it exactly, you know? Doesn't she leap to the eye – the fairly vulgar woman that the Gillespie girl saw?"

She did. I could see her yellow hair and her fierce make-up and hear her shrill voice in those absurd syllables.

"How'd you find her, Tolefree?"

"Don't know that I ought to tell you, Farrar," he said with a smile. "Shameful business. Yet – we have no secrets from each other, have we?"

I was about to say, "Of course not," when I remembered the appointment with Cossor.

"Don't tell me anything you don't think discreet," said I.

"Discreet! Well – it was discreet enough," he chuckled. "I just suborned one of Yonge's clerks. Or rather, trapped him while he lunched. Stood him a drink. Said I had a message for what's-the-name-of-that-young-woman, you know – the one with the golden hair and the shrill voice? He fell for it in a moment. Oh, said he with a grin, I meant Miss Poppy de la Valle. Of course I did. So I scribbled a note and left it to be given to her if she called at Yonge's today, or posted to her if she didn't."

I laughed.

"It's almost too easy, Tolefree."

"Looks so, doesn't it? But you know the sniggling attitude of clerks towards that sort of client."

"What did you put in the note?"

"I told her, anonymously, that if she would be at Antonelli's in Old Compton Street at 9.30 tomorrow evening she would hear of something to her advantage. In the meantime I hope to hear of something to her disadvantage. So we're going along to Yonge's now to see what we can dig out of the sphinx."

"But," I exclaimed, "tomorrow evening? You remember we have an appointment. You'd not risk bringing Miss Gillespie into that company, Tolefree!"

"Why not? She never saw Miss Gillespie, and won't know her from Queen Elizabeth. Whereas Miss Gillespie can point her out to us. And then – well, we shall see."

We went along to Adams House in Bishopsgate Street, ascended in the elevator to the offices of Thomas Yonge, Solicitor and Commissioner of Oaths. We were ushered in to his presence after a ten minute wait. The tall man with the long face and the sleepy eyes looked up from his table between two mountains of documents and files.

"Hello, Tolefree," said he. "How do, Mr. Farrar? Find chairs. Now, who's been misbehaving this time?"

"Who hasn't?" said Tolefree. "It's a wicked world, Mr. Yonge. However, you may be able to help me with a little information."

"Any legal information cheerfully dispensed on the usual terms, Tolefree. But don't tell me you of all men are going to spend any money on lawyers!"

"I won't tell you anything so silly, Mr. Yonge. It isn't legal information I want. Just a few particulars about a client of yours."

"Ah – a client of mine? Nothing doing, Tolefree. You ought to know me better. The relations between a solicitor and his client are – well—"

"Sacred to the *N*th degree of sanctity," said Tolefree. "Don't want to know anything about them. But the client—"

Yonge shook his head.

"No, sir! I steer clear of all criminal business. Now – try Hunt and Chivvy on the first floor. They're your mark, Tolefree."

Tolefree smiled patiently.

"This isn't criminal business, Mr. Yonge. Perhaps a mere peccadillo – I don't want you to say anything about that. But it may have some bearing on a crime."

"Ah?" said the lawyer, as though Tolefree were stating an interesting zoological fact.

"I mean the murder of your client, Mr. Burnet."

The sleepy eyes opened wide for an instant, and then half closed again.

"Ah, poor Burnet! But I understand Burnet's solicitors are Menzies, Warren and Kitson, in Lincoln's Inn Fields. You've come to the wrong address, Tolefree."

"I know about Kitson's firm," said Tolefree. "Kitson read the will after Burnet's funeral. It contained a highly peculiar clause, Mr. Yonge."

"You think so? That shows you haven't had much experience of wills, if I may so, Tolefree. If there's one document in which, more than another, a man will insist on expressing his worst peculiarities, it's his will and testament. At least, that's my observation. Wills are the most eccentric exhibits in all literature."

"This, however, was a peculiar clause – not for any eccentricity of the disposition, and it was expressed in a most conventional way. I should, in fact, attribute its authorship to the ineffable and immaculate Kitson. Its peculiarity lay not in what it said but in what it didn't say."

"Ah, Tolefree – you know, if you're going to explore all the possibilities of peculiarity that lie outside the terms of a document, that's a pretty wide field, isn't it?"

Mr. Yonge looked at his watch.

"Your name was mentioned in the clause," said Tolefree.

"Indeed? I've heard something about it from Kitson. But you know, the will's not yet proved, so I can hardly discuss it, can I? Then – there's the question of *locus standi*, you know."

"Mine?" Tolefree asked.

"Yes. Where do you come in?"

"As a person charged by Burnet's heir to discover any facts that will possibly tell us what it was that Burnet feared a day or two before his death – the thing that made him call me in to a consultation that couldn't take place because Burnet was killed before I saw him."

Again the sleepy eyes opened wide to take a straight stare into Tolefree's across the table.

"Facts?" he echoed. "I'm afraid I know of no facts that have any bearing on the question."

"You'll remember that I suggested a possible bearing," said Tolefree.

"Ah – possibilities! But that's even a wider field than peculiarities, Tolefree. Now, my dear fellow, you don't really expect any help from me?"

"Indeed I do. You're a legatee, or trustee, of the sum of £500 under this clause of the will, to be expended according to Burnet's directions in the matter of Miss Poppy de la Valle."

The lawyer shook his head.

"You're romancing, Tolefree. You oughtn't to try it on a case-hardened shell-back like me! Why, Kitson read me the clause, and there's certainly nothing in it about the lady – what did you say her name was? It sounded – well—"

But Tolefree persevered.

"We're neither of us very unsophisticated persons, Mr. Yonge," he said. "I put it to you that Burnet is now dead, and that if you tell me what I want to know he at any rate will be quite indifferent about it."

"Ah – poor Burnet, yes! But you know, Tolefree, the affairs of a dead client are as sacred to a lawyer as those of a living one."

"No doubt. But if I put it to you that you can help me to bring home to the murderer the crime of Burnet's murder by giving me the information I want — ?"

"What information do you want?" Yonge said, abruptly.

"Just this: what were the relations between Burnet and this woman who calls herself de la Valle? When did they begin? And why did Burnet provide £500 in his will for her?"

Yonge traced patterns on his blotting pad for a few moments. Then he threw down his pencil.

"You're too vague, Tolefree. You're fishing. I'll do a straight deal with you. At present you have hypothesised a woman, a connection between her and Burnet and Burnet's instructions to me, and some link between this hypothetical woman and your hypothesis of Burnet's murder. I admit nothing and I'll say nothing. But come to me again in two days' time with a spot of evidence to tincture all this hypothetical stuff – and then I'll see."

Yonge rose to put an end to the interview.

"I take you at your word," said Tolefree. "Saturday before noon, Mr. Yonge – if by that time I haven't all the information I need."

"I expect you will, Tolefree. In fact, I expect you have it all now if the truth were known, eh?"

He ushered us to the landing, rang for the lift, and bade us goodbye.

"Crafty old man," said Tolefree. "But let's meet craft with craft."

The first display of Tolefree's craft was a visit to the clerks' office on the floor below, where he called out the victim of his lunch-time guile. He encountered some delay. The clerk was engaged at the telephone. When he came to us, Tolefree asked,

"Has she called?"

"No, Mr. Tolefree. She won't be calling today."

"How do you know?"

"Well – it's curious, but I was just phoning her telling her not to call. Boss's instructions."

"Oh!" said Tolefree. "Well – just address that note to her, will you, and get it in the post?"

And the second display of Tolefree's craft to walk to the end of Bishopsgate Street and return, and in ten minutes to be in the clerks' office again, with second thoughts about the note: he would withdraw it after all and send her a wire. I waited for him in the street.

"49, Blisworth Mansions, Charing Cross Road," he said, reading the address. "What'll you bet, Farrar, we don't need to bother friend Yonge on Saturday morning?"

We parted, having arranged to meet at dinner at the club in the City.

I approached the time of Cossor's appointment with a sense of excitement. It was not easy to guess what made him seek me out. All sorts of possibilities suggested themselves. Moreover I had an uncomfortable feeling of doing not quite the right thing in seeing Cossor without Tolefree's knowledge.

However, I meant to straighten that out at once.

Cossor was shown into my private room on the stroke of half past four. Tall, cool, alert, rather splendid – he shook hands and took a chair opposite me, talked about disconnected things, – the rarity of his visits to the City, the transformation wrought by modern buildings in Moorgate Street, the depression in the freight market, and all the time weighing me up, taking me in, placing me. And...

"Well, Mr. Farrar, I didn't come to talk of ships and sealing-wax, and I mustn't waste your valuable time."

I murmured something.

"You were a great friend of Burnet, I believe," said he.

For twenty years, I told him, we were very close friends.

"So that you knew his life intimately."

"I thought I did. Now I'm not so sure."

"Exactly," said Cossor.

He paused, looking intently at me.

"Exactly," he ingeminated. "I've had a long experience of the shady side of things, Mr. Farrar, and I've come to the conclusion that no one knows anyone intimately. It's impossible."

"If you suggest that there was anything shady about Burnet—" I began.

"No, no. You misunderstand me. All I intend to suggest is that none of us can be sure he knows everything even about his closest friend. For example, I should judge that you never had even a suspicion of the reason for that weekend party at Midwood and why your friend Tolefree was invited to join it."

I stared at him. It was an extraordinary thing for him to say – unless he meant me to understand that he himself did know and was about to reveal the secret. After a moment's silence, I rejoined,

"I certainly had no suspicion. But had you? Because, if we knew what that reason was, we'd not be far off the explanation of Burnet's death."

"Very true, Mr. Farrar. No – I cannot say I was definitely aware. But I will tell you this much: I expected other things to happen during that weekend, and I think they would have happened but for Burnet's death; and I think, further, that Burnet's death was procured in order that they shouldn't happen!"

I continued to stare. Cossor relaxed his gaze with a laugh.

"I daresay you think that's a bit of – let's say forensic expansion of something that was quite plain before," said he.

In a sense it was, of course, because we all knew there must have been some reason for murdering Burnet. The question was: how much, if anything, did Cossor know of the reason, and how far was he prepared to go in revealing it? His next remark made me very wary of Mr. Cossor.

"If you'd enlarge – or illustrate your point—" said I.

"Ah! You hardly expect me to do that in the circumstances – do you? Unless—"

"Unless what?" I asked, as he checked.

"Unless – Well, presently, Mr. Farrar. First, I want to ask you if you know Tolefree well."

"Fairly well. He's a pretty familiar figure in the City."

"Yes – as an inquiry agent, no doubt. But Tolefree himself? Is he just an inquiry machine? Or has he the bowels of a human being? Is he a detective robot or a man like another? And what precisely is his *locus standi* in this?"

Here was a curious echo of Yonge's question. I considered before replying.

"Tolefree," I said, "is acting on the instructions of Mr. Gillespie, I understand."

"But is he in collusion with the police?"

That was another remarkable expression for a lawyer to use.

"I don't quite follow you," said I. "He's not working for the police officially; but I'm quite sure he wouldn't work against them."

"Not even in the interests of humanity – or, let's say, chivalry?"

I was going to be plunged into deep water if this conversation went on long. Every instinct in me bristled up against the vicarious inquisition into Tolefree's character.

"I'm not a very subtle person, Mr. Cossor," I said. "I'm not able to see a parallel between murder and chivalry. What Tolefree would say in answer to such a question I can't tell you. But why don't you ask Tolefree yourself?"

He looked long at me before replying.

"Why don't I? I came to you to try to judge for myself whether it would be possible to do so. Look here, Mr. Farrar, – it's not subtlety we want; it's just plain common sense. Things happened at Midwood that night which can't be explained by any subtlety, but only by plain common-sense. I've had to deal with a great many of the cases you see described as mysterious – stupid word! D'you know what I've always found? That if a thing was impossible you couldn't make it possible by being subtle about it. If it couldn't happen this way, then it didn't happen this way, and no amount of subtlety will alter the fact. You know, and I know, and Tolefree knows, that things are said to have happened at Midwood which couldn't have happened any more than you could have delayed the rising of the sun on Sunday morning. I should be ready to talk to Tolefree about this – but only on conditions."

"Let me ring up Tolefree and ask him to come here," said I. "That'll clinch it."

"No!" The syllable rang out sharply.

"But you don't say what you've just said to me for fun, Mr. Cossor. You must have a theory of not only of what didn't but of what did happen."

"Theory!" There was a note of ironical scorn in his voice. "Everybody has a theory – or six. Catterick has. I expect all the millions who've read the reports of the inquest have. The conception of theories and the search for facts to fit them – that's a time-wasting amusement. No: I have more than a theory. I have a certainty. I know where the evidence could be obtained to prove it. But I'm not going to look for it except on conditions. Given those conditions, I will help Tolefree to solve this problem in two days. Without them – well, he'll have to do the best he can. But I implore you to try to persuade Tolefree to agree to act on conditions. That's why I asked you to see me."

I was too astonished to find words immediately.

"But—" I commenced, and stopped to reflect on the amazing fact that Cossor claimed to know the truth about Burnet's murder, but also claimed to keep the knowledge to himself unless conditions were granted. Then, on a sudden, I was seized with a kind of rage against the cool presumption of this clever lawyer who came to make a fool of me – for that was how it looked. And at once I lost my excitement and he became less formidable.

"Mr. Cossor," said I, "here's an honest-to-god common-sense question: do you know who killed Burnet?"

That got him right in the solar plexus. It was evidently the last question on earth he expected to be asked. He shrank back as if I had hit him. But his answer came instant and pat.

"Certainly not!"

"Then in spite of what you said about subtlety, you are being subtle, aren't you? I'm rather a simple sort of chap, and don't know anything about law. But I've a dim memory of hearing – or I may have read it – that all members of the bar are officers of the courts and that they are bound on all occasions to assist the course of justice to the very limits of their power."

I found myself saying this with a touch of surprise at my own temerity – lecturing a King's Counsel about his duty! But my surprise was not a patch on Cossor's.

"Why, of course," he said. "You aren't suggesting, are you, Mr. Farrar, that I am lacking in my duty to the law – for instance, that I'm impeding the course of justice?"

There was something very cold and menacing in Cossor's face as he leant across the table to say this to me. But somehow I felt certain of my cue.

"It would be most presumptuous of me to suggest," said I. "But I've a recollection of the impression you gave us last night at Midwood. Didn't you rather indicate that you had fallen for the theory that Burnet was killed by some hitherto unsuspected person who got into his room by means of a ladder against the balcony?"

"If I did?"

"Well – you seemed to be convinced that Catterick was on the wrong trail. Would it be consistent with your duty as a lawyer to leave him there when you could put him on the right one?"

Then Cossor said the most astounding thing of all.

"Mr. Farrar – you're entirely wrong about my position as a lawyer. I have no status as a lawyer in this case. I'm a citizen only. I will grant you that it is a citizen's duty to assist the police if he can – at least not to obstruct them. And now I will stagger you. I'm perfectly certain that within a few days Catterick will have wormed out every fact there is and taken steps which from my point of view would be – shall I say, deplorable? I am more anxious than I can tell you that Catterick shall not worm out these facts. I would do almost anything to prevent him!"

"Good God!" I cried. I could scarcely believe I was hearing him right.

"Quite so. Now you know why I want to make terms with Tolefree."

"But I don't!" I protested.

"You're not a fool, so you must. I tell you I can help Tolefree to his solution of the problem at once. In two days he can make it unnecessary for Catterick to turn another stone. But there must be terms."

Cossor, under his aspect of icy precision, was eager. He could not quite keep the tremor out of his voice. My own excitement had quite gone. I was now extremely aware of Mr. Cossor. I sat for a little while cogitating my answer to him.

"On that showing," said I, deliberately, "I am a fool. I cannot see it. Am I to suggest to Tolefree that you can put him on the track of some outsider who's murdered Burnet on condition that all investigation of what happened inside the house is brought to an end? Because I'm perfectly certain Tolefree would never agree. Tolefree has other fish to fry than Burnet's murderer."

The electrical effect which I had thought to produce in Cossor by this statement completely failed to come off.

"Naturally," said he. "You misunderstand me. I don't want the investigation stopped. Clearly if the murderer came from outside he had an accomplice in the house: that's been plain from the first. I want merely to make terms with Tolefree about his investigation. However, if you won't agree to put this up to him, I needn't waste more of your time. Think it over, Mr. Farrar. And remember that both Tolefree and Catterick will be needlessly handicapped if they have to spend days in looking for clues with which I can supply them – on terms."

He got up and held out his hand to me.

"I shall faithfully report to Tolefree what you say," I told him.

"That's kind of you. My telephone numbers both at my chambers and at my rooms are in the Directory. Good afternoon, Mr. Farrar."

Twenty

Tolefree did not use either of Cossor's telephone numbers. When I met him at dinner he was full of a scheme which he had hatched after making some explorations in Charing Cross Road. He listened to my account of the interview with Cossor. But he said, in effect, "Thank you for nothing, Mr. Cossor."

"Can't be done, Farrar," he declared. "I'm not going to hamstring myself by making terms with Cossor. I bet I know all he has to tell me. What's more I bet I know why he wants to make conditions. Why, Jehoshaphat! The man's in a panic. Let him stay there. When we come to making terms, I'll dictate 'em."

It was true, as Tolefree said, that the real horror of poor old Burnet's fate was in danger of being lost to view amid the confusion of personal fears and suspicions created by the circumstances with which the murder was surrounded. Tolefree was not going to lose sight of it, however, and whatever withers were wrung by his discoveries he meant to chase up every clue. The two chief clues were in London, he said. One was the identity and history of the woman with the absurd name. The other was the scrap of paper which Burnet had clutched as he died, for which so much risk had been run with so much daring during the night after he died. He would not discuss Cossor's theories of the collusion of a person inside the house with a person outside.

"Cossor's got skill in the art of throwing dust in people's eyes," said he. "Wants to limit the investigation, doesn't he? He's every reason to try to stop it altogether. He'll have to explain several things himself when I've fitted the facts together. There's a whole lot of his time Mr. Cossor will have to account for. Drop him, Farrar, and turn to something important!"

The thing to which Tolefree wished me to turn was not much to my taste.

"Thursday night," said he, "and we've got till Saturday morning to make good my boast to old Yonge. We'll have to divide the job. I'm going after that scrap of paper. I want you to go after Miss Poppy what-d'ye-call-her."

"Tolefree! I'd rather go after a mad tiger," I exploded.

But he made light of my objection: he hadn't yet heard Miss Poppy de la Valle, and I had. It was, he declared, perfectly simple. He had ascertained the habits of the lady. She might be expected to arrive at her flat in Charing Cross Road at any time between midnight and one in the morning. She would not be accompanied. The flat was one of a bunch in a big building which had only one entrance. In the lift lobby on the fourth floor I should find a sofa on which I could deposit myself to wait for her. And then the rest was easy. I was to discover from her all she knew about Burnet.

"But, my dear Tolefree," I protested, "it's preposterous. I'm absolutely no good at this game. I couldn't extract anything from a schoolgirl, let alone a person like Poppy."

"Point of fact, Farrar," he replied, "you're the only man who's at all likely to get anything out of her. You're a friend of Burnet's. She liked old Burnet in her own fashion. You've got all the cards. You know all that any detective could know: her association with Cossor, her journeys with Burnet, the legacy, her visits to Yonge's office. Blow it off on her gradually and make her think you know a lot more. What you want to get from her is when she first met Burnet, and where, and what their relations were, and who if anybody besides Cossor was aware of them.

Make her talk. You're far more likely to succeed than I – and I must get that hotel traced tonight if possible."

I prophesied to the contrary. I foresaw utter failure and a highly undignified failure. But Tolefree would have none of it. He saw success right ahead.

In the beginning it seemed that Tolefree was right and I was wrong. I sat on the predestined sofa in the dingily lit lobby of the fourth floor of Blisworth Mansions from midnight till half past, the object of indifferent glances from the lift attendant as he went up and down and from the few people who passed along the corridor. At half past twelve a woman stepped out of the lift and said good night to the attendant. She had yellow hair under a black hat. She was wrapped in a fur coat. She took no notice of me, but went on to No. 49, three doors down the corridor, put a key in the latch and entered.

Miss Poppy de la Valle.

I walked after her and rang at the door. A sleepy-eyed maid opened.

"Miss de la Valle?" I asked.

"Yes – but Miss de la Valle cannot receive a visit at this time of night," said the maid, and would have shut me out.

I declined to be shut out.

"Pardon me, but please give my card to Miss de la Valle, and apologise for the lateness of the visit. Tell her the business is urgent."

The girl looked suspiciously at me, but took the business card I had given her, read it, and hesitatingly went into the flat. Through an open door, I heard two sentences.

"Middle-aged man. Looks respectable. Here's his card."

"Farrar? Well, I'm damned!"

Then the door of the room shut. I could have sworn that the expletive was in a man's voice. I waited.

Two minutes may have passed before the maid returned.

"Please to step this way," she said, and led me into a tiny sitting room, switching on the light and closing the door upon me.

There immediately arrived the shrill-voiced woman still in hat and coat.

"Mr. Farrar?" said she. "You wanted to see me?"

A woman with dyed hair and a blatantly artificial complexion, dark brown eyes, and that high loud voice which I had heard on Cossor's staircase. She sat down. There was a little table between us.

I apologised for calling at such a time, and pleaded the urgency of my business.

"You were acquainted with the late Mr. Wellington Burnet," said I. "He was my greatest friend. You know he has been killed in a dreadful manner, Miss de la Valle. I am seeking information which may help to clear up the puzzle of his death."

She nodded.

"How did you know I was acquainted with him? Did he tell you anything about it?"

"Unfortunately not a word," I replied.

"He wouldn't. You're a man of the world, I suppose. You wouldn't expect him to go shouting about it, would you? Now, you can guess I've got no information that'll help you in any way."

"I think you have," I urged. "Let me put it to you this way: you could hardly have been glad that Burnet was murdered."

"I should think not!" she exclaimed. "He was an old fool, but rather a nice old fool. The dirty dog that did him in ought to swing for it. But I don't know anything about it. How should I?"

"Of course not. But you could help a lot if you'd answer a few questions."

"Depends on the questions," said she. "Fire away, Mr. Farrar."

"Then will you tell me when and where you first met Burnet?"

"When? Some time last May, I think. Where? At the Wigwam Club."

"Casually?"

"Quite. He happened to be sitting at a table with a crowd I knew and I joined in. Absolutely casual."

"And was it then you struck up an acquaintance? There must have been something—"

Yep. Your friend was fairly sozzled, Mr. Farrar, and whether it was the hair dye or the rouge or the lipstick or what – there certainly was something. Maudlin! – but I'm not telling you about that."

"I want to know nothing about that," said I. "What I meant was that the acquaintance continued, and there must have been something – you see, I knew Burnet. He wasn't often sozzled: in fact, I never saw him sozzled. And you saw him several times afterwards when he was quite sober."

"How d'you know that?"

A hard look in the bold eyes.

"I happen to have heard it."

"If you think I'm going to tell you what he said when he was quite sober, you're thinking wrong," said Miss de la Valle.

"I'd not dream of being so indiscreet," I assured her. "But perhaps you could tell me how often you met, and when the last time was."

"Four or five times. I haven't seen him since the end of July. You know, Mr. Farrar, you're barking up the wrong tree. I'm not the right woman."

"You're connected with the stage, aren't you?" I asked.

"Never seen the bright side of the footlights in my life."

"But you had some thought of the stage as a career?"

"Never a bit of it."

How I wished for Tolefree's knowledge of physiognomy! I could not tell whether this woman was lying or not.

"If you're not the right woman do you know who is?"

"If you don't, then I'm sure I don't."

"You've not seen Burnet with this other woman?"

"Certainly not! You're playing with me, Mr. Farrar. How could I have seen him with her? I ask you!"

Something in her tone and look brought the dawn to my intelligence: she was speaking of Mrs. Burnet. I felt sick. Was the ghastly truth that Burnet, "maudlin," as she said, had discussed his marital troubles with this creature? And was that the explanation of her knowledge of Cossor? But these were things I could not possibly ask her. I harked back.

"Did you see Burnet at the Wigwam Club more than once?"

A grim sort of smile spread over her face.

"No, sir! First time was enough Wigwam for Burnet. He was only sorry once that he went to the Wigwam – for ever after!"

"I believe," said I, "a number of theatrical people went there?"

"Yep – all sorts went there, till the busies closed it up."

"And some of them were in the party where you met Burnet, weren't they?"

"Very likely. Yes – come to think of it, there was a guy talking stage to him when I got there. But you know what that sort of crowd's like – or, no, I suppose you don't! Hot stuff at the Wigwam, Mr. Farrar."

"Yes, so I imagine."

It was a world as alien to old Burnet as his wife's world. How scurvily fate had treated him in his relations with women! How much happier for Burnet if he had stuck to me and the Club and our Thursday evenings and given superfluous wealth to a Home for Stray Dogs! The reflection darted through my mind as I watched the woman getting bored with the talk and wishing to put it to an end. But there were two things I must ask her.

"My friend Burnet," said I, "was one of the most generous men on earth."

"Really!"

"I always found him so. I hope you did," I suggested.

"What do you want to know? How much he paid me?"

I blushed fiercely.

"I trust you'll think nothing so insulting," said I. "You haven't heard anything from Mr. Yonge, the solicitor?"

She gazed at me with a suspicious, puzzled frown.

"I may and I may not. If I have I expect you know it. What's the game, Mr. Farrar?"

"No game, Miss de la Valle. I merely mentioned the matter as an instance of Burnet's characteristic generosity."

"That? My God! – I should have said it was an instance of his morbid sense of remorse. Did you ever hear of conscience money? If you'd said your friend Burnet had a tender conscience—"

She hoisted the fur coat round her shoulders. It was my turn to look puzzled.

"If that's all, Mr. Farrar—"

"One other thing. You have an acquaintance with Mr. Cossor?"

She took the question like a blow between the eyes. She sprang to her feet, and for the first time I heard and saw the real shrill-voiced woman.

"Who are you?" she shouted. "I don't believe you're Farrar at all! You're a busy – a dirty, lowdown busy. I'll soon see!"

She flung open the door, ran across the hall, and burst into a room.

"Here!" she cried. "Come and see who this is that says he's Farrar."

"Not Farrar? Then I expect it's our friend Tolefree in masquerade."

The man followed his voice into the hall.

It was Cossor.

"No – not Tolefree, I see, but veritably Mr. Farrar in the flesh. How d'e do? We didn't expect to meet again so soon, eh?"

I walked towards the flat door. "Don't let us keep you, Mr. Farrar."

I opened the door somehow and got out while they stood side by side watching my undignified exit.

Twenty-One

HOW intolerable at times is the tyranny of personality! It depends not at all on character or virtue or intellect. A nameless something will make a decent man feel like a worm in the presence of a scoundrel...

Cossor had personality.

I had discovered Cossor in a compromising place and dubious company. Mine should have been the accusing finger; his the indignity. But I sneaked away from that lamentable flat feeling like some naughty boy caught out in some sly misdemeanour. The inferiority complex entangled me till I felt the cold night air on my face in Charing Cross Road, now almost deserted and silent but for a few echoing footsteps and the roar of an occasional belated car. It was half past one in the morning.

The normal atmosphere of a familiar street restored my self-assurance. I looked up at the tall building with dislike and consigned Cossor to the devil.

"Well, Farrar?"

I started as a touch fell on my arm.

"You here!"

"These two hours," said Tolefree. "Waiting. Saw you come. Hung about for you. No knowing what queer folks you might meet in such a place. Been on tenterhooks. I'd have given a tenner to be behind the arras, Farrar, when you found Cossor in Poppy's flat!"

"Tolefree! How the devil did you know Cossor was there?"

"Saw him go in. It marches, eh?"

"Come along to my rooms, Tolefree. The thing's getting on my nerves. Where are we going to end up?" I groaned.

"On top. Cheer up, Farrar. A great day's work."

And so it seemed when we compared notes in my rooms in the quiet house in Manchester Square, and Tolefree listened attentively to my tale.

What did he make of it?

He lit his pipe and jerkily, between the puffs, put his thoughts into order.

"I'll tell you now," he said, "that I'd settled the whole thing in my own mind three days ago. Only the process I used won't pass muster in a court of law."

"You mean you've guessed?" said I, incredulous.

"Guessed is the word."

"You mean you've guessed the murderer? You *know*?"

"No, I don't know. Guessed is the word. And I've not guessed the murderer, but people who were concerned in the murder."

"People! Then – you've adopted Cossor's theory of an accomplice."

"Or accomplices," said Tolefree. "But that didn't need much guessing, did it? From the first it didn't look like a one man job."

"N-no," I stammered. "I suppose not—"

"But I'm not going to start speculating now. I'd like just to run over the things we've found and the inferences we can draw from them. Then I'll make an appointment with you for tomorrow morning, Farrar. Meet me at eleven at Masterton's Hotel, will you? That'll be crucial."

"Good heavens!" I cried as Tolefree absolutely chuckled this out. "You've found the hotel?"

He was enjoying my astonishment.

"I think so. In fact I'm certain. But we'll see in the morning. Then I'll tell you how. For the present, where are we? Let's hammer it out."

This, according to him, was where we were:

Burnet's one-time uneventful life has been subject to two disturbing influences. Up to his marriage, humdrum, respectable, commonplace. Marriage carries him into an entirely new country, where he is a foreigner: First disturbing influence, said Tolefree.

In that country, the people in whom we are concerned include Mrs. Burnet and Cossor. They are the only persons of social position at Midwood at the time of the crime. Noted that Mrs. Burnet is a relative and was an old flame of Cossor's. Noted also that for a considerable time Burnet has not been happy in his marriage.

Not being happy in his marriage, Burnet seeks distractions away from home. He returns quite needlessly to the treadmill of his business in the City. Finds no anodyne there. Nor in a futile attempt to restore his old relations with me. He is driven to more violent drugs.

Hence the Wigwam Club and its sequels: Second disturbing influence, said Tolefree.

In that underworld the people in whom we are concerned include Miss Poppy and young Annesty. Perhaps there is another woman. On the face of it almost certainly another woman – if Miss Poppy's statement is true that she never had any connection with the stage. Annesty's experience shows that Burnet was trying to get some woman established on the stage.

But there's a puzzling link between the disreputability of the Wigwam Club and the social gorgeousness of Midwood. It's Cossor: he has some relations with the Poppy woman, at present unknown.

In one or the other of these circles, then, Burnet has come a purler. He has come down so hard that it becomes necessary to send out an S.O.S., and Tolefree is called in. Do we get a hint of the disaster from the Poppy woman's remark about conscience money? That's a word with a nasty ring for Tolefree. If the money bequeathed to old Yonge to administer for Miss Poppy is regarded by the lady herself as conscience money, then Burnet's adventures in the Wigwam world must have included some episode of which he was so mightily ashamed that he wasn't content to let his remorse die with his body, but provided for keeping it alive afterwards. It must have been something pretty terrific – or he must have thought it so, for when he made this provision in his will presumably he had no ghost of a notion that anybody was going to murder him.

"So, you see," said Tolefree, "we've got two hefty forces bearing on Burnet's conduct. First, there's the persistent force that lies in the social background of Midwood and in Cossor's old relations with Mrs. Burnet. Given certain circumstances that might be a tremendous force. Then, there's the force of demoralisation that plays round the soul of everyone who dips into the Wigwam world. That's a regular hell's kitchen of a world, you know, Farrar."

"I don't know. I can only imagine," said I.

"Anyhow you can take my word for it. And then – you've got these two new and utterly alien forces in Burnet's life after he's reached the set, staid ways of middle-age. Without both or either of 'em, Burnet's life would undoubtedly have gone on smoothly and conventionally. And you see where we get? – in one of 'em we shall find the cause why Burnet was murdered. Isn't it next door to a certainty that when we've seen the missing part of that hotel bill, we'll know which of the two it is?"

Tolefree displayed a little unaccustomed elation as he ended his review.

"Mr. Edward Cossor, K.C., wanted me to make terms with him, didn't he? Tomorrow, Farrar, he'll be wanting to make terms with me!"

But when I met him next morning, Tolefree's effervescence had disappeared. He was cold, wary, slow of speech as usual. Until I inquired my way there I had never heard of Bastin Street, W.2. When I reached it I had a shock of surprise. It was one of the narrow streets in the angle formed by Edgware Road and

Praed Street, and, like all that region seemed to be a dependency of Paddington Station. It consisted mainly of third-rate hotels and boarding houses wearing a sort of vagrant bed-and-breakfast air, and Masterton's Hotel was one of them – a little larger than the rest, but true to type. I had passed its door when a taxi drew up in front of me and Tolefree alighted. He had another man with him.

"You're on time, Farrar," said he. "This is Inspector Pierce, of the C.I.D. He's lent himself to me for an hour. We may want him – to use as a corkscrew if the bottle proves stubborn. But he thinks not. He's made a few inquiries for me already."

"You oughtn't to have any trouble, Tolefree," said the Inspector. "It's a respectable place, with a railway trade. I know nothing against it."

"What beats me," I observed, "is how you fixed on it."

"Five hours hard work with the Hotel Directory and the Telephone Directory," Tolefree replied. "I had to look for an hotel bearing the name of its proprietor – or some former proprietor: the possessive's settled that – in the W.2. district, and it had to be an hotel whose telephone number ended with the numerals 31."

"You made a telephone number of that? I thought it must be the end of the date – 1931."

"And I at first; but you know in hotel bills the dates are generally in a series across the tops of the columns. So I took the hypothesis of a telephone number – and it worked. It had to be an hotel with some number ending in 31. It also had to be an hotel that kept its accounts with a mechanical calculator. I got Masterton's Hotel with the aid of the two directories and a first-class headache. Pierce got the adding machine for me by having a call made last night. So we're there, Farrar! It's the place, beyond a doubt. The question is whether we can get a look at their carbon duplicates – or, if they're destroyed, the book in which the account is entered. I've no right to demand it. That's why I asked Pierce to come. They won't refuse him anything."

"But you understand, Tolefree," said the Inspector, "that I'm not in on this officially? Our friends at Midwood haven't asked us to help them—"

"Catterick? Help?" Tolefree grinned. "Not much! You're just the persuader, Pierce. These people will know nothing except that we want to examine an account with your approval."

And that was exactly how it happened. We walked into a dingy lobby and approached a wicket in a glass screen labelled "Office." The whole place was drab and uninviting. Tolefree asked the woman inside the screen to send his card to the manager. Presently we were ushered into a cupboard of a private room and the manager, who was a lady of uncertain age but decided manners, appeared to us there. "Yes?" she said, very much on her guard. "Which of you is it?"

Tolefree treated her admirably. She might easily have believed, had she been that sort of woman, that it broke his heart to put her to the slightest inconvenience. But she wasn't. His tone mollified her severity, but did not quell her suspicions. It was a trivial matter from her point of view, said Tolefree, but important from his. He would be grateful for a glance at the duplicate of a certain account which the hotel had issued.

"Certainly not!" she said. "It's unheard of. Why should I show you an account? You don't expect me to jackal for you in a – private inquiry, do you?" – and she looked at Tolefree's card as though it were a cockroach.

"My dear madam," said Tolefree, "you misunderstand me altogether. I wish merely to be able to confirm the accuracy of a statement that a certain account issued by Masterton's Hotel was issued on a certain date. Unfortunately the date has been torn from the original."

"No – it's no good. You can't smarm me! I see no reason why I should show you anything. And if that's all, Mr. – er – Tolefree—"

She took another look at the offensive card.

"By no means all, madam," said Tolefree, with his best smile. "I'm sure we shall end with a good understanding. I didn't want to distress you about it, but I assure you that this is a highly important matter. Will you, Mr. Pierce—"

The Inspector took a card from his case and handed it to the lady. It made all the difference. She looked angry, but repressed her wrath.

"I told Mr. Tolefree," said he, "there was never a breath of suspicion of any sort about Masterton's, and he thought if we could avoid making an official business of this, so much the better. You understand? We were trying to save your feelings. It's a matter of great importance, as he says. Of course you'll assist Mr. Tolefree. Let him see this account – or if you haven't got it, confirm it by your books. There's no reflection whatever on your hotel. And now, Tolefree, I'll leave you."

The official touch worked like a charm. Whereas Tolefree's card was a noxious source of offense, Mr. Pierce's was a magic wand.

"What account is it?" she asked when Pierce had departed.

"The series number," said Tolefree, consulting his pocket-book, "is R 1067."

"Well!" she cried. "That thing again?"

"Oh?" Tolefree raised his eyebrows. "Somebody else curious about it?"

"That's no business of yours, anyway," she snapped. "Wait here."

Whether Masterton's Hotel deserved all the eulogy of Mr. Pierce or not (and I daresay it did) its business habits were highly methodical. Within two minutes she was back, bringing a box file labelled "R 2." Tolefree gave no outward sign of inward eagerness as she opened it and rustled through the flimsies with which it was filled. But as for me, I could hardly suppress my excitement. She withdrew a leaf and looked at it.

"R 1067?" said she. "The date is the 5th May, 1931. Is that all you want to know?"

She made as though to restore the paper to the file. I gasped, for it was certainly not half that Tolefree wanted to know. But he still betrayed no feeling.

"The 5th May? Let me see, – what day of the week was that?" He looked into his pocket-book. "It was a Tuesday. M-m – R 1067 – may I compare?" I gasped again, as he looked up brightly and held out his hand.

At last the paper was in it.

Tolefree glanced from it to his book and back again, and murmured, "Yes – yes. That's it – 5th May. You see, Farrar? Not the day you thought."

He passed the document to me. My hand shook a little as I held it for an instant, pretending to examine the date. Two words leapt up and two words only. They burnt my eyes. They were undoubtedly the words for which Burnet had been murdered, and here we were at the end of our quest.

"No – that's not the day," said I, hoarsely, and passed it back to him.

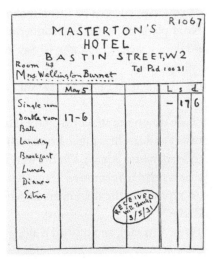

Tolefree handed the paper to her with a word of thanks and apology for having troubled her to no purpose, We were outside the cupboard and in the lobby before my hand ceased trembling. Tolefree was in no hurry. He stopped to pass the time of day with the porter, who swung open the glass door and followed us out on to the steps. There Tolefree lingered, and I saw a ten-shilling note fluttering from his fingers. It seemed to act as a magnet upon the eyes and the feet of the porter. He followed Tolefree down the steps and a yard or two along the street.

"How long have you been at Masterton's, porter?" said Tolefree.

"Matter of five years, sir," said the man.

Tolefree parted with the note.

"When do you get an hour off?"

"Two to three, sir."

"I guess you're not a very talkative chap?"

"I guess not, sir."

"What floor is Number 43 on?"

"Third floor, sir."

"Well, I keep a few of these things at Paddington Station for emergencies. If you happened to be there, looking at the first bookstall on No. 1 platform, with the chambermaid who takes care of the third floor – well, what about it? Say half past two?"

"That'll be all right, sir."

"Good. Now go down to Praed Street and call a taxi, will you?"

The porter rode up on the step of the taxi. The manageress was in the doorway and saw him touch his cap to us as we drove off. We rode to Manchester Square. On the way Tolefree asked me not to talk: he wanted to memorise. In my room he sat down immediately to reproduce the document of which the series number was R 1067.

"That's it, Farrar," he said, and pushed it along the table.

Twenty-Two

While Tolefree kept his appointment with the porter, I went to my office and tried to put this horror out of my mind by attending to business.

It was hopeless. The vision of that evil piece of paper clutched in old Burnet's hand as he faced his death obscured everything. It seemed to bring the last scene in Burnet's life into the clearest perspective – a struggle for its possession, desperate, relentless. Just for that and nothing else, whether the murderer was this person or that, hired assassin or member of the household, and by whatever means he came at Burnet.

There was no need now to speculate between the two forces that had disturbed Burnet's life. We knew.

The affair of the Wigwam Club and the flat in Charing Cross Road was disreputable enough. If Burnet had not been miserable in his marriage he would never have fallen for anything of that sort; but, amazing as it was in Burnet, the vulgar story was nothing out of the common. Such things happened every day. He had behaved in a fashion that caused him remorse, and he had done what he could by way of practical repentance. So, at any rate, I read that shrill woman's allusion to conscience money. But that had nothing to do with the document Burnet held in his hand on Saturday evening and nothing to do with Burnet's murder. It was the other force, the Midwood force, that we had to disclose and circumvent to find the murderer of Burnet.

Being a rather conventional person with utterly old-fashioned notions of propriety, I think at this moment I was more stricken with horror and hatred of the intrigue revealed by the hotel bill than by its fearful implications. That a fastidious and highly cultured woman like Mrs. Burnet should choose this sordidness... that Cossor, cynical and blackguardly as his conduct on the previous day had seemed, should be involved in it! Cossor, whatever his character, had the outward habits of a gentleman... and – Masterton's in Bastin Street!

And why was the bill for two persons made out in the name of Mrs. Burnet? It was surely quite unusual. But then the whole thing was outrageous. If they were this sort of people, what they did in the trivial matter of the hotel bill could have had no importance whatever for them. One needed to be shameless...

These reflections see-sawed through my head while I sat staring at shipping documents without seeing them. And then suddenly an idea blazed up – some reminiscence of things read in newspapers. Formal evidence for the purpose of divorce proceedings, – how did it go? Hotel bills were often produced as the *pièces de conviction*. Parties offered to supply evidence to support the other parties' application. It generally took the form of hotel bills. And according to the manageress, other people had been curious about this particular bill.

I pushed the papers aside and jumped up. That was it! Everything would be explained if Mrs. Burnet had come to London on the 5th May, engaged a room at this inconspicuous hotel, stipulated for a double room, and either stayed there or not stayed there, but in either case paid the bill. It would absolve her from the worst inference of the beastly thing – and I wanted her to be absolved at any rate from that. How this theory could be reconciled with the tragedy in Burnet's study I could not clearly see; but it would explain the single name on the bill itself.

I had difficulty in containing my impatience to present the suggestion to Tolefree. When he picked me up at half past five, I almost threw it at him.

"Well, I'm damned, Farrar!" said he. "You've worried that out? Thought of a divorce action as the mainspring of all the trouble? That's clever of you. Because you're right. It was."

"Ah – by gosh, Tolefree," said I, "you know that for certain? Be hanged to the cleverness – but I'm jolly glad. I couldn't believe that woman would—"

I stopped with my mouth open, for Tolefree shook his head and looked strangely compassionate.

"Don't rush to conclusions," he adjured me. "Queer ground this. You can't be sure what any woman will do on such queer ground. I'm more befogged now than I was before. No doubt in the world an action for divorce was on the cards. But – I'm sorry to disappoint you, Farrar – your theory is wrong. Two persons were in No. 43 on May 5th."

So did Tolefree destroy my short-lived castle in the air. No doubt I looked as crestfallen as I felt.

"But," he said, "that's next to no matter. The important thing is that they were playing up for a divorce. To tell you the truth, Farrar, I've got a curious sense of being on the verge of something new – and decisive. Listen! The wretched story of Room 43 and the hotel bill are nothing compared with what I learned this afternoon, almost, as you might say, accidentally. There's another connection between Masterton's Hotel and Midwood than what happened on May 5th. Close the door and I'll tell you."

I slid the bolt across the door, telephoned my head clerk that I might be late and no one need wait, and returned to listen to Tolefree.

The porter was as good as his word. He was standing by the bookstall when Tolefree reached the platform, and with him a woman, plainly a servant in her going-out dress, but young and intelligent. He took them into a waiting-room, pledged them to secrecy, and began his catechism about Room 43 and May 5th. The porter honestly confessed that he could remember nothing. The maid, however, remembered everything – not the date, for there was nothing to fix it in her mind, but the circumstances. They were strange, and aroused her curiosity. The two people came in not very late – about eleven o'clock, she thought. About a quarter of an hour afterwards she got a ring from 43. The lady met her in the doorway and demanded to know whether a second room could be obtained. She said all the rooms on the third floor were full, but she would inquire at the office about a room somewhere else.

"Why did she want a second room?" Tolefree asked.

"She said the gentleman insisted on having a separate room," the maid replied.

She went down to the ground floor. The office was temporarily closed in the absence of the clerk, and some delay occurred in getting at the room register. In the end she found a vacant number, and went upstairs with the information. The lady then said it didn't matter. As they were talking at the door the gentleman pushed by them. He had his hat and coat on and carried a little suitcase. He took no notice of them, but went downstairs, and left the hotel. The porter was off duty and knew nothing of this; but the maid, wondering, descended to cancel the second room, and found the office in a flurry. The gentleman had gone out, flinging over his shoulder the words, "Mrs. Burnet will settle." As the suitcase carried by the gentleman was the only luggage they had brought in, the office was somewhat concerned about Mrs. Burnet's solvency. But she put their doubts at rest within five minutes by coming down fully dressed and announcing that she had decided not to stay, demanding her bill and settling it, ordering a taxi and driving away.

When Tolefree reached this point of his narrative, I broke in,

"Why, after all I was right! They were just faking evidence."

"Certainly you can read it that way. Or you can read it differently. It was strange, you know – sort of improvisation. Doesn't look as if they'd rigged it up beforehand. It puzzles me, Farrar. It doesn't assort with your dainty woman theory, does it? But that's as far as we can get with it. Now, listen to the porter. He's been all ears for the maid's story, and I've seen his eyes growing bigger and bigger, and his mouth bursting with speech."

One couldn't have guessed that morning at Masterton's, as Tolefree said, that the insignificant porter for whom a ten shilling note was an irresistible magnet, would supply what might prove to be the master clue to Burnet's tragedy. But it seemed quite possible that this might be so. When Tolefree had come to the end of his questions, the porter said to the maid,

"Look here, Alice! – can you mind whether that dam' skunk Flint was about that night? Or was it after he left?"

Yes, the girl answered, he was there. He made some beastly remark to her about it, and she told him he was a nasty-minded brute.

"Who's Flint?" Tolefree asked.

Flint, said the porter, was a dirty dog. Flint had been for a few months the head-waiter at Masterton's, and he was such a dirty dog that he poisoned the atmosphere. He got himself hated by everybody. Never, it appeared, had there been such rejoicing among the staff of Masterton's as when Flint gave a fortnight's notice and took himself off.

"What made you mention Flint?" Tolefree demanded.

"Well, sir, – it was the name."

"What name?"

"Name of Burnet."

"Why should the name of Burnet bring Flint to your mind? And if it did, why not before now? I thought you said you knew nothing about what happened on May 5th?"

"Neither I did, sir," said the porter. "Never heard of it till now. But 'twas the name of Burnet – have you read about that murder down in the country – man of the name of Burnet?"

"Yes, of course. But what's that got to do with Flint or Masterton's Hotel? The name of Burnet is common enough."

"Yes, sir. But the name of Mr. Burnet's house – what is it? Midwood? Yes – that's it. Seemed familiar to me all along and I couldn't place it. But now I know why. Flint was bragging before he left about getting a job in a slap-up country house instead of a rat's-hole like Masterton's, and the name of the house was Midwood. And now I'm wondering whether he hadn't got something at the back of his wicked head when he made insulting remarks to Alice."

It was patent, said Tolefree, that the porter was prepared to believe any villainy of Flint, and there was a real fire of excited hatred in his eyes when he had linked up Flint, as he thought, with a house where murder had been committed. But of actual information he had no more. He knew nothing about his *bête noire*, whence he came, what his character; only that he detested him.

"Yet you see, Farrar, that this chance mention of a name in his hearing may be a vital thing for us."

"Why – there's no Flint at Midwood," said I.

"There may be. We heard nothing of any recent change of servants. And what's in a name? A scoundrelly fellow gets to know of an episode such as that of Room 43. He's the kind of man who finds advantage for himself in everything that other people wish to hide. 'Look here, Mrs. Burnet, I know a secret you want to conceal. The price of concealment is so-and-so. I shall be pleased to take charge of your pantry for you—'"

"Good God, Tolefree! You mean Elford—"

"Yes, I think so. In fact I don't doubt it. The porter describes Flint for me, and he gives me a speaking likeness of our friend Elford."

"A blackmailer! – in the house—"

"That seems quite on the cards, doesn't it? 'Mr. Elford, your peculations in the household are becoming so brazen that Mr. Burnet cannot fail to take notice of them. He's a very particular man about accounts.' – 'Madam, I have not the slightest fear of

Mr. Burnet. I rely on you to protect me from him.' Doesn't it go something like that, Farrar?"

"Then Elford," I exclaimed, "finds that Burnet already possesses knowledge of the Room 43 business, and his power of blackmail is gone. He's threatened with exposure to the police. And then—"

Tolefree considered this.

"You see all that?" he said. "I can't go quite so fast. There's a lot in it that wants more explanation. But our theory of the murder – in fact our knowledge of it – requires an accomplice, doesn't it? Here we have a little light on that. Mark this, Farrar: I've said it before. If that murder was done from the outside there must have been more than one accomplice. Elford was not in the house, but safely guarded at the police station when that trick was played in the middle of the night. It wants investigation. We'll learn something about him tonight, or I'm a Dutchman. Now I'm going to put it across Miss Poppy Whatsername good and hard. Don't forget – nine o'clock at St. Bride's. If I'm not about when Miss Gillespie turns up, take her along to Old Compton Street and I'll meet you there."

My eruption into the garden at Midwood where she walked with Denley had left some displeasure in Margaret Gillespie's mind. She was not at ease with me. That showed in her manner when she found me pacing St. Bride Street alone just after nine. She was very silent in the taxi. She seemed indifferent when we plunged into the queer, exotic atmosphere of Antonelli's. But a hand waved from a table at the end of the long narrow room. Miss Gillespie immediately came to life.

The presence of the owner of the hand surprised me. How or why Tolefree had got hold of Denley for this occasion I did not know. I thought, for a fleeting moment, that it was not too scrupulous of Tolefree. But if the girl suspected any ulterior plan in Tolefree's mind, she gave no sign. She seemed to be just grateful to him.

We supped. We sat over coffee and cigarettes till the place was empty, and we were still in conference when gentle intimation came to us that Antonelli's was about to close.

It was a strange conversation, full of half meanings and reserves on all sides. Tolefree, for all his whimsical courtesy to Margaret Gillespie, had Denley on the operating table all the time, probing him mercilessly. He certainly stood it well. Whatever Denley knew about that Saturday evening at Midwood – and Tolefree evidently believed he knew much – he kept it to himself. Tolefree began suddenly to grill the young man after a long spell of desultory meandering round the subject.

"Well, Denley," said he, "you'd do much better to tell the truth – spill the beans, 'cough it up,' as Catterick would say."

"I'm not conscious of having told anything but the truth."

He pushed back the dark hair from his forehead, and sat up.

"No," said Tolefree. "But there's such a thing as inferential lying. All right if it's in a good cause – I'm enough of a casuist to give you that. But cloaking a murder isn't a good cause. And you're cloaking a murder."

"Nothing of the sort."

"Oh, but you are. I'll prove it. Will you answer me a few questions now – straight, without any prevarication whatever?"

"Depends what they are. I'm not going to promise in the dark."

"There! Exactly," Tolefree sighed. "All I want to do is to uncloak a murder. And you say you're not cloaking it!"

"False syllogism," said Denley, quietly. "Ask your questions. If I can't answer them candidly, I'll say nothing. Then you can't accuse me of – what was it? Inferential lying?"

Tolefree's eyes gleamed.

"Very well," he said. "I'll begin with this question: What did you hear when you listened at the door of Mrs. Burnet's room on Saturday evening – just before Gillespie found you in the corridor?"

"Nothing."

"What had you heard or seen before that which induced you to listen at the door?"

No answer.

"Jack!" cried Miss Gillespie. 'Don't you see where this—"

"Excuse me, young lady." Tolefree intercepted her. "I'm quite content with the terms Mr. Denley has made."

"Of course you are – but I don't think it's very sporting of you to trick him—"

"I hate you to think ill of me," said Tolefree. "I'm quite a good sportsman, really. However, I'll drop the catechism. Instead I'll state a few facts, and he can pull me up if I'm wrong. Now, Mr. Denley – I think you must have heard something which brought you into the corridor, and that you must have seen something there which puzzled you, and you listened at Mrs. Burnet's door on the chance that your ears might help to solve the puzzle. Remember the time when this happened: it was a very few minutes before Burnet was found murdered a few yards away. You hated to be found in this posture by Gillespie, and you shooed him off when he spoke to you. Afterwards you thought better of it, and went to look for him. But before you found him the murder was discovered, and then – why, it was too late."

Tolefree paused. Denley stared at him without speaking. "When you were questioned at the inquest, you said you'd not been out of your room. That wasn't a lie by inference. It was a whopping lie direct. You'll pardon me for using words of one syllable. Now, a man of your sort doesn't tell lies aimlessly. So I'm justified in assuming that you had what you thought a sufficient reason for committing perjury."

Denley remained silent.

"I don't suggest that it wasn't a sufficient reason," said Tolefree invitingly.

Denley still remained silent.

"Well – no answer to that. Let's pass on. In the night – or rather early on Sunday morning – the lights all through the upper part of the house suddenly went wrong. I don't know how you discovered that they'd gone wrong – unless you'd put 'em out of action yourself."

"I certainly did not." Denley shot the denial at him.

Tolefree leaned forward with his elbows on the table, gazing hard into his eyes.

"So," said he. "That's interesting. Now, it is highly important for some person or persons that the lights should be out of action for a certain time – *odit lucem!* A desperate thing is attempted while the lights are off. I shall not ask you whether you know who put them off. Nor will I ask you how at such an hour you know they are off; nor why you put on your dressing gown, and steal down to the first-floor corridor, and switch them on again; nor why, when you realise that you are being watched, you flee in great haste back to your room—"

"Jack!" The girl's exclamation was a hoarse reproach, under her breath. Denley said nothing.

"I perceive," said Tolefree, "that you had not put Miss Gillespie wise to this little incident. Perhaps it was just as well. But if you were prepared to tell the candid truth, Denley, you'd admit that all this wants explanation. As an intelligent man you must have realised that I could not account for the murder of Burnet without supposing the existence of an accomplice – perhaps more than one. You must also have seen that I was bound to look for accomplices, and for any motive whatever which might be attached to them."

Denley continued to look straight across the table at Tolefree, with set lips.

"I daresay, also, you have observed that murderers more commonly give themselves away by what they do after the crime than by what leads up to it."

No answer.

"Anyhow, it is so. Oh, by the way, no doubt Miss Gillespie has told you of those occasions when she saw her uncle with Miss Poppy de la Valle—"

"Who?" said the girl. "That creature! You know? You've found her?"

"Mr. Farrar has," said Tolefree.

She looked at me with increased distaste.

"Well – I won't ask you whether you've informed her of your own meeting or meetings with the creature. Oh, my dear young lady," said Tolefree, placing a hand on her arm as she uttered an angry exclamation, "there's not the least need to be peeved. I don't doubt that Mr. Denley disapproved of her even more deeply than Mr. Burnet – or you yourself. That's not the point. But, Denley, you will remember the hurried trip to London you took on the evening after the reading of Burnet's will, when you went from Charing Cross to the Temple Station, and thence into the Temple, and then into Paper Buildings, and had an interview in Mr. Cossor's chambers with this creature, and afterwards saw her at Blisworth Mansions in the Charing Cross Road."

"You're pretty good at spying, aren't you?" said Denley at last, with a curl of his lip.

"Beastly trade," said Tolefree. "But at least confess that if we'd had your confidence from the start, there'd have been no need to spy. I'm looking for the tracks of accomplices in a murder. I come across Mr. Cossor, Mr. Denley and Miss Poppy Thingembob all tangled up with each other and with the man who was murdered. You won't think me indecently curious if I speculate a little on that, will you? Or if I itch to know why Mr. Denley hides up any number of things? Now – are you going to spill the beans?"

"Not on your life," said Denley.

"Very well. Let's drop the subject. Miss Gillespie – he don't ride well on the curb, does he?"

"No – but he goes straight," said she with a toss of her head.

"Straight!" Tolefree exclaimed.

"That's what I said. You don't know everything, and you aren't half so clever as you think. You don't think you can possibly make a mistake, whereas I'm dead sure you're up the wrong street all the time."

Tolefree gazed at her attentively.

"So?" he said. "Wish I could be dead sure of anything. Another cigarette, Miss Gillespie?"

"Not one of yours," she sniffed. "Jack – you pay for my supper, remember!"

Twenty-Three

On Saturday morning, when Tolefree came to see me, a little excitement peeped from under his mask of sententiousness. He had already telephoned Yonge. He now told me, a gleam in his eye, that I must dispense with the joy of his society over the weekend, and said I might expect a summons from Catterick to be at Midwood on Monday afternoon for the resumption of the inquest.

This was startling. The adjournment had been *sine die*. Catterick would certainly not have got the coroner into action again so soon unless he had made some vital discovery.

Tolefree shook his head over this.

"I'll tell you, Farrar, but it's a deadly secret. This is a regular frame-up, and I'm responsible. I've given Catterick a pointer or two, and to oblige me, as I particularly want all the crowd at Midwood on Monday night, Catterick's agreed to subpœna the lot!"

"You, Tolefree? Why d'you want them at Midwood?... I say! – you think you've got to the end of the road?"

"Oh," he answered, "wait a bit! That's far too sanguine. Put it that if a little experiment comes off on Monday we may possibly see to the end of the road then. I want to force Denley to say who it was he saw in the corridor just before the murder. I want to trap the man who was eavesdropping on the terrace on Wednesday night. Then, Farrar, I'll have a chain linking up

Masterton's Hotel with Burnet's study – and at the end of it we may find the man who killed Burnet: that is, if Catterick's not allowed him to evaporate in the meantime."

He would say nothing more definite. I pumped him in vain.

Denley? When I taxed him with the brutality of the scene at Antonelli's he did not deny it. But, he declared, it was necessary. Denley deserved no mercy: whatever his motive he was lying thirteen to the dozen. Why drag the girl into it instead of playing Denley privately? Because, he said, smiling at what he called my "romantic susceptibility," he had hoped the girl would make Denley squeak. She wanted him to squeak, as anyone would see. She was terrified by the possible results of his obstinacy. Nevertheless she was quite a plucky girl. Tolefree admired her.

But even if Denley had owned up, what then?

Ah – if Denley had owned up, we should have saved days. No fear then of losing our man – whereas now Tolefree was not so sure. Denley could have told us, if he had been frank, who was the jackal without whom the murder could not have been done.

The jackal? Elford?

Possibly Elford, he said. But not certainly. Or not Elford alone. Because Denley was running great risks, and obviously he would run no risks for the beautiful eyes of Mrs. Burnet's but-ler. Denley's pig-headed silence screened someone else. What Denley and Cossor and Elford and Mrs. Burnet knew between them would provide the master-word of the conundrum. There must be some powerful motive for silence. Tolefree meant to force his way to it however brutal he had to be.

And on this he breezed away, telling me to look out for Cat-terick's message.

I did in fact get a telegram from Catterick within the next hour, demanding my attendance at the Institute in Midwood village at four o'clock on Monday. And then, to my great sur-prise, about half past eleven came a telephone call from Cossor. He wished to see me, either in my office or at his chambers. I chose to go to the Temple: my clerks, in common with other people in the City, expected to be clear by noon on Saturdays.

That Cossor, after what passed in our former interview and the humiliating scene in the flat at Blisworth Mansions, should now seek me out again could mean only one thing: Cossor by this time knew all about the grilling of Denley last night.

If I had been wary of him before, I got behind a double guard now. Whatever Cossor's connection with the tragedy at Midwood, if indeed he counted for anything in it, he had undoubtedly taken alarm at Tolefree's inquiries, and a man of Cossor's stamp in a difficult place was likely to be difficult himself.

When I was shown into his room by a grave, elderly, soft-footed clerk, Cossor sat at a table piled with documents in a corner where books behind glass cases reached from floor to ceiling. He rose to meet me, pulled two chairs up to the fire, and passed me a box of cigarettes. He seemed at perfect ease. Next to impossible to believe that this cool, self-possessed, distinguished man-of-the-world had anything to fear from hotel bills, or from demi-mondaines in dubious flats, or from any common human being. And he said not a word about Denley.

"Very good of you to come, Mr. Farrar." He held a light for my cigarette. "I suppose you've received notice from Catterick that the inquest will be reopened on Monday? Yes? And I also. Of course your friend Tolefree is at the bottom of this. I won't ask you whether you know. It wouldn't be fair. But no doubt Tolefree has now obtained enough lights to show him where this thing will end, and I gather from the symptoms that he will bring on a crisis at once."

"Symptoms?—"

He had said the word with the glint of a smile and in a tone of irony.

"I have a very observant clerk, who informs me that yesterday and today certain persons have taken an unobtrusive but unremitting interest in my movements."

"You can't mean – detectives?" I exclaimed. "You're being watched?"

"Kept under observation is, I think, the official formula. Yes. Didn't you know?"

"Good God – certainly not!"

"Ah, then, as you're Tolefree's right-hand man, he plainly lets not his right hand know what his left hand doeth! However, I assume that if I am being kept under observation, the same process is being applied to other people. That means that Tolefree doesn't intend to have any witness missing when his moment comes. I deduce the conclusion that the moment is near. By the way, Tolefree's not a detective in the common run of the business, is he?"

"Hardly. He never did anything but private business inquiries until now. And in this affair, as you know, he's no official standing. He has no responsibility for discovering the murderer of Burnet. He's merely commissioned by Gillespie to find out, if he can, what it was that upset Burnet last week and caused him to call for Tolefree's help."

Cossor lay back in his chair and blew a cloud of smoke to the ceiling.

"Need we split hairs?" he said. "Tolefree sees very well that the two things are inseparable. What I meant was that the common inquiry agent is generally a rather lamentable person. Tolefree struck me as a cut above him."

It was remarkable that Cossor, reclining there and contemplating the ceiling, should take the trouble to pay compliments to Tolefree for my delectation. My wariness grew. Yet Cossor had an air of candour.

"Distinctly a cut above him," he repeated. "I've acquired respect for his ability. Now I want to test his humanity. That's why I asked to see you. The question is: will Tolefree listen to reason?"

"I've always found him a most logical man," said I.

Cossor twisted a smile out of his face.

"I said reason – not logic. I needn't expound the difference to you, for you're a man of mature experience. Mr. Farrar" – he sat up, threw the stub of his cigarette into the fire, and leant towards me – "there's time between now and Monday to prevent a tragedy if you can persuade Tolefree to listen to reason."

I answered him with deliberation.

"It's quite unlikely that I shall see Tolefree before Monday."

"But you can get in touch with him—"

"I hardly know that."

Cossor regarded me closely for some moments.

"You yourself, the friend of Burnet – do you think to do his memory a service by going over the past with a muckrake?"

"At present," I said, "I'm concerned with the past only so far as it can show why Burnet was killed and who killed him."

"But aren't you also concerned with the consequences in the present and the future? You are, whether you think so or not. I'm as anxious as Tolefree to get the foul mess cleared up. You don't believe it. You have a theory of the crime. It's not very flattering to me, but I don't resent it in the circumstances. I see Tolefree's plan perhaps more clearly than you do. Now, will you give him a message from me, a proposal – call it anything you like? Tell him I understand what he's driving at. Say I think he has probably got at the main truth, but that in one respect he's hopelessly astray, and that, if he doesn't realise this before he pounces, he will do an inhuman thing – a gratuitous, brutal thing."

I tried hard to get a concrete meaning out of Cossor's elusive speech. There was only one way.

"Inhuman to whom?" said I.

"To whom? Well – say, to me for one."

"You don't mind if I'm quite frank? I can tell you that I think that won't cut much ice with Tolefree. You see, he has decided views about what happened at Midwood on Sunday – I mean about certain conduct – and I fear his humanity is hardly equal to the strain you put on it."

Cossor laughed grimly.

"Spoken like Torquemada!" said he. "I should give that for Tolefree" – he snapped his fingers – "if it were not for—"

He broke off.

"But this is perfectly futile!" he said, and rose with a sudden impatience. "I asked you two days ago to tell Tolefree I would help his investigation on terms. Your answer to that was to follow me to a woman's house—"

I rose too.

"Pardon me," said I. "That is incorrect. I had not the faintest idea you were in the house till I was leaving it."

"Then why the devil did you go there?"

We were now in the attitude of two bantam cocks ruffling their neck-feathers.

"I'm not called upon to account for myself," I replied. "No doubt you heard all about it from the lady. But I might ask you in turn why the devil you were there! – and that's one of the questions Tolefree would like to have settled."

Cossor turned away with a show of petulance.

"Do you both take me for a born fool?" he snapped out. "Tolefree knows perfectly why I was there. But it's useless to go on wrangling. If he's determined to be a brute – well, he'll be a brute, I suppose, and the consequences will be what they will be. Still, I implore you to try to get in touch with him and put it to him as I've put it to you. He can prevent a tragedy and do a decent thing if he will listen to me. That's all. I've taken up a lot of your time—"

Cossor had spoken in riddles; I could not refer them to Tolefree; I did not mean to let Cossor involve me in any undertaking whatever by coming the superiority complex over me. Therefore he took up no more of my time. I wished him good morning and went.

Tolefree's proceedings between then and Monday were unknown to me. I did not see him; and he was not at his rooms, for telephone calls brought no answer. Not till I got into my old

place in the improvised Coroner's Court on Monday afternoon
did he come into view again. I had driven down, had to change
a wheel on the road, and arrived a little late. Outside the village
institute I saw the constable on duty talking with three men
who eyed me closely as I passed in. I did not take the meaning
of their presence then. Inside I found the coroner explaining
to a puzzled jury why he had called them together again so
soon. There was a full assembly of the people who had been
at Midwood, looking as puzzled as the jury – all save Cossor.
Cossor, sitting beside Annesty, sent me a sardonic glance as I
slipped in and took my seat with Tolefree. Mrs. Burnet was
there, her pallor accentuated by her black dress; Gillespie and his
sister, apparently wondering what it all meant; Denley, eyeing
Tolefree with a touch of resentment in his look; Elford, standing
beside Peters at the back of the room; Catterick, seated by the
coroner's side.

When I arrived, the coroner had reached the end of his ha-
rangue.

"This new evidence may be crucial," he was saying. "I cannot
yet suggest whether it will be enough to enable you to return a
verdict – but at any rate it will materially help our inquiry."

Catterick handed him a foolscap sheet.

"Call William Elford," said he.

I stole a look at Tolefree's face. It was utterly expressionless,
even when Elford, who had gone white as his name rang out in
the sharp tones of the constable at the door, stumbled rather
than walked forward to the table and sank on a chair facing
Catterick.

"You've already been sworn, Elford," said the coroner.

"I want to ask you a few more questions."

"Very good, sir."

But there was no conviction in his voice. Elford thought it
anything but good: he regarded the coroner with an air of re-
proachful martyrdom, and avoided Catterick's censorious eye.

Elford certainly had no idea at that moment of the ordeal he was to undergo; but he was extremely uneasy.

"First, Elford, how long have you been employed at Midwood?"

"Since last June."

"Who engaged you? Mrs. Burnet?"

"No, sir. Mr. Burnet."

"How did you get into touch with Mr. Burnet about this situation?"

"I applied for it in person."

"No letters passed between you and Mr. Burnet, then?"

"No, sir."

The coroner consulted his foolscap sheet.

"Now, Elford – you can answer the remainder of my questions or not, as you like. You are not bound to say anything that will commit you in any way. You understand?"

"Very good, sir."

"Well, you have hardly told me how you got into touch with Mr. Burnet about this situation. You say you applied for it in person. But you would hardly have come down to Midwood on the off-chance that Mr. Burnet wanted a butler and offered yourself for the job. What I want to know is how you obtained either an introduction to Mr. Burnet or the knowledge that there was a job to be had."

"I heard of the job," said Elford, "and I went to Mr. Burnet's office in the City and saw him about it."

"Yes? And how did you hear of the job?"

"I can't quite remember, sir. I heard talk of it."

"From whom?"

"That I can't say now."

"Where?"

"I can't remember that either."

In these few moments Elford's look, as his eyes shifted from the coroner to the stolid face of Catterick and back, was sheer terror. Perfect silence prevailed in the room. The jury's air of bepuzzlement had given place to one of intense curiosity.

"You can't remember either how or where you got this information. Very well. Now, Elford, is this your first job as a butler?"

"No, sir – but my first employment in a private establishment."

"Ah – and where were you before you came to Midwood: your last employment, I mean?"

"At an hotel."

"What hotel?"

I held my breath, staring at Mrs. Burnet while I waited for the answer.

"It was at a small hotel – Masterton's in Bastin Street."

She did not twitch a muscle. Cossor had perfect command of himself. So far as he was concerned, it seemed, Masterton's Hotel might have been in Constantinople or California.

"What position had you at Masterton's Hotel, Elford?"

"Head-waiter, sir."

"But you had been a butler, I understood you to suggest. Where was that?"

"At a Club."

"What Club?"

"The Wigwam Club, sir."

"Oh! I seem to remember that the Wigwam Club was recently struck off the register at the request of the police, don't I?"

"Yes, sir; but that was after I had left."

"I see. Where were you on May 5th, Elford?"

I got another jerk as he sprung the fatal date on Elford.

"Fifth of May?" Elford repeated the question as if searching his memory. "I was at Masterton's all through May, sir. That's where I must have been on the 5th."

"Nothing recalls that date to you particularly?"

"No, sir."

"You can't remember anything out of the common happening on the night of the 5th May? No visitor to whom your attention was specially drawn?"

"No, sir. My duties did not bring me into contact with visitors much, except in the restaurant."

"You are acquainted with a maid at Masterton's known as Alice?"

"I believe there was a chambermaid of that name there at the time."

"And a porter, known as John?"

"Yes – I knew him."

"Now, Elford – what is your name?"

"William, sir."

"William Elford? Then why were you masquerading as William Flint at Masterton's Hotel?"

He did not flinch: he had been prepared for that.

"You know, sir, that employers have curious ideas about names for servants, and I thought Flint was not a very good name for a butler in a private house."

The coroner took a long look at him.

"Are you Flint, or are you Elford?"

"Flint is my real name, sir."

"Was that the name you were known by at the Wigwam Club?"

"No," said he, his hands clenched on the table.

"What, then?"

"I was known as Miller."

"There was a William Miller charged at Bow Street Police Court last January with stealing a purse belonging" – the coroner looked at his foolscap – "to a Miss de la Valle. Was that you?"

Elford nodded.

"When you applied to Mr. Burnet for a situation, were you Miller, or Flint, or Elford?"

"Elford, sir."

"And did you tell him any of these things?"

"No, sir."

"I suppose Mr. Burnet did not engage you without recommendations?"

"He would have," said Elford. "In fact he did; but he told me afterwards that Mrs. Burnet insisted on recommendations."

"And you supplied them?" Catterick handed some papers to the coroner. "Are these the letters you supplied? Look at them. I will put the question direct, to save time. Are they genuine, or false?"

"I had no chance of getting the sort of recommendation that Mrs. Burnet wanted." He glanced across at her.

"Then, they are false?"

"Yes."

"You invented the letters and the persons who wrote them, didn't you?"

"Yes."

"Had you ever seen Mrs. Burnet before you came to Midwood?"

"Never."

The coroner had come to the end of his foolscap brief. He folded it up.

"Now, Elford – you are the chief witness in the matter of Mr. Burnet's murder. Did you tell the jury last week all you knew about it?"

"Everything."

"You do not know who killed him?"

"No."

"You do not know who fired that shot from the garden the other night?"

"No."

"You are certain about the time when you received Mr. Burnet's last telephone message on the Saturday evening?"

"Quite certain."

"Tell me exactly what message Peters gave you. That must have been almost the last thing Mr. Burnet said in life."

"Peters said I was to go up and ask Mr. Annesty to call and see Mr. Burnet on his way down to dinner."

"You yourself were to go? Wasn't that strange when Peters answered the call?"

"I don't know that it was. Anyhow that was the message. I packed my books away in the desk and went right upstairs."

"And is that all you can tell the jury?"

"That's all I know."

The coroner paused again and took a long look at Elford. The eyes of everyone in the room were fixed on his ghastly face. Everyone felt that the ordeal was not over.

"You told us last time that your accounts were in confusion," said the coroner. "More than confusion, wasn't it?"

"How do you mean, sir?"

"Isn't it a fact that you'd been robbing your employer right and left? I have a statement here. It shows deficiencies amounting to hundreds of pounds. But it also shows that you were drawing large sums almost from the day you arrived at Midwood, with Mr. Burnet's knowledge. Look at that statement, Elford. Does it state correctly the amounts you drew between June and November?"

He passed a paper.

"I expect it's right," said Elford dully.

"Well, can you suggest any reason why you were able to obtain all this money from Mr. Burnet during those months, and why suddenly in September it stopped and you began to muddle your accounts?"

"Mr. Burnet was master of his own money, I suppose."

There was a momentary flash of defiance in Elford's face.

"That's the question, Elford," said the coroner. "With regard to this particular money, drawn between June and September, was Mr. Burnet the master of it – or were you?"

"I don't understand—"

"Well – have you ever seen the document of which this is a duplicate?"

The coroner took up a sheet of paper that had lain face downwards on the table, and held it out to Elford. I caught a glimpse of the printed heading, "Masterton's Hotel." It was the flimsy Tolefree and I had inspected on Friday morning. Somehow or other Tolefree had coerced the determined lady into parting with it.

Elford stared – murmured that he knew nothing about it. The coroner replaced it and he told the jury it would be put in evidence later on. Its production did not disturb Mrs. Burnet. She watched the proceedings at the table, quite composed. "So you say you know nothing of any document like that? Never seen it before

"I know nothing! What do you mean? How should I know?"

Elford raised his hoarse voice, and there was a tremor in it. He fidgeted in the chair. The blackmailer driven into a corner was an ugly sight. The coroner bent to listen to a whisper from Catterick.

"Now, Elford," he said, "whether you are speaking the truth about these things or not, I'm bound to put this to you. According to the law, a person who conceals knowledge of a crime is an accessory after the fact. To withhold information about a murder makes that person equally guilty with the murderer, and equally liable for the consequences. You understand that, and you still say there is nothing more you can tell us?"

In the painful silence that followed the question, a motion of Catterick's made a sound that seemed like a cannon shot. But he had only twisted his chair and beckoned to the constable at the door.

Elford said, in a dull voice, "Yes, I know," and bending over the table put his right hand behind him.

Catterick whispered to the coroner again.

"Good God!" said he, and, turning sharply to Elford, exclaimed, "What are you doing, Elford? Constable! – come round!"

In an instant, the room was in uproar. Elford leaped up, knocking over his chair, and stretched out his hand with a revolver in it. The women cried out, the constable dashed round the table.

"Stand back!" said Elford. "I'm going to save the hangman a job!"

Before the constable could reach him, there was a flash. A shot crashed. A shriek and a second shot followed, and immediately the constable, stumbling over the fallen chair, went to ground with Elford under him.

"Keep away!" Catterick's voice commanded. "Tolefree! – the door."

Tolefree leaped up and stood with his back to the door.

The constable rose. Elford lay in a heap on the floor. Catterick stooped over him, the coroner standing by.

"He's dead," said Catterick, and immediately turned to the side of the room where the witnesses had been sitting. "Anyone hit?" he cried.

"No, Inspector," said Cossor; "but it was a near thing."

Catterick stepped over. Cossor pointed to a hole in the match-boarding.

Annesty, standing by, examined it, sat down in his chair and put his head against the wall.

"That was a close call, Mr. Cossor," he said. "The shot must have passed between your head and mine!"

Twenty-Four

The suddenness of the tragedy was petrifying. We stood in the attitudes into which the shooting and the shouting had thrown us, looking in a kind of paralysis at Elford crumpled on the floor, at Dr. Fleming now kneeling beside him, and at Catterick examining the bullet hole in the wall.

Dead silence followed the uproar.

The coroner rose and with a gesture indicated to Catterick that it was all over with Elford.

Then Catterick burst into a storm of activity which broke the spell. He issued orders rapidly. After a word with the coroner, told the jury to dismiss and the witnesses to remain. Tolefree stood aside from the door; the jury bustled out. Catterick called the constables who were on duty inside and outside; three men came and removed Elford's body. He turned to Mrs. Burnet.

"Will you take Miss Gillespie back to the house, please?" And to Gillespie: "You know what's wanted, Mr. Gillespie. Perhaps you'll see them home?"

The three departed. Tolefree closed the door after them.

"Mr. Cossor, Mr. Annesty, Mr. Denley," Catterick's glance went from one to the other. "Mr. Farrar, Mr. Tolefree, – I shall want your help. Kindly wait here while I have a word with Dr. Fleming."

He took the coroner out of the room. In three minutes he was back. A glance of understanding passed between him and Tolefree.

"I shall be glad if you will all go up to the house presently," he said. "Mr. Tolefree has something important to tell us. This business" – he gave a glance at the end of the room and the stain on the floor where Elford had fallen – "upset all my plans. But it may quicken things up."

The strain eased off. We began to talk to each other.

What everyone observed was the strange and fortunate fact that the wild firing in that small and crowded room had done no damage except to the suicide. But the most astonishing thing was the suicide itself. Catterick said ruefully that he hadn't believed Elford had "guts enough for that" or he would have had him searched for arms.

"A pity," said Tolefree. "But it might have been worse, Inspector; he nearly bumped you off."

"Yes, by gum! – he did. His first shot whizzed right past my ear. Too excited to shoot straight, or I guess my number would have been up."

"Fine for you, Mr. Catterick," said Annesty, "and I'm very glad for you. But—"

He pointed at the hole in the wall and shivered.

"Aye, that's so!" Catterick said. "A mere toss-up between me and you and Mr. Cossor – and death."

We shivered in sympathy with Annesty.

"I can hardly believe it even now," said he.

"What – that you almost stopped a bullet?"

"No – that confession of Elford's. It was a confession, wasn't it? – saying he would save the hangman a job?"

"That's the way it looks. Why can't you believe it?"

"Because I never could see where Elford came in – how it was possible for him to have killed Mr. Burnet. Tolefree, wasn't it you that said if he did he must have done it in less than no time?

Yes, I remember you did. And, like you, Inspector, I thought he hadn't enough guts to kill anyone."

"Well," said Catterick, "I was mistaken, and so were you, for he's killed himself right enough! As Mr. Tolefree knows, I had my own theory of Elford from the first five minutes – and now he's saved me the trouble of proving it. Shall we move on, gentlemen?"

I drove Cossor, Annesty and Tolefree up to the house in my car.

Probably there never was a much stranger scene in a country house than the one Tolefree staged that evening at Midwood. After a scratch meal we gathered in the drawing room, in a semi-circle before the fire. The prevailing feeling appeared to be just curiosity about Tolefree's promised statement, but we were soon to learn what fires of passion and suspicion raged beneath that mild exterior appearance.

Cossor pointedly made for himself a place beside Mrs. Burnet. They occupied the settee where Tolefree and I had sat on Wednesday night, and faced the broken mirror. Denley as pointedly took a seat by Miss Gillespie. We thus fell queerly into two groups – a Midwood group and a group of interlopers.

Catterick cleared his throat.

"Before anything is said, Mr. Catterick—"

Cossor's quiet, cold tones broke into the Inspector's preparations for speech. He desired to know what purpose this conversation was meant to serve, and particularly whether it was to be regarded as a private conversation. Catterick passed the ball to Tolefree. In turn Tolefree said his purpose was to avoid needless further inquiries, and perhaps the production of needless evidence in any future proceedings.

Within a moment it became clear that this was a duel between Tolefree and Cossor; each was measuring up the other.

"I shall reserve the right to object at any point to the continuance of this – er – performance," said Cossor, deliberately, "and to withdraw from it, or to advise other persons to withdraw."

Tolefree made a sign of acquiescence.

"But," he said, "I feel sure no such thing will happen, Mr. Cossor. I anticipate the greatest frankness between us all in clearing up the points about Mr. Burnet's death which the suicide of Elford leaves still in doubt. I think no one realises better than you that Elford's suicide is not the last word in this affair."

"I expect I realise all you realise, Mr. Tolefree," said Cossor, with elaborate formality. "Nevertheless I may have different views about the proper way of saying any word."

"Well," Tolefree replied with equally elaborate geniality, "we shall discover that as we go along, shan't we? Let's get to business. Any jury dealing with Elford's case will want to know a lot about what led up to this act of desperation. Annesty, you, for instance, weren't convinced, even when Elford shot himself, that he was the man who murdered Mr. Burnet."

"Couldn't see how it was possible, even then," said Annesty.

"Well, I agree with you. Even now I'm quite certain Elford did not murder Mr. Burnet. All the circumstances point to at least two accomplices in this crime. Elford was one. We have yet to find the other. More: Elford was certainly not the killer. What drove him to his suicide was the coroner's warning that an accessory to murder was equally guilty with the murderer. Elford was a tool – a willing tool, no doubt; but the master criminal is the man who handled him."

"Do you know that man?" said Cossor.

"I think I do," said Tolefree.

"Then why don't you denounce him at once?"

There was contemptuous challenge in Cossor's voice.

"In due course," said Tolefree.

"Have you told the Inspector whom it is you suspect?"

"Mr. Cossor," Tolefree answered, quietly, "I have not your familiarity with the law; but common sense tells me to say nothing till I'm sure. That's why we're here – to make sure."

Cossor sat back with the air of one who washed his hands of the whole thing. He did not again interrupt. Tolefree then put his case ingeniously, turning for confirmation of his points first to one and then to another of us. This trouble, he said, went far back into private places of Burnet's life and affected several people. At some point the paths of Burnet and Elford crossed. Elford was a crook with a bad record. No one could possibly believe the fantastic tale he told of his engagement by Mr. Burnet as butler at Midwood. Burnet must have known of Elford's character and, for some reason yet to be unfolded, must have deliberately placed a crook in charge of his household.

"Mrs. Burnet, – you can throw no light on that?"

"None," said she, in a startled voice.

"Then I'll see what I can do. Farrar, you can help. There's a short cut to the truth if Mrs. Burnet will allow us to take it. If she'll admit that for some time past she was only outwardly on good terms with her husband and that there'd been talk between them of divorce—"

"I will answer that," said Cossor. "There had been talk of divorce. But – go carefully, Mr. Tolefree! or I shall break up this irregular – er – inquisition."

"As you please." Tolefree shrugged. "I want to get at the truth, no more. There was this strain in the relations of Mr. and Mrs. Burnet. How it began does not concern us – probably in the character of Burnet and the circumstances of his marriage. He was a fish out of water in Midwood. Farrar was one of the first to perceive that, and to see Burnet's character deteriorating under the strain. Unhappiness of this sort has devastating effects on some men. It cracked Burnet. A very sober and abstemious man began to drink. A rather conventional man began to do riotous things. Farrar, he came to your rooms in Manchester Square one night last Spring in a very damaged state?"

I nodded.

"Annesty, the club where you told the coroner you made his acquaintance was the notorious Wigwam Club. You did not pay any particular attention to the company he kept that night, but later on to your surprise you learnt that he wanted to get a certain woman a job on the stage, and that was why he so unexpectedly interested himself in your proposals."

Annesty nodded.

"So! We have Burnet cracking up when Elford comes into the picture. He has got entangled with a woman. Miss Gillespie, – you saw him three times with that woman?"

Margaret Gillespie nodded.

"And each time they got into your train at the Temple Station?"

"Yes," said Margaret.

"No one present wants to volunteer any information?"

Tolefree said these words looking straight into the fire. No one did volunteer any information. Cossor sat gazing in front of him. Denley eyed Tolefree with the same resentful stare that he had worn at Antonelli's restaurant.

"Then," said Tolefree, breaking the silence, "if there is nothing more to be said about that, we have Burnet in the toils of a strange woman last Spring, and shortly afterwards taking a crook into his house as butler. The butler is manifestly concerned in the murder. He may be concerned with the woman. The woman is certainly concerned with persons in this room. But they do not volunteer any information."

He stopped for a full minute. The only sound in the room was the crackling of the fire.

"In that case," Tolefree said, "we had better go on to another element in the story. Take the facts of the murder itself. There has been a great lack of candour about what happened that Saturday evening. All the emphasis falls, or is forced, upon Elford. We are left to suppose the impossible. To believe that this frightful violence could be done in a room in the middle of a houseful of people, and that no one could hear it. That the corridors and staircases of Midwood were empty and silent during exactly the time it took to murder Burnet, and that no one saw and no one knows anything. It is untrue. It is preposterous. I don't believe it. I have never believed it. Now, does anybody want to volunteer information?"

Tolefree paused again. The circle remained silent.

"Mr. Catterick," he said, "you observed my statement? It is not denied, but no one offers to tell the truth. I will come to closer quarters. Mr. Denley – I want an explanation from you. I've asked you for it once before. You refused. Are you going to speak? Will you tell the Inspector what you saw and heard on that Saturday evening?"

Denley sat speechless, his dark eyes full of wrath.

"In your evidence at the inquest you did not tell the whole truth. Tell it now. What you heard, what you saw, what you did."

Denley made no answer.

"It's a serious thing to obstruct the course of justice, Denley. Mr. Catterick – tell him so!"

I saw Denley grab Margaret Gillespie's arm. She shook him off.

"I'm going to speak," she declared.

"Margaret—"

"It's simply silly," cried the girl. "If you don't answer, I will."

"There's no need, Miss Gillespie," said Tolefree. "I won't have you distressed. I know very nearly all I want to know. Denley – you heard something which caused you to leave your room and go into the corridor. When you got there, you heard something more – in Mrs. Burnet's room. You knew what those sounds meant. You were seen there by Mr. Gillespie, listening at the door. You pushed him off without explanation, and you have never said anything of this to anyone except to Miss Gillespie. A few minutes afterwards, Burnet was found murdered. You must have some strong reason for keeping silence. What is it?"

Denley did not answer. He glowered at Tolefree.

"I know what the reason is, Denley. You had a nasty suspicion before you heard that Burnet was killed; afterwards it became a ghastly one. I've told you already that you're helping to cloak a murder."

"Jack!" – Margaret Gillespie appealed to him. In vain.

"Shall I say what you heard and what you suspected?" asked Tolefree.

"No! I will say it!"

A gasp of astonishment burst when Mrs. Burnet broke in upon Denley's silence with her low, clear voice.

"Ah!" said Tolefree.

"He suspected, or knew, that—"

"Alison!" Cossor rose and stood in front of her. "I forbid you to say another word!"

He turned from her to Tolefree.

"Enough of this!" said he. "Catterick – you know this is perfectly improper – outrageous."

"Nothing to do with me," said Catterick.

"Nothing whatever," Tolefree rejoined. "Mr. Catterick has no responsibility. Nor has anyone any liability. It's quite open to anyone to speak or be silent, or to stay or go."

There was an extraordinary look of contentment on Tolefree's face as he spoke. Cossor saw it and stared at him with a steely look in his eyes.

"You're a damned ingenious devil," said he.

"I'm not asking for bouquets from you, Mr. Cossor, but thank you all the same. It is pretty ingenious, isn't it? You see that by this method we're bound to arrive? Having narrowed down the possibilities so far, and having a card or two up my sleeve, I'm quite confident of arriving before any of us leave this room. In fact, if you come to reflect upon it, Mr. Cossor, no one can leave this room now, can he?"

"Damn you!" said Cossor.

But Cossor sat down again on the settee beside Mrs. Burnet. He was to regret the curse.

"I am sorry to disturb Mrs. Burnet in any way," said Tolefree. "She must put it down to the purblind folly of people who ought to have known better than to think any fact bearing on the murder of her husband could be successfully concealed. Let us go on. The evening of the murder, Mr. Cossor was with Mrs. Burnet in her boudoir. A perfectly innocent meeting – no doubt to talk about the divorce case which was pending. Mrs. Burnet's maid was in the suite most of the time. But for some reason they wished to conceal the fact of Mr. Cossor's presence in the room. The reason will probably appear before we are through. The inquest revealed that a footprint had been made on the balcony outside Mr. Burnet's room that afternoon. The footprint was Mr. Cossor's."

"Good God!" Annesty and Catterick exclaimed together. They seemed to be the only persons in the room who were unaware of Cossor's footprint.

"But how could Mr. Cossor have been on that balcony if he was in Mrs. Burnet's boudoir?" Catterick asked.

"It's an easy step of four feet from one balcony to the other," said Tolefree.

Catterick looked at the silent and glowering Cossor, and shook his head.

"No, sir," said he. "That won't do. We found the marks made by a ladder, both on the stonework and in the gravel below. The man who made that footprint climbed up from the outside."

"Not so, Mr. Catterick," Tolefree told him. "I know how the ladder marks were made. Now – you saw that footprint; it was made by a boot or a shoe with a leather-composition sole, stamped in circular patterns, wasn't it?"

"That's so," said Catterick.

"Well, Mr. Cossor wore that shoe. He won't deny it. He was kneeling beside Mrs. Burnet when I reached the head of the staircase, and the first thing I saw as I went up was the sole of that shoe. I've a curious memory: it unconsciously records these things."

Catterick said no more.

"Mr. Annesty," Tolefree asked, "what time did you say you left Burnet's study finally?"

"I didn't notice the time," he answered. "Burnet must have telephoned Elford almost immediately after I went, for I'd only just had time to get into the bath when Elford came with the message asking me to call at the study on my way to dinner."

Tolefree considered. "Give it ten minutes," said he. "That would just about account for the movements of everyone concerned. If Mr. Denley would say what he knows, we could fix the moment when Burnet was murdered, but he won't. Anyhow, within that ten minutes he must have come out into the corridor and gone back again, and Mr. Cossor must have left the boudoir to go to his bedroom – or at any rate to reach as far as the landing where you found him when you rushed out of your room. Anyhow, these were some of the important facts known to Mr. Cossor, Mrs. Burnet and Mr. Denley. Neither of them volunteered any information. Instead, they all closed up like oysters."

He was taunting them to speech. They sat tight.

"Mr. Catterick and I know why Burnet was killed. It was because he had possession of a document which his murderer wanted. You've got a corner of it, Mr. Catterick."

Catterick took out his wallet and extracted a triangular scrap of paper.

"That's it," said Tolefree. "I have a good memory, as well as a peculiar one. When I first saw Burnet's body that rag of paper lay close to his hand. I memorised the few marks on it. You went through the room with a comb just after, Mr. Catterick, and you found that and took it. But Burnet's murderer did not know what you'd done. He had possession of the rest of the document, grabbed and torn from Burnet's hand, but he had left behind that one small clue. I felt certain he would go back for it, and he did. Some time after one in the morning he was in that corridor and switched off the lights of the bedroom floors. Then he waited to see whether the fact had been noticed. It had been. But too late. Farrar and I got there after he had paid his visit to Burnet's study – and after he had frightened the footman into a fit. Then there were three queer things.

"First, Mr. Denley suddenly appeared in the corridor and switched on the lights again. He ran away immediately: we saw him running.

"Next, at that time, Mr. Cossor was not in his room: I went to see.

"Last, there was a terrific how-de-do at the top of the staircase, outside Mrs. Burnet's boudoir, but it did not disturb her.

"If I conclude that Mr. Cossor was in the boudoir, and did not want the fact to be known, but that Mr. Denley knew or guessed it, I think I am not far wrong. They can say. I think I know why Mr. Cossor was there, but in the circumstances, it's not for me to speculate."

Tolefree would have fallen dead if a look of hate could kill. But Cossor did not speak.

"That document for which Burnet was killed was an hotel bill," said Tolefree. "A duplicate of it was produced at the inquest this afternoon. Elford said he had never seen it before. He told a lie. It was a bill issued by Masterton's Hotel in Paddington for a double room hired there on May 5th. It was made out to Mrs. Burnet and settled by her."

"By me!" exclaimed Mrs. Burnet.

Cossor turned to her with a strange and startled look.

Tolefree leaned over, his glance darting between them.

"By me? I have never even seen Masterton's Hotel," said Mrs. Burnet.

Twenty-Five

Tolefree looked almost terrible during those few intense moments while he bent over menacing them with his eyes. The contest with Cossor had wrought him into a being quite unlike the mild and philosophical Tolefree I knew. He was relentless.

"If you never saw Masterton's Hotel… By the way, Mr. Cossor has not said whether he ever saw Masterton's Hotel—"

Cossor made no response to the invitation.

"If you never saw Masterton's Hotel, Mrs. Burnet, at least you will not say you never heard of a bill issued from Masterton's Hotel with your name on it. Never mind the answer. I know. Mr. Burnet died for that hotel bill, and I don't think I should be far out in saying that he died to save his wife's honour."

Upon that I thought Cossor was going berserk. He rose, his face distorted with rage, and thrust across to Tolefree, crying,

"You filthy scoundrel!"

Catterick stepped between them.

"No breach of the peace, if you please," said he.

Cossor's madness was momentary.

"You're right, Inspector," he said, and went back to his seat.

Tolefree's calm remained unruffled.

"I have a great respect for Burnet because he did what I have said – died for his wife's honour."

He paused as if awaiting another outburst. None came.

"I have no respect at all for people who, out of whatever personal motive, hid any truth that might have led to the quick discovery of Burnet's murderer. I have very little knowledge of the law, and this is the first criminal matter I ever touched. But I will venture to tell Mr. Cossor, eminent as he is, what I should have done if I'd found myself in his place.

"Let us suppose that at some time after his cousin's marriage he learns that it is a failure. Burnet, the rather elderly and unsophisticated man of business, is no man for her, and she no woman for him. There's talk of divorce. Burnet, with his old-fashioned, conventional middle-class ideas, utterly refuses to manufacture a divorce. Some time or other, let us continue to suppose, Mr. Cossor receives an offer of evidence which will enable Mrs. Burnet to divorce her husband. He is not satisfied with it. But he explores it. He discovers the woman. So far from satisfying him, she confirms his doubts. He does not know that she is acting in collusion with Burnet, and that each evening after leaving Mr. Cossor's chambers she is meeting Burnet, for whom she has a sort of contemptuous liking, and reporting to him the progress of the plot."

"Plot!" Cossor exploded, as it seemed involuntarily.

"Well said Tolefree. "Not a nice word; but whether Mr. Cossor likes it or not, it is a plot against the peace of Burnet. But in truth no evidence can be had that will divorce Burnet, and Mr. Cossor knows it – for there is no better appraiser of evidence than he. Things go on getting more unbearable at Midwood. Then suddenly, not long ago, Burnet himself learns that there is evidence being bandied about which would put the boot on the other leg and enable him to divorce Mrs. Burnet – the bill issued from Masterton's Hotel."

"It's a damned lie!" cried Cossor.

"We are talking at cross-purposes," Tolefree said, quietly. "I put a supposititious case. And anyway it's not a damned lie, for he has it in his hand when he's killed. Let me go on supposing. Suppose, for instance, that his eccentric engagement of Elford, a thorough crook, who has been employed at Masterton's Hotel, is explained by that bill, or by the episode that occasioned the payment of the bill. Suppose the bill to be valuable material for blackmail. Elford is not above blackmail. There must be someone else too, who is not above blackmail – of a certain sort – for it has always been clear that there were two people in it. These things crowd in on him; Burnet finds himself in a hopeless tangle; and he calls me in. Before I can see him, he is murdered.

"Now the circumstances of the murder are very awkward for Mr. Cossor, who is also in a terrible tangle. I will not trouble to describe what Mr. Cossor does, or how plainly he shows his dislike of my appearance on the scene. But I will suggest to Mr. Cossor what he might have done to avoid the unpleasantness of this evening when, as I remarked just now, not one of us can possibly leave this room until the question of Burnet's murderer is settled. Not one."

Tolefree looked round the stupefied group, his eyes resting for an instant on one face after the other.

"Catterick," said he, "hadn't you better call in two of your men? No – three!"

I gasped.

The Inspector went to the door and called into the hall. Three men in plain clothes filed in. He placed them at the end of the room.

"A demonstration in force," said Tolefree. "Those men are armed." He spoke in a matter-of-fact tone. "They may as well go out in the hall and wait, Catterick, now that we've had ocular proof of their existence."

They filed out again. It did look rather like a performance, as Cossor had said. But Tolefree was speaking again.

"Let me pursue the argument as to how their presence might have been avoided. If Mr. Cossor had made as good a case for himself as he has made for a thousand clients, he would have done this: As soon as he had an opportunity, after Burnet's body was discovered, he would have told the truth about his own movements. He would not have allowed himself to be rattled into a course that could only bring suspicion on him. He would have said: 'I was a fool. I missed my chance. I was in Mrs. Burnet's room talking to her when the murder was done. I heard it done, though I did not know at the time. I heard a violent noise in Burnet's room next door. I did not want to be seen leaving the boudoir until I was sure the coast was clear, and as the maid had gone downstairs we had no one to put on watch. I slipped out on to the balcony and hopped across to Burnet's window. But the curtains were drawn. I could not see into the room, and I heard nothing more. I slipped back, waited to make sure that everything was quiet, and then left her and went up to my room. I had hardly reached it when I heard her scream.' And then, if he had been asked why he made such a secret of so little, he would have said, 'I had a great delicacy about Mrs. Burnet's honour. Burnet, if not suspicious, was jealous.' That would have been a good case."

"And however you discovered it or calculated it, that is the exact truth," said Cossor.

"I know it is."

"Then why the hell have you done this?"

"I had a purpose. In five or ten minutes from now it should be plain to you. Take your mind back to Annesty's evidence – about his meeting with Burnet at the Wigwam Club. You said he didn't seem to be in the company of any particular woman, Annesty?"

"No – I told you there was a crowd."

"Well, there was a particular woman. I don't know whether she's an actress or not. Probably not. Know of her, Annesty? – Miss Poppy de la Valle?"

"No – but didn't I hear that name somewhere recently? It sounds familiar—"

"It was the woman Elford robbed," said Catterick.

"Ah, yes—"

"That was the woman," said Tolefree. "You know her, Mr. Cossor." Cossor nodded. "And you, Mr. Denley, as I understand. Well, Burnet that night at the Wigwam Club was sozzled. He went off to Masterton's Hotel. As soon as he got there he thought better of it and fled, leaving her with money to pay the bill. She paid it as Mrs. Wellington Burnet."

I heard Gillespie swear a guttural oath under his breath.

"Elford was in the place as head waiter. Elford saw his chance. What a chance! To such a crook it must have seemed like manna dropped from heaven. Wellington Burnet, the well-known City man, the shipping magnate, the wealthy owner of a big estate – Wellington Burnet caught out by his own conscience, terror-stricken and with shame of what he has done! Wellington Burnet will be a good thing, a fat living for Elford. But Elford, crook as he was, hadn't brains enough to work this game as it was actually worked. He couldn't have known of the chance of doubling hearts – couldn't have invented a two-handed scheme of blackmail. He went into partnership with a cleverer man who presently turned up. Only a very astute intellect could have devised a plan for blackmailing both husband and wife. And only someone who was in a position to discover what could be discovered about the state of things at Midwood. I don't think in all your inquiries you ever saw this man, Mr. Cossor? It must have been an inconspicuous third party who put up the case to you?"

"It never got farther than anonymous letters to me, but they inadvertently gave me the name of the hotel, and the rest was easy. I had seen through Elford long before you came into it," said Cossor.

"Ah – very likely. But you didn't know the ramp was being worked with Burnet as well? That while they pretended to you to believe the lady who paid the bill was Mrs. Burnet, they themselves were playing off the other woman on her husband?"

"I suspected something of the sort, but Burnet naturally did not confide in me. And even the woman herself did not know."

"Oh, but she did," Tolefree declared. "She's a queer creature – a certain loyalty. She was in communication with Burnet all the time. The pity of it was that the crooks succeeded. Burnet paid a considerable sum to get hold of that hotel bill."

"Why in God's name I can't understand," Cossor exclaimed.

"No? In a purely quixotic spirit of delicacy, I should think. He did not want his wife's name hawked about on a Masterton's Hotel bill."

"But he'd not been too delicate to negotiate with Annesty for putting some woman on the stage – this one or another!"

"Ah – there's that," said Tolefree. "I'll come to it presently. But he did pay, and I think that was the reason. I think also, that if he had lived long enough to see me, that bill would have passed into my keeping, and there'd have been a pretty prosecution for blackmail in due course, after which Elford and his collaborator would have gone into retirement for a time. As it is Elford has retired permanently, and as for his collaborator—"

Tolefree turned and glanced at the door. Our eyes followed his. I seemed to see the three waiting figures in the hall. The tension was rapidly growing to breaking point as realisation came of the incredible thing Tolefree was suggesting.

"Elford's collaborator was rather clever," he went on, "indeed, devilishly clever. But he left rather too many traces, and he began to get nervous and give himself away – especially when he tried to kill Elford."

"To kill Elford?"

Two or three of us cried out together.

"Yes – that night when he broke your mirror with his bullet, Mrs. Burnet."

"But Elford? – Elford wasn't there, Tolefree," said I.

"Oh, yes he was. I saw him myself. It was Elford who pushed the window open and Elford who listened, and Elford who kicked me in the stomach. I had no doubt about it; but Elford didn't know I'd recognised him, and I didn't want him to know."

"Elford," I persisted, "came up to the drawing room with the other servants. It was he who found that the window was unfastened."

"Naturally, as he'd unfastened it himself! You remember his coming into the room and walking round just as we got here?"

"But if he was outside at the time of the shooting—"

"After the shooting, he ran down that alley towards the stables, and no doubt he was round in the kitchen by the time the alarm was up. There's no mortal doubt about it, Farrar. I saw him quite plainly. The point is that blackmailers always quarrel: Elford's collaborator meant to put him out. And that's one thing that gave him away."

"You knew all this! – and yet you chose to submit Mrs. Burnet to this evening's martyrdom—"

Cossor's eyes flamed with anger.

"To say nothing of Mr. Cossor," said Tolefree.

"I told your friend, Farrar, the other day that you were going to do a brutal thing. I asked for a meeting with you to prevent it—"

"And I declined. I was too busy on serious work. I don't know why, Mr. Cossor, but you resented me from the first – and at last you compelled me to resent you. I detest deceit and you chose to try to deceive me. I will tell you now that I knew in my bones who had murdered Burnet half an hour after I set foot in this house."

"Psha!" Cossor spat it out.

"I am rarely mistaken in a physiognomy. I knew. I have ever since been finding my way to evidence. Will it be admitted that the man who shot at Elford is the man who killed Burnet?"

"If so, how do you discover him?"

"By his footprint under the cedar."

"It could not be identified."

"But he was afraid it would be, so it was obliterated before a cast could be taken."

"Well—"

"Well – it meant that I knew my man for the first time that night with perfect certainty. When you know a man, it's easy to get his biography. It's always more reliable than his autobiography – which in this instance is chiefly fiction."

A glance of understanding passed between him and Catterick.

"Mr. Catterick, I think there's a draught from one of those windows."

Catterick rose and went round to the back of the circle.

"They're all closed," said he.

"Ah – perhaps I'm unduly nervous. Will you stay where you are in case a window should be opened? As I was saying, the man who shot at Elford is by inference the man who murdered Burnet. It was a duel, in which Elford fired the last shot. Annesty, you thought that remark of Elford's was a confession – you know, when he said he would save the hangman a job. But it wasn't a confession. It was an accusation. He meant to kill his accomplice before he died himself."

"His accomplice — ?"

"He only just missed you," said Tolefree.

Catterick's great hands had gripped Annesty's arms before he could stir.

Twenty-Six

Two minutes of sickening, almost intolerable excitement. Then Catterick, and his prisoner, and his troop had gone.

"Annesty! But it's impossible, Tolefree. Some ghastly error, man!"

Gillespie removed the paralysis that had fallen on us. His bronzed face, which had gone pale, now flushed and his blue eyes shone indignation.

"Sorry, Gillespie, to have dashed your faith. But there's no error. Ask your sister: I think she alone in Midwood saw through Mr. Annesty."

We all looked at Margaret Gillespie.

"I certainly thought him very cheap and couldn't understand what he was doing here. But I didn't know I'd worn my feelings on my face," said she.

"And you, Mr. Cossor — ?" Tolefree turned to him.

But Cossor confessed that he hadn't a glint of the truth till the last few minutes. When he had told me he could help Tolefree to his solution, he merely meant that he was aware of Elford's character, and was willing to tell Tolefree what he knew – on condition that Mrs. Burnet was spared all the agony of publicity. Annesty had signified nothing to him. He had taken Annesty at his own valuation, as the rest of us had done.

"I thought as much," said Tolefree. "I couldn't risk it. I had to nurse Annesty up to the last moment, or he'd have slipped through Catterick's fingers. I had, in fact, to get him into this room under the confident impression that I was a blundering fool about to accuse you. I'll offer you any apology you care to accept, and, so far as it can be done, I'll stave off publicity – or Catterick will."

Cossor acknowledged this with a stiff nod. "I'm curious to know how you got at him," said he.

"But, Tolefree, – damn it all! I can't believe it even now," Gillespie burst in. "How the deuce could he have done it?"

"Did you see his face when Catterick pounced on him? Wasn't that answer enough? You don't study faces hard enough to make a good detective, Gillespie. Figures are more in your line, eh?

"I'll answer Mr. Cossor's question this way: I got at Annesty through his face. I had the extraordinary bit of luck to see him immediately after he had done this thing, before anyone knew there was a murder, and before he understood who I was. You remember his rushing into the billiard room, Gillespie? There was panic in his eyes. After the discovery I never ceased to watch him. He's a marvellous actor! He had me guessing many times. But first instinct came right. By the way, he's not an actor at all."

"Not an actor?" Mrs. Burnet questioned. "But my husband—"

Tolefree smiled the suggestion away.

"No – Burnet was never deceived. He had great experience of the world. He knew his man. You remember that woman at the flat, Farrar, telling you about somebody discussing theatre business with Burnet when she saw him at the Wigwam?"

"She said something about a guy talking stage to him."

"Well, the guy who talked stage wasn't Annesty. No doubt it was some other innocent youth, really bitten by the theatrical bug. Enter during the séance Mr. Annesty, *chévalier d'industrie*. I've had him taped off: ne'er-do-well son of a good family, well-educated, but a crook by instinct, or atavism, or something. Of course, Annesty is not his real name. I daresay he has as many aliases as Elford. I will keep his family out of the case if I can. So, enter Annesty. He sees Burnet with one over the eight inside him, watches him, notices that he falls for the yellow-haired woman, picks up his identity somehow – you know what men will give away in their cups. You can imagine the rest of that revolting night's business. It ended, no doubt, in a joyous reunion at Masterton's, after Annesty had watched the principals off the premises, between him and Elford, alias Flint, alias Williams, whilom steward at Mr. Annesty's favourite club. Burnet is fair game for the precious pair."

"But how do they get hold of the hotel bill?" asked Gillespie.

"That's plain enough," Cossor put in. "When the woman left the hotel, she tells me, she threw down the money on the bill and left it."

"The point had puzzled me," said Tolefree. "But she solved it. As you say, she glanced at the bill, put down the cash, and departed. How Elford secured it I don't know. But he did. Common larceny on the spot, probably, either after or before the uprising of Mr. Annesty. It's to Annesty that the full value of the find becomes apparent. He lets no grass grow under his feet. He comes down on Burnet sick and ashamed of himself. What tale he pitches I don't know – threats of exposure of Burnet, accusation of Mrs. Burnet, perhaps both. Anyhow, Burnet pays. And Burnet knows he'll have to go on paying if he's to save himself from disgrace and keep tragedy out of Midwood. You remember what you told me, Gillespie, about the day your uncle introduced you to Annesty?"

"Yes, quite well. What of it?"

"Your uncle said he wanted you to know Annesty because you'd probably see a good deal more of him. Poor old Burnet! He knew! But of course that didn't strike you as it struck me when I heard of it, because you hadn't studied Mr. Annesty's face just after he'd done a murder. Then, Burnet pays. He pays Annesty four times; he pays Elford even more often. Think of that – the dirty scoundrel always at hand to leer at him on the sly and remind him of the toils in which he's caught!"

Mrs. Burnet shuddered.

"You recall Annesty's effusive gratitude to your uncle for subscribing a thousand pounds to his imaginary theatrical production? A clever conception! It covers his tracks, for Burnet did actually pay him a thousand pounds in all, and he thought no doubt he might some time or other be called on to account for it. But not in a lump, or by cheque. Between June and September Burnet draws four cheques to self, each for £250 – a previously unheard of thing at Burnet's bank. The two beauties think they've invented a gold mine! But the lode suddenly gives out. No pay-dirt after September. Evidently Burnet is prompted by something to stop payments and consider means of punishing these fellows. Elford is getting impudent and beginning to peculate, but I don't think that's the main reason. There must be something else. I wondered whether Mrs. Burnet could enlighten us."

Cossor looked to Mrs. Burnet. She bent her head.

"You're very astute, Tolefree," Cossor said.

"There was something? May I guess it was that you had by that time discovered what happened at Masterton's Hotel, and that you put it forward in the discussions about – well, the future?"

"I told Burnet that this thing was being said of his wife, that he knew it was false, and that it was up to him—"

"Well," said Tolefree. "That settles the whole question. Burnet has been wounded in two places: there's the attack on his wife's honour, and there's the threat to him. But the blackmailers have overreached themselves. They've not reckoned on any understanding or even on any communication between the two sides. Burnet sees his chance. He stops payment. He calls me in to discover – what I've since discovered for myself."

"All that's very well," Gillespie burst in. "But—"

And Gillespie's "but" echoed the doubts I felt and no doubt Denley as well. Whatever Annesty's character and record, how could he have killed Burnet? It was physically impossible.

"I don't question he's the world's worst skunk," said Gillespie. "But you haven't proved it and I don't see how you can."

"Proved? That depends on what you want for proof. If you ask me to bring an eyewitness, I can't. No eye but Burnet's saw him strike. But you don't want eye-witness proof to satisfy the rules of evidence. Nearly every murderer is convicted on circumstance. And here there's circumstantial evidence literally overwhelming. He can't get out of the net. Mr. Cossor, don't you agree?"

"There's just one thing that bothers me," said Cossor, "but go on."

"Well, I deduce the unknown quantities from the known. As to what happened before the murder, I deduce from Burnet's bank accounts that he suddenly stopped payment to his blackmailer, and from that again that the blackmailer had suddenly lost his hold. I find from your statement that it occurred when he learnt that both you and his wife were aware of the escapade at Masterton's Hotel. From the fact that he had invited, or more probably commanded, Annesty to be here that weekend, I deduce an ultimatum to Annesty, and terms including the surrender of the blackmailing instrument – which was the hotel bill. Any flaws there, Gillespie?"

"No, but—"

"But let us come a little closer. As to what happened on Saturday afternoon, I deduce this from the actual movements of Burnet and Annesty: that Burnet gave him his ultimatum when they entered the study after tea – demanded that the hotel bill should be handed over. Annesty went to his room to get it. He hung about. Burnet lost patience – sent Elford to hurry him. Lord knows what Annesty and Elford may have said to each other then. But Annesty came down with the document and gave it up. Then I can only imagine that Burnet was indiscreet.

Having secured the paper, he flourished his victory, perhaps threatened Annesty with the police—"

"Or insisted on restitution of the money," said I.

"You think he may have done that?"

"I think he's pretty certain to have done it. Burnet was a man of most generous impulses, but he would have been implacable to anyone who had tried to do him down."

"Perhaps. But, however it happens, there is a struggle for the possession of the paper. Annesty in a panic. Seizes the heaviest thing at hand. Burnet goes down. That's the end."

Cossor had given assent to each point as Tolefree made it.

"But still," said he, "there's one thing that bothers me."

"Same thing I can't see, I expect," Gillespie remarked. "How could Annesty have got upstairs and into his bath in the time? He couldn't possibly have done the murder and then all the other things he must have done afterwards between the time when Uncle Wellington made his last telephone call and the time when Elford got to his door to deliver the message."

"That's the point," said Cossor.

"Nevertheless, he did. And not only that, but he removed from the study the one thing, as he thought, that could possibly betray him – the candlestick. That would bear fingerprints, and it must not be found there. So far as he can judge, if he escapes unnoticed from the study, there is only one man at Midwood who will suspect him – Elford. But he has undoubtedly put himself in Elford's power, and he knows his Elford. He must deal with that later on. And it's when he comes to deal with Elford that he presents me with the absolute evidence of his guilt. He tries to kill Elford—"

"Even now," Gillespie protested, "I don't see how you get that. You say it's the footprints. But Annesty was there and measured up his footprints with the rest of us."

"He did. You know I suggested that each member of the party should be warned of the experiment we were going to make? I asked you to inform Mr. Cossor and Annesty, who had gone upstairs. We waited till they came down. Well – Annesty was the only one of the seven of us who had changed his evening shoes for walking shoes."

"Gosh!" Gillespie sat back.

"There is," said Cossor, "the question of the return of the candlestick. He must have obtained access to the study during Saturday night. But how?"

"Ah," said Tolefree. "It puzzled me more than anything else – and you were responsible for that."

"I?" Cossor exclaimed. "How do you fasten any responsibility on me?"

"You made me doubt for a time whether it really was Annesty who'd been in the study. I'll tell you."

Tolefree related our experience after the derangements of the lights, and his visit to the bedrooms of the upper floor.

"When I looked into his room," he said, "Annesty was apparently fast asleep. He deceived me thoroughly – put me right out of my stride. And when I looked into your room and you were not there, you can imagine that I began to have my doubts as to who it was put Peters to sleep! You shared my suspicions with Mr. Denley, whom I saw in the corridor."

"Mrs. Burnet and I had a great deal to talk about after the grilling we received from Catterick," said Cossor.

"You had, of course," said Tolefree with emphasis. "Having made the initial mistake of concealment – well, I needn't platitudinise on that, to you of all men! But it was a mistake for Mrs. Burnet not to hear that din outside."

"She and the maid and I sat trembling lest a knock should come at the door."

"I thought of knocking," Tolefree grinned. "Fortunately, I conquered my impulse: after all, I couldn't quite see you in that galley. But there it was. Between you and Mr. Denley, Annesty seemed to be slipping out of my grasp. I'm curious to know what Mr. Denley was doing—"

"Making an officious ass of myself," Denley replied.

"As how?"

"Imagining things – as I'd done in the afternoon. I may as well make a clean breast of it now, Tolefree. Just after Annesty had gone to his room, as you suppose to get that paper, Mr. Burnet summoned me to bring him two letters to sign. Exactly as I passed Mrs. Burnet's door, it was opened a little way, and I caught a glimpse of Mr. Cossor, who immediately shut it again. I found Mr. Burnet in a black temper. He almost bit my nose off. Knowing something of his troubles and Mrs. Burnet's, I began to fancy things. It was when I was on the way back to my room that I paused a moment outside Mrs. Burnet's door, wondering whether Mr. Cossor had gone, and hoping he had, and then you came on me, Gillespie. Then again – in the night, it was the same thing. I was reading, trying to forget the horror, when my light suddenly failed. Went out to explore. Found all the lights off. Heard voices in Mrs. Burnet's room. Imagined further stupidities. Did a bit of damning. Footled about with the switch at the head of the stairs, and, just as all the lights came on, heard a door open and did a bolt. That's the extent of my folly, Tolefree. I'll always take a woman's advice in future: Margaret wanted me to tell the whole story from the first."

"Loyalty seems to be a quality shared by the Gillespie and Denley families," said Tolefree, dryly. "Only they carry it to excess. However, you blow away the last wisp of fog. My instinct about Annesty was right, and my senses of sight and hearing were deluded, that's all. Mr. Cossor was asking how he got access to the study. It could only be one way. He had the key."

"But Catterick had locked the place up overnight," Denley objected.

"That's so. But when Farrar and I rushed up from the billiard room to the corridor with Annesty immediately after the murder, one of the first things I observed was that there was no key in the door. You remember, Farrar? And Catterick had to get Elford's keys to lock up. That might have meant nothing, though it was unusual. But in her evidence at the inquest Mrs.

Burnet mentioned knocking at the door, getting no answer, and *finding that it was not locked*. From which it was to be assumed that Burnet usually had a key in the door. Who could have taken it but the man who killed him?"

"It's well constructed, Tolefree," said Gillespie. "But yet it doesn't meet my point. You won't contend that all this could have been thought out and done, and Annesty undressed and in his bath in five minutes?"

"No, I won't. There's no need."

"Then I'll be hanged if I can see what you're driving at. The murder was certainly not done before ten minutes to seven, because Uncle Wellington telephoned for Elford at that time. And it was done before five minutes to seven – you worked out the times yourself."

"That would be a good objection if you could believe Annesty. But why should you? He's a consummate and most artistic liar. I'll suggest to you what probably happened – no, what certainly happened. The murder was done some while before Burnet sent that last telephone message—"

We all stared at Tolefree as though he had gone mad.

"Or rather, before the message was sent. It was done soon after Annesty went into Burnet's study with the document. Now think of him, sick with fear, looking down on Burnet with the candlestick in his hand. It's a terrible thing to have done, even for a crook like Annesty. He looks – and he listens. Is there an alarm? Has anyone heard? Gradually he gets his nerve again. No one has heard! He does some quick thinking. Burnet is dead. He makes sure of that. Up to now he's the only man who knows Burnet is dead. An *alibi* – how can he get it? What will give him away? The candlestick, – no doubt with fingerprints, and an ugly stain on the base of it. That was to go. Nothing else that he can see. But it is known to everyone that he has been with Burnet in the study. Can he invent anything to prove he's not there now? He looks round. The telephone! – he can ring up Elford! He probably locks the door before he takes up the telephone receiver and presses the button marked 'Butler's pantry.' He gets the answer. He says, 'Is that you, Elford?' He has a shock when he hears, 'No, sir, it is Peters.' But he's equal to it. Peters has mistaken him for Burnet! He feigns Burnet's tone. 'Tell Elford to go up to Mr. Annesty and say I shall be glad if he will call in on me on his way down to dinner.' And Peters says, 'Very good, sir.' I think that's the explanation of the telephone message and the consequent confusion of times. It gives Annesty his alibi."

"Seems rather far-fetched," said Gillespie.

"I not only think it. I know it."

"How can you possibly know that?"

"Because I suggested to Catterick that he should have the telephone receiver tested for fingerprints. If Burnet had used it there would be fingerprints. Even if he had not used it that afternoon there would be fingerprints. Then Catterick found, as with the candlestick, that there were no fingerprints whatever. The receiver had been carefully cleaned since it was last handled. Annesty is so clever that he is too clever. He wipes the telephone receiver clean to show that he has not used it – and does not reflect that he is proving at the same time that Burnet hasn't used it. He takes the candlestick, but he remembers that he will have to get rid of it somehow, and it had better go back to Burnet's desk before it is missed. So he takes the key of the door. Perhaps twenty seconds after he has spoken to Peters he's up in his room again. He has just time to strip for a bath when Elford arrives."

"On that showing," said Gillespie, "Elford was not a party to the murder."

"He certainly was not accessory before the fact – but after! Up to the neck in it. He must have known the truth the moment he saw Burnet's body. It gave his partner in blackmail into his hands. The idea of those two beauties thereafter watching each other, crossing each other, trying to kill each other! Can you beat it?"

"But," said Gillespie, "how does the candlestick get back to Burnet's desk?"

"Annesty brings it back – that night. He's got two urgent reasons for getting into Burnet's study – that one, and another which he's discovered during the evening. He finds that in the struggle for the paper a corner of it has been torn off. He must recover it if he can. Catterick has greatly increased his difficulties by the brilliant tactics which removed Elford from the premises for the night; but I expect he's had a word with Elford while Catterick is examining his witnesses – arranges with Elford to switch off the lights for a sufficient time to do the job. But now he has to go through it alone and risk what will happen when he has blinded the house. Darkness of course is absolutely necessary to him. He brings it off.

"Apparently the disappearance of the lights has disturbed no one – not even the police sentry," said Tolefree, with a smile. "He is in the room; the candlestick is back on the desk; but the paper is not to be found. That's worrying, but he cannot delay. Then some noise made by Peters must have alarmed him. That's the only way I can account for his neglect to relock the door. He gets ready for a dash in the dark, but Peters strikes a match to look at the fuse-box. When it flickers out he has his opportunity. Now if he is challenged, he can say the extinction of the lights brought him down. But it is actually simpler than that. He gets behind Peters as he strikes his second match, blows it out and speaks. Peters collapses. In the next instant he is round the corner, up to his wing, and in bed. When I arrive he is apparently fast asleep. Mr. Annesty has an *alibi* again. And for a time he succeeds in throwing me off the scent – with the assistance of Mr. Cossor."

It may have been a little humiliating to Cossor to be expected to explain to a private detective what had seemed suspicious in his conduct. But as we all looked to him to round off the case he did it good-temperedly enough. His motive throughout was a passionate desire to keep Mrs. Burnet's name clean. He had some acquaintance with the Wigwam Club and had met the yellow-haired woman there. When the threatening letters about the incident at Masterton's Hotel began to reach him (which was not till after Elford had been established at Midwood and obtained an insight into things there), he investigated it closely with the help of Denley, and soon picked up her tracks and those of Elford. They realised that Elford must have a confederate; but Annesty had never come into the picture.

"He was far too clever," said Tolefree. "Even the woman was not aware of him."

"A queer creature. In her way she developed an admiration for Burnet, and I've no doubt, after what you said about her meetings with him, that in all her appointments with me when we were trying to get at the bottom of the blackmail threats, she was in fact acting on his behalf. After his death she suspected everyone, except me, whom she knew – even poor Mr. Farrar – of playing him false. She had an almost comic conception of him as a sort of innocent child lost in a naughty world."

That made me smile.

"Burnet! – why I never knew a man so absolutely in command of his world – at least, till—"

Then I saw Mrs. Burnet looking at me, and pulled up with a jerk.

"All the same, she was right," said Tolefree. "That was Burnet exactly. In her very naughty world he was indeed a lost child. He knew the City inside out. He could hold his own in any business with the smartest lawyer or the cleverest financier. But in her realm of jazz and cocktails, sex and crookery he must have been as perfectly alien as an icicle in hell. It was his one experience, but it just seared him. That's the only word for it. I've seen Yonge. He'd told Yonge he could never forgive himself – not for the peccadillo, because getting tight at a night club was no such great thing, but for developing the frame of mind in which it was possible for Wellington Burnet to go so low. And, in his innocence – it's a thing that makes me respect Burnet's memory

– he thought he'd hurt the yellow-haired woman in some way. He was for lifting her out of it – setting her up respectably. Poor old Burnet – you should have heard Yonge on the Don Quixote of Moorgate Street! But Burnet was in earnest – so much in earnest that he'd left Yonge instructions for looking after her in the event of his death. The thing's amazing."

"Not amazing if you knew Uncle Wellington," said Gillespie. "It's almost a pity that – yes?"

Gillespie spoke to a servant who had entered and come up to his chair.

"Mr. Tolefree's wanted on the telephone, sir."

Tolefree went out.

"Must be Catterick, I suppose," Gillespie said.

We kept silence. In two minutes Tolefree came back.

"Catterick," he said. "Don't know whether to be glad or sorry – the hangman's to be cheated of a job after all."

"What!" we cried.

"Mr. Annesty preferred diethylbarbituric acid to hemp, so—"

"What the devil are you talking about, Tolefree?" exclaimed Gillespie.

"That's veronal," said Cossor.

"Yes. Had it all ready for emergencies, it seems. Must have swallowed enough to put a regiment to sleep as soon as they got outside the door. Was unconscious before they reached the station, passed into coma, and has now joined Elford where Elford tried to put him this afternoon. So we shall have another inquest instead of a trial for murder."

"You don't really regret it, I expect," said Cossor.

Tolefree took a look at the Midwood group – Mrs. Burnet, showing signs of wear, Cossor not so formidable as he had been, Denley and Miss Gillespie regarding him with less hostility, Gillespie himself manifestly relieved.

"No," said he, "perhaps on the whole it simplifies things. And it won't matter two hoots to poor old Burnet, will it, Farrar?

Visit our website to explore the list of great Golden Age books and sign up to our infrequent Newsletter to be told of our latest titles first:

www.oleanderpress.com/golden-age-crime

<u>OREON titles in this series</u>

The Crime of a Christmas Toy
Henry Herman

Death of an Editor
Vernon Loder

Death on May Morning
Max Dalman

The Hymn Tune Mystery
George A. Birmingham

The Essex Murders
by Vernon Loder

The Middle of Things
J.S. Fletcher

The Boat Race Murder
by R. E. Swartwout

Murder at the College
by Victor L. Whitechurch

The Charing Cross Mystery
by J.S. Fletcher

The Doctor of Pimlico
by William Le Queux

Who Killed Alfred Snowe?
by J. S. Fletcher

The Yorkshire Moorland Mystery
by J. S. Fletcher

*Fatality in Fleet Street **
by Christopher St John Sprigg

** Free ePub on sign-up to the
OREON GA newsletter:*

ND - #0142 - 040724 - C0 - 203/127/14 - PB - 9781915475176 - Matt Lamination